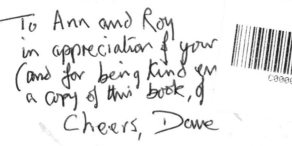

To Ann and Roy
in appreciation of your
(and for being kind) en
a copy of this book, of
Cheers, Dave

D.E. Toft grew up in Salford and eventually studied English at Cambridge University. He later spent much of his life in education and taught in the East End of London, industrial West Yorkshire and Greater Manchester.

He now lives with his wife, Josephine, on the edge of Kinder Scout in the Peak District. He is chair of the Hayfield Kinder Trespass Group, which keeps alive the spirit of the 1932 Mass Trespass. He loves photography, playing guitar in a band with his wife and friends, walking on the wild moors of the Dark Peak and travelling around the globe.

He believes that as well as revealing great beauty in strange and exotic landscapes and architecture, travel also allows us to experience people living their day-to-day lives in different cultures and societies. And despite everything that governments and religions do to divide us, people everywhere share more in their common, caring humanity than ever separates us. After all, we all live on this tiny planet, whirling through a cold, dark, empty universe and we need to look after each other. There are no lifeboats for anyone if this ship sinks.

'Give me books and French wine...'
    Keats

Here's the book - wine to follow
on completion of a 5* Review!

P.S. Roy - there's a character from
    Liverpool in it !'.'

D.E. Toft

STILL POINT

AUSTIN MACAULEY PUBLISHERS™

LONDON • CAMBRIDGE • NEW YORK • SHARJAH

A CIP catalogue record for this title is available from the British Library.

ISBN 9781398400382 (Paperback)
ISBN 9781398400399 (ePub e-book)

www.austinmacauley.com

First Published (2021)
Austin Macauley Publishers Ltd
25 Canada Square
Canary Wharf
London
E14 5LQ

Neither ascent nor decline. Except for the point, the still point,
There would be no dance, and there is only the dance.

T.S. Eliot
Burnt Norton

Between breathing in and breathing out
There is the still point
Yoga.

Prologue

He looked down again to check that the magazine was full and, as he pushed it back into the handle of the gun, he felt sick and dizzy but at the same time somehow clear-headed and strangely detached. It was as if he was no longer part of his own body, like watching his hands through the viewfinder of a video camera. He knew with absolute certainty that he was dying, knew there was no way he was going to survive and for a moment wondered if perhaps he had already become...dead. He wiggled his fingers. His hands looked so small, his legs felt cold and numb. He glanced around the dreadful, dingy cellar, lit only by an unshaded, dirty, sixty-watt bulb, vomiting its stale light onto the damp, yellowing walls. Everything looked so very far away, yet sharp and clear, like peering the wrong way down a telescope. All perspective on time had gone. How long had it been since the nightmare started, when had it all begun? If he could find the thread and untangle it all like a writer has to, where would it be, when you could say, "Chapter one... Once upon a time, there was this undercover customs and excise officer..." He eased himself carefully back into the armchair. There was no longer any pain now, but he was terrified of starting it off again. As his back felt the firm support of the chair, he carefully allowed his muscles to relax a little but winced at the very prospect of more pain – and heard himself make a sound somewhere between a sigh and a groan. There was a moment of relief that the sheer physical intimidation of the pain had not materialised, but he couldn't tell if he was still bleeding. For a moment, he was tempted to look down at his wounds and check, but he knew he couldn't, absolutely mustn't. Once had been dreadful enough. He couldn't even remember how many shots had hit him, but he knew it was a mess, knew there was no hope. He tried to force his thoughts in another direction, grasping at any chance to stay awake, to hang on to some semblance of reason in the darkening room. He focussed on what would happen next – which way would they come at him? Carefully creeping along the hallway to the cellar door, gesturing in silent mime to each other, giant shadows flickering onto the walls like a gothic '50s' film noir as they crept onto the creaking stairs down to the cellar; or American gung-ho, smashing through the door and rushing the stairs in a shower of exploding splinters and stun grenades? But most likely, he knew, it would be closer to the first and end not with a bang but a whimper. But it would end. It was all so desperate and part of him just wanted it to be over, though a deeper part would just not let go...so he tried something else, something more demanding, forced himself to build some sort of structure, a framework for the events that had culminated in him being here, a narrative imposing order on the fragmented chaos that was his mind. How had it all come to this, dying in this squalid room? That was what he needed, get back to that, the events, the order...

He had to stay awake, he was barely conscious and he sensed an imminent, impotent panic that at any moment the cloying, inky blackness lapping around the edges of his mind might suck him under once and for all into a smothering eternal darkness. He had to stay awake, had to fight, had to rage against the dying of his light, not because of any courage in the face of his own death and suffering, but the complete opposite – through the weariness and pain he was astonished to feel not welcoming relief at the prospect of the end but absolute terror of a point where he couldn't breathe, ever again. In fact, he wasn't actually thinking in any recognisable way at all. He had given up on everything, but parts of his mind and body just wouldn't let go. In spite of his complete lack of belief in anything outside of physical existence, he had entered on a desperate, primaeval battle to survive as long as he could, dredging deeply from somewhere in the darkest recesses of his being, a strategy for staying alive – keeping his mind in some kind of consciousness. He glanced around the room, which seemed steady and clear again, but his mind was still whirling with the shock of what had happened to him in the last hour, perhaps with the pent-up anguish of all that had happened in the last few days, weeks, months... God, was that all it had been, a few months? He couldn't be sure but less than a year for certain. Pictures of events began to form in his mind, in no particular order, shuffling into consciousness from the murkiness of his memory. He shook his head, trying to fix the images, to put them into some sort of order...that night in East Ham when the copper had been shot; the lead into the Salter case; gunshots, Euston Station, Manchester, the demo ...and above everything else, Val...yes, yes, that night in East Ham, that was sort of where you could start... Yes, that was the beginning of the Salter case, there in that dark street in the East End, that was where if you were a writer you could say 'Chapter One...'

Chapter 1

The badly lit street was quiet and still, in that edgy, orange streetlight way that is as quiet and still as it ever gets in London. Edwardian terraces, two stories, small front garden with a larger one at the back, bay windows. To Derek Brown, watching the street from the passenger seat of a standard-issue grey ford Sierra, they reminded him more of neat rows of seaside guest houses than the meaner back-to-back industrial terraces of his northern childhood. Small houses, small lives, small minds, narrow horizons – a spark of sensation rather than thought flickered through his mind, kindled by some remembrance of childhood. Then, like a spark, it was extinguished by the cold and dark as quickly as it had fired into existence. It was too late in the night, or early in the morning, for hanging on to anything. It was all he could do to stay awake through the successive, sapping waves of tiredness that swept over him every few minutes. All he really wanted to do was to let go and sink down into the warm, welcoming darkness of deep, dark sleep. Nearby, the clock on East Ham Town Hall struck four o'clock and somewhere a few streets away, as if it had been waiting for the last of the chimes as a starting signal, someone fiercely revved their car engine and accelerated off at speed, holding low gears as long as they could, the noise splintering the silence of the night. He jerked back into what passed for full awareness and blinked. He wiped a hand over his tired eyes and resumed watching the row of bumper-to-bumper parked cars, checking again the position of the van involved in the raid, with the four Armed Support met officers and one of his men in it. He could now feel the first of the adrenaline seeping into his system and with it the involuntary tightening of the stomach around what felt like a thousand potential little pinprick ulcers. No matter how often he did a job like this, it never got any better, never became just a routine. When he had first been selected for the Customs and Excise Special Team and all this had been new to him, there had at least been excitement – late-night action, a feeling of involvement with something mysterious, dangerous, thrilling, certainly more spine-tingling than the boring office jobs most of his other friends from university were doing. But now he just felt deeply bored with the whole played-out process, and at the same time infuriated by his inability to assert his consciousness over his physical reactions to it. So he was left with the worst bloody combination he could think of in the circumstances – all the edginess of physical fear without any of the compensating thrill. He looked at his watch – five past four. Nearly time. God, he wished this was over, it wasn't even his job. The bugger who'd planned it all had just gone on extended leave – heading for early retirement on grounds of ill health – whatever that meant – probably a more serious version of 'gardening leave' – and it had fallen to Derek to see it through, with only a day to familiarise himself with the plans. It had, of course, crossed his mind that the sudden, mysterious disappearance of the officer concerned at this precise moment might be linked in some way to the operation, but he'd had no time to start asking questions. And his bosses had been absolutely insistent that the raid should go ahead.

"Ten minutes, Bill," he spoke quietly to the middle-aged man sitting behind the wheel, who simply nodded in reply. "I'd better let the local nick know – it's too late even for those leaky bastards…isn't it?"

"Well…how long does it take to pick up a phone?" Bill's gruff, stereotypical Glaswegian accent added a hard edge to his only half-joking reply. Derek hesitated, microphone in hand. "Seriously, Derek, I'd give it another minute." Derek nodded. Bill was technically his superior but wasn't in field command on this one, so the decision still rested with Derek. But he knew as well as Bill how many jobs they'd lost because of the Met. The new Armed Support groups were tight enough but local nicks were notorious for leaking. On the other hand, they had to notify them at some stage, because they'd need local co-operation once the arrests were made. What's more, in less than five minutes, seven men, four of them armed, were going to smash down the door of a house and storm in screaming and shouting like banshees from hell to disorientate those inside. Even in London, neighbours were bound to react and phone the police, and the last complication Derek needed would be another van load of plods arriving with another armed support group – talk about friendly fire, Christ it didn't bear thinking about. Urban myths about such incidents were legion in the Customs, who detested working with the police, especially the Met., who they regarded as endemically corrupt and incompetent at just about every level. Unfortunately, fields of operations overlapped significantly and there was inevitable use of police facilities, especially the armed units which were more and more often a necessity nowadays. Customs Officers had arms training but it was much more effective to use the greater resources available through the met, hence the four with them tonight, two for the front, two for the back. They'd had to brief them, of course, but they'd made sure there was no opportunity for them to get in contact with anyone since. Mind you, Derek thought, they wouldn't want to jeopardise the chance of a good old shoot 'em up anyway, so they were safe enough – if safe was the right word. Derek looked along the street and again at his watch. Ten past four. He glanced across at Bill, shrugged and made the call, complete with verification code. His heart rate was up now and he could feel a shakiness in his voice as he spoke, asking them to have an arresting van standing by if possible – it would make it easier, and they'd have to use Forest Gate nick for the questioning anyway. *If* they arrested anyone. *If* there was anyone in the house. *If* there was any heroin in the place. As it wasn't Derek's case, he had no real idea how thorough and reliable the intelligence was, only that someone up top must have been convinced it was worth it to have been so adamant that it should go ahead despite lack of very much on the case notes. To Derek, it all seemed… a bit heavy-handed.

"Let's give it a couple of minutes now. I'll tell you what, Bill, I'm still feeling a bit uneasy with all this – did you look at the file?"

"File is a bit grandiose, isn't it? Fucking flimsy – and what about the missing page torn out of the notebook?"

"No idea, or why they insisted on it all going ahead so soon. There's just nothing remotely near the threshold for this sort of raid. I just keep feeling there's something they're not telling us."

"Well, nothing new, there, Derek." They both smiled.

If he'd been allowed more time, he'd have wanted to start again from the beginning, but he didn't have the time and at the end of the day you had to trust there were sound operational reasons for it all. And anyway, it didn't matter now, because it was too late for doubts. He gave the police the code he would use to summon the van, which they promised would be on standby and again checked his watch. Nearly there. Seconds stretching with tension now. Right. Four fifteen. Derek raised the mic to his lips and pressed the transmit switch. "Code, The Hammers – go, repeat go."

The second 'go' was pretty redundant – the van doors were already opening as Derek climbed out onto the pavement and reached back inside to lift out the 'sergeant's key', the 15 lb hammer he would use on the front door.

The officers converged like giant, cartoon bats drawn to the streetlight in front of the house, swarming into one great black shadow at the gate of number 29, an end-terrace with a narrow entry at the side. Without any word or pause, two of the armed police and Ron Macartney, the third customs officer, hauled themselves over the shoulder-high fence that blocked off the side entry. Unusually for this area, it wasn't wreathed with razor wire, and as soon as they were over Derek strode purposefully up to the front door, paused to weigh up the swing and without further ceremony smashed at the door with the hammer. The first blow left it splintered but still closed, the second shattered it wide open. Inside he could already hear the first sounds of reaction. Everything was happening very quickly now, the release of tension into action, Derek like the others functioning without conscious thought, with no awareness of the passing time, like adrenaline-fueled robots.

Simultaneously, a crackling and spitting from his radio told him the team at the back were in place, and then loud in his ear, "ARMED POLICE, come down with your hands on your head." Derek jumped slightly. He hadn't noticed the copper push past him as they'd bundled into the dark hallway, but there he was, blocking their way up the stairs and causing a bottleneck in the hall, knees slightly bent, completely still, 9 mm handgun braced with both hands. This was against all accepted practice and not what they'd gone through at the briefing – the idea was for one of them to go down the hall and clear the ground floor, and one to get upstairs before anyone could react, fast and furious. But he could hardly start arguing now, and the moment of advantage had already passed. But now he, Bill and the second copper were trapped behind this guy in the hall. For a short but seemingly infinite split second, everything seemed to stop, like someone had pressed the pause button on the video. Nothing happened, nobody moved, no sounds. And then from upstairs:

"Christ! OK, OK, fucking hell, you bastards. We're coming down. Stay cool, stay cool."

Despite feeling distinctly exposed and uneasy at the imposition of these new tactics, Derek and Bill exchanged amused smiles, it sounded so unlikely, like clichés cribbed from a badly written episode of 'The Bill'. The policeman didn't move or react in any way. "How many?"

"Three, no pieces, we're clean, man, take it easy." The voice was frightened, high, shaky. Derek barked another code word into his walkie talkie summoning an arresting van and almost immediately they could hear a siren, followed by the screech of tyres as it pulled up outside. Derek again smiled at Bill. "Bloody Sweeney – got a lot to answer for."

The second armed officer had manoeuvred himself into position to cover the first as well as he could but only the one in front had a clear line of fire.

Bill again grinned but they both felt it was all a bit dangerously crowded at the foot of the stairs now. Derek resumed watching the policeman, who appeared to have hardly moved a muscle. Only the sweat on his forehead betrayed any humanity beneath the expressionless exterior, as the first of the suspects appeared and began to descend the stairs, hands already on his head. He looked very young, pale, underfed Derek thought, but with an overlaying age ingrained on his face, which was grey and drawn with shock and fear – and years of taking drugs, if their intelligence was even half accurate.

"Slowly, very slowly, one step at a time, when I tell you. No sudden movements or I'll shoot."

"OK, take it easy." The young man looked completely bewildered. He came down one step.

"Right, next one…another."

Derek glanced around the shabby hallway where he was standing, for the first time taking in the details of the place. The nerves of earlier had gone, though he was still unhappy about the bloody copper, and the rush of adrenaline was still whizzing around his veins leaving him with that strange feeling of clarity and detachment. Everything seemed normal enough, but in a strange, heightened way that threw his tired perceptions out of true. Here he was, standing in a normal enough hallway in a normal house on a normal street while not two feet away there was a man with a gun pointing at another man who had his hands on his head. The whole scene had a dream-like quality to it like one of those Salvador Dali paintings, everything real, but nothing quite right. He could see the man on the stairs clearly now as he neared the bottom, dressed only in a pair of blue jeans, no shoes or socks, no top. As he reached the hall, shivering, vulnerable, the armed officer moved backwards carefully, keeping out of reach of any sudden lunge for the gun, his eyes constantly flicking from the man to the landing above. Two uniformed officers from the recently arrived arresting van were already at the door. They pushed through and grabbed the suspect with an apparently unnecessary level violence, pinned his arms behind his back and bundled him out of the door, one of them shouting the equally superfluous, "Right, you fucking bastard, you're nicked." Derek nearly laughed out loud.

The armed officer took up his position again at the bottom of the stairs.

"Right, next one, very, very slowly, I'm getting really twitchy here." A young girl about nineteen appeared at the top of the stairs, jeans, black T-shirt, hands already on her head. They hadn't expected her, they'd been told only two would be in the house that night, and the one they were really after was still upstairs. Derek again felt a sense of irritation and concern that the details he'd been given were wrong, even in such a minor way. Things were seldom as neat and tidy as expected in the field, but working to someone else's intelligence was edgy because you couldn't even be sure what it was you were supposed to have expected. And anyway, it should have all been over by now if they'd gone in like they should have.

Following each command, she began her descent. *Only one more to go*, Derek thought, the whole process making him impatient now, then another half hour to get them into the van and search the house – and sort out that wounded copper. Another wave of tiredness swept over him, but he knew you couldn't rush anything now they were in this situation. He glanced over his shoulder at Bill, standing behind him in the narrow hallway. Bill, his face pale, eyes red with sleeplessness, always at its worse in these hours of dawn, raised his eyebrows in a sympathetic gesture of weary agitation. Then he glanced back at the officer with the gun, covered from the doorway by his colleague.

Suddenly, there was a tremendous bang, and the officer at the bottom of the stairs collapsed heavily to the floor, gasping. The girl was screaming, "Jesus, Jesus, Jesus," and then the other armed officer was at the bottom of the stairs firing – two shots, then two more, each so loud that Derek was lying flat on the floor before he had any real sense of what was happening. His eyes had taken it all in, but his mind hadn't sorted it out into any meaningful pattern. He looked up, found his radio already in his hand, and reacted quickly and automatically.

"Alert, alert, officer down, officer down, get an ambulance here now! Ron, watch yourselves at the back." His hand was shaking badly, and as he warned his colleague at the rear of the house, he suddenly realised how vulnerable and exposed he was in the hall. If the bastard upstairs decided to go out in a blaze of glory, down the stairs and out the front door, all that stood between Derek and sudden death was only one bloody copper with a pistol and from his mate's record that was no fucking reassurance at all. The one who'd been hit was still alive and making a dreadful groaning now but not moving. There was blood everywhere, thick and sticky, on the wall, on the carpet. Derek was suddenly unsure how long he had been lying there. A strange silence had settled like fine dust over the hallway – or rather a stillness. There was, in fact, a great deal of noise, crackling radios, the man groaning, his wounds bubbling sickeningly away, more sirens outside and another, deep pounding sound that Derek couldn't place, until he realised it was the sound of his own heart thundering in his ears fit to burst his chest. *Oh, Christ, that's all I need, a fucking heart attack.* And he had a sudden vision of ending his days, now, lying in a bloody hallway, grasping desperately at his chest while the muscles of his face twitched and shuddered with spasmodic shock. He was over the numbness of the first shock now and the fear was kicking in – he was so frightened, he knew he was on the edge of an actual 'run for the door and keep going' panic. But then he took a deep breath and used his experience to assert control over himself. He knew that he would be more at risk if he gave way to his primal instinct and did a runner. He forced his attention back to the scene before the vision became a self-fulfilling reality, and made himself take in the details everything that was happening as a way of calming himself and maintaining steady control.

The armed policeman, stepping carefully over their colleague, was now advancing up the stairs. Still no reaction from up there. Derek knew that the policy now should have been to cover and contain and wait for more back up, but the copper was already near the landing and nothing would stop him now. Derek certainly wasn't going to try – and he was probably right that it would be quicker for his mate if they could get upstairs and finish it off double-quick like they should have done in the first place. He took another step. Derek edged forwards on his elbows to watch and saw that the girl was now sitting on the stairs, wedged upright against the wall, her eyes wide open, as if she couldn't quite believe what had happened. Apart from that, she looked OK except, oh Christ, he couldn't look, but couldn't look away – part of her head, above her right eye, was completely missing. There was blood all over the wall behind her. What held his gaze with morbid fascination though, was the *neatness* of the wound. He couldn't find any other word for the precise line of the edge of it, like someone had surgically trimmed away the whole section. Only the wall behind told the real, sordid truth, splattered with blood and what Derek realised with horror were bits of bone and hair and brains.

Outside, someone was shouting orders and swearing, and, in the distance, he could hear more approaching sirens. Then, outside at the back there was a shout, loud, followed by two shots, each one making Derek cower down. Another shout, another shot, a pause… then Derek's radio crackled into life. "Derek? Ron here. Christ, we've got him, back window, we've got him. Dead, he's dead, I think. Bastard. Jesus Christ." Fear, excitement, relief shaking his voice.

"OK, stay there but don't touch anything etc. etc. – wait for the plods, it's their game now. And keep out of the way until they arrive – he might not be the only one left up there."

As if in confirmation of this, the policeman on the stairs resumed his intense, methodical progress upwards until he'd disappeared from Derek's view. Derek was still on his hands and knees, and now aware of a growing nausea. Christ that's all I need, puking up. He turned to Bill, still on the floor

19

behind him. Bill looked up and smiled a wild, manic grin which threatened to unnerve Derek completely. Derek knew that he was still only holding on to his very sanity by the most tenuous of grips and that at any moment he could let go and plummet into a fit of sheer madness, start screaming and never stop. He'd been near to this edge before, on some really fucked up operations, but he'd never been as physically vulnerable for what felt like such a long time. The sight of the girl had shaken him to the core and shattered the calmness he'd managed to impose before. He was terrified again but at the same time felt a disturbing and unsettling fascination like if you stand on the edge of a sheer drop, fear and fascination, fear of the fall, fascination with the magnetic temptation dragging you towards the cool emptiness of the jump. The temptation of Christ... He knew what he had to do – talk, externalise, distract his mind outside of itself, that always worked for him. The only chance.

"Jesus, the shit'll hit the proverbial for this one, Bill. Where the fuck did we go wrong?"

"Less of the 'we' white man!"

"Hey, come on, I only organised the knock – like I said before, I knew there was something wrong about it all – what the fuck is this all about, Bill? And Christ, that stupid bloody plod fucked it all up and..."

"Look if it's all the same to you, or even if it isn't all the fucking same to you, I'd rather we had the post mortem, if you'll forgive the terminology, when I've got a rather better outlook than my nose stuck up your arse."

"That's what they say about doing 69, isn't it?" Derek responded.

"What the fuck are you talking about?"

"There's only one thing wrong with 69...and that's the view."

Derek started to giggle.

"Jesus Christ, I don't believe you, Derek."

Derek began to laugh now, and he could hear Bill starting to as well. Within seconds, they were both shaking with laughter like a pair of drunks, their nerves translating fear into hysteria. He kept his eyes away from the pool of sticky blood still oozing from the slumped body of the policeman, feeling not revulsion but a shiver of precarious gratification at his own escape.

Then 'ALL CLEAR ALL CLEAR ALL CLEAR...' from upstairs and the bedlam rush of people bundling into the hall – stretcher-bearers, paramedics, armed officers in flak jackets, jostling around Derek and Bill as they struggled to their feet. They both pushed their way out against the tide into the front garden, gulping in the cool fresh air that greeted them. For a second or two, neither of them could move, stunned by the circus that was playing itself out around them. The quiet street they had left behind not thirty minutes before was now filled with blue uniforms, yellow jackets, headlights, flashing lights, floodlights, all the fun of the fair, with a jerky soundtrack of the aggressive spitting and cackling of radios and raised voices. Photographers were flashing away and although he couldn't see it, he knew that behind the bright orange tape that sealed off the area would be the darkness and the shadows and the voyeurs.

Standing at the gate of the small front garden was a group of senior police officers. One of them looked up as Derek blinked his startled eyes in their direction and, too late to avoid contact, he saw one of them point in his direction. He glanced at Bill, hoping that by looking away, he would become somehow invisible – if he couldn't see them, perhaps they couldn't see him. It was worth a try.

"You, the customs man, over here please."

The voice was more than loud and insistent enough to ensure that Derek heard, and, while a little gruff and coarse around the edges, full of that natural authority that would brook no refusal.

"Oh dear, oh dear, I think someone wants a little wee word with you Derek," Bill smirked,

"Oh. Fuck, beam me up, Scottie."

"Too late for that, laddie – you're doomed. When Malone finds out what's going on, it'll be a no anaesthetic vasectomy for you, for sure. And with all your enemies, he'll probably put it out to competitive tender. In fact, come to think about it, I might put in a bid myself…"

Derek moved towards the gate, light-headed, ecstatic to be alive, but with a growing unease at just how far out of his depth he was with all this. He stepped back to let the first of the stretchers out, carrying the covered-up body of one of the night's victims zipped up tight in the blackness of the body bag.

He turned back for a moment and smiled at Bill. "You see, Bill, there's always someone worse off than yourself."

Chapter 2

i

Derek jerked awake, dry mouth, disorientated, wrecked. He'd got back to his flat around six thirty, had two huge brandies and crashed out on top of the bed. The team had agreed an afternoon meeting, 2 pm, no one would have been fit for anything earlier, but they couldn't leave it much later. There would be investigations galore now – police would need statements, Customs would want to know what the fuck had gone wrong and so did the team, so did Derek – what the fuck went wrong and why the fuck he'd been given the case. He blinked and shook his head to try to shake off the deep urge to just go back to sleep. But he knew he wouldn't actually be able to. He looked at his watch – eight thirty, barely two hours tossing and turning, his mind whirling and he knew he was still in deep shock at the events in East Ham.

Always someone worse off…he remembered his parting words to Bill and smiled. It was a standing joke between them, but it certainly served as a pick me up sometimes when he was getting things out of proportion. Let's face it, we all accumulate worries and anxieties that are relatively petty in the scheme of things but which loom large in our own universe, real risk versus perceived risk. Is the food cooked properly, will the plane crash, will I get cancer? To say nothing of the anxieties that dominate day to day existence – promotions, personal life, and for Derek the claustrophobia that made a drama of every trip on the tube. None of it was rational. Bill always used the example of Lockerbie – you live in a small village miles from big cities, far from fears of crime and terrorism and a plane blows up and lands on the village, victims of a global intrigue thousands of miles away. Hamming up his accent, he would always end with "So, laddie, if you're in the wrong place at the wrong time, well you're in the wrong place at the wrong time and there's fuck all you can do about it – you're doomed!"

But in the end, deep down inside, we all know that there will come a day when there isn't anyone else worse off – because we are all actually in the process of dying and will one day actually die and as we struggle and gasp for that last breath, it is as bad as it gets. And in the process of arriving there, most of us will gradually crumble with age, go lame, start dribbling, suffer pain. We might give birth astride the grave but the pain of birth isn't ours, we just slide out. But our own death is uniquely ours and ours alone, and it will never be easy and seldom quick. And suddenly a wave of sadness and self-pity swept over him already all on his own, directionless, approaching forty and absolutely clueless where he was heading or how he'd suddenly got where he was, from bright young spark to washed-up washed out lost cause…But he was caught in the trap - life was stale for him but it was still life. He looked down and realised his hands were shaking and he flinched at a sudden flashback of the dead girl's face. He poured another large brandy, lit up a Marlborough and sucked desperately hard for the nicotine kick, gulping the brandy down in one, sighing as the first fire subsided into a soothing glow, first in his stomach, then glowing through his muscles and relaxing his mind. And the shaking stopped. And his rambling thoughts slowed down, leaving him just tired and bewildered. This simply wasn't like him, not at all. But what was worrying was that somewhere in the confusion and exhaustion, he had the unsettling feeling that it wasn't all just to do with last night. There was the distinct possibility that while the events of last night had certainly jarred and shaken him up, something much darker and deeper than shock had been stirred up into the mix. It was as if some distant doubts from the periphery vision of his brain had been circling like vultures and were now peck peck pecking into the foreground of the swirling, twisting tornado that was his consciousness.

Everything spinning and whirling. Except for the girl, clear, sharp and dead on the stairs – quiet and still in the eye of the storm. He shook his head again and made a coffee.

ii

The run-down Victorian HQ building he'd nicknamed 'Victory Mansions' was even worse inside than out. Bleak corridors, bare lightbulbs, the very lowest end of 'utilitarian'. But today it matched his mood exactly. He walked up to the third floor where his team were based and into the large room where they met for briefings. It was just two o'clock and abnormally quiet on the floor. As he walked into the room, the six people already there, all reading or writing notes, looked up at him. Four of them were sat at the high table at the far end, two uniformed senior Met officers and two besuited senior officers from Customs – his well-respected Senior Investigating Officer Phillip Manson and the sleek, well-manicured Assistant Chief Investigating Officer David Maloney. Phillip was respected because he had been a good field officer and understood the pressures of the job. He didn't over socialise with the teams, kept a polite distance – but you instinctively knew that he *understood what it was all about.* The job, the sense of public service, the essential duty to protect the country. Malone, on the other hand, was so far up the ladder the rest of us would need oxygen just to breathe up there.

The other two people already there were Bill and Ron McCartney, the one who'd been round the back of the property. They both looked as bad as he felt and before either could say anything, Maloney started the meeting, "Good, well, that's everyone, so let's convene this meeting."

"What's the status of it?" Ron's incisive Liverpudlian accent had just the right amount of challenge in the tone.

"Status?" asked Maloney.

"Yes. Is this part of a formal investigation or informal debrief or what?"

"Aye," said Bill. "Is it to be minuted – and if so by who and for who?"

Maloney looked down at the papers in front of him. "This is simply a debrief, not part of a formal investigation."

Derek sensed some evasion is Malone's answer and asked, "So no minutes, no record of what's said here? Nothing attributable?"

"I thought it was clear what I said," replied Maloney, clearly annoyed by all this, undermining his authority in front of the Met officers. "Now can we begin…"

"No, not yet," said MaCartney, "We know there will be an internal police investigation and also a criminal investigation into the case and the deaths. We know Customs will have its own internal investigation and I'm sure I speak for us three that we want to help in any way we can, obviously, but we don't know what part if any today plays in all that. I for one don't want to be saying things today that might be somehow used against me. We're knackered and in shock at what went down last night. If there's any doubt in my mind about today, I'm out until my staff rep is present."

"Absolutely," said Bill, and Derek nodded emphatically.

Malone came back in a much less formal tone, "There's absolutely no need to worry. We thought we'd have an informal debrief while it is all fresh in your minds and we really appreciate you coming in after that ordeal."

"So why are the Met here?" Derek knew he needed to tread carefully but it was the elephant in the room and a bloody big one at that. "The operation was Customs and Excise. I know the criminal investigation is a police matter but surely the debrief should just be us at this stage."

He noticed that Phillip Mason hadn't once looked up from his papers but just sat twiddling his pencil. Neither of the policemen looked up either. Malone replied, sounding even more conciliatory.

"Yes, yes, I do understand exactly what you're saying and why, but we are all working together. It's a terrible ordeal for all of us, especially you three but let's remember, we can't separate everything out as neatly as you're implying, Ron –

the Armed support with you last night were, of course, Met officers and one of them has now died..." he paused, and Derek sighed, looking down at the floor, "...so the force have a keen interest in how the events unfolded."

"I'm not surprised – their guy fucked it up and put us all in mortal danger," growled Bill. "I don't want to speak ill of the dead but we'd been through everything with them and he just didn't follow any of it."

The older of the two police officers looked up.

"Well, that's exactly what we want to know. David, do you mind if I just say something? Listen, let's be absolutely clear – no minutes, no record of the meeting whatsoever – unless any of you want particular points to be recorded, OK? We honestly need to know as soon as possible the train of events. What happened at the back of the house seems to be completely straightforward – that was you, I think Mr McCartney? But Messrs Brown and Haggerty, you and the second 'front of house' armed officer were the most prominent witnesses to what happened in the hall. We just need to know as soon as possible what went wrong there. Something obviously did – and in no way are we thinking in terms of the operation at that point that it in anyway reflects on actions by Customs Officers. We would at some point be interested in the nature of the intelligence that led to the raid..."

"Me too..." said Derek. Malone lowered his eyes.

"...but for now, we'll all just have to trust each other..."

Bill snorted and for the first time, Mason lifted his head. "Come on, Bill. There are two dead suspects and a dead policeman. I know you guys are shattered but let's do everything we can to help, eh? It's a mess and we need to get it sorted for everyone's sake."

"Thanks, Phillip, well said. I hope we can. It all probably looks too formal, us sat up here," said the policeman and stood up. "Come on, let's just get rid of the table and sit down and talk through the whole things. No minutes, no secret mics, no formal record. I will take notes but not attributable to individuals and I'll let you see them before we leave. Is that acceptable to everyone? If we don't, details will get lost that might help us all, we need as much as you can recollect at this time. Good. Now before we start, Any chance of some coffee, David?"

"And biscuits?" asked Ron, and it was the chance for everyone to step back and relax, smiles all round.

Two hours later and the police had left. "OK," said Malone, "thirty-minute break and then we'll just finish off our side of all that. An hour at the most – guillotine at 5.30, seriously. It's a terrible situation, we're all tired and upset by it all – and you three look completely done in – but we need to get a couple of matters sorted out."

iii

Malone started off the final session. "Our main concern now is to sort out any loose ends at our end. Before we do that, I'm well aware Derek that you must be feeling particularly fed up with all this, being put on the case so late and the case file being so…slim."

Derek nodded, unsure where all this was going. Malone continued, "Last night the police view was that the whole thing had gone wrong because we weren't properly organised and hadn't done our homework. It didn't take long for them to realise that it was their guy on the ground that fucked it up, nothing to do with the intel."

"Or lack of it," Derek said.

"Or lack of it," Malone agreed, to everyone's surprise. It might have been exhaustion on their part, but all three of them were surprised at how reasonable and even compassionate, Malone was sounding. Derek thought he even saw a glimmer of approving surprise flicker across Phillip's face.

"The truth is that I insisted on following through with the operation because what little information we had suggested it might be crucial in taking a huge shipment of heroin off the streets. I know we normally try to follow the goods and get the whole chain rather than take out just a few foot soldiers, but I had reason to believe that this was so big that we couldn't risk losing sight of it. Unfortunately, that wasn't the case and, in the end, it wasn't worth it on any level.

"So you guys are completely in the clear and will be fully exonerated by any enquiry. It will not appear as a blot on your records. You will have to appear as covert witnesses in the police investigation and probably in court but as far as David and myself are concerned, the matter is closed with Customs and Excise. I'm just glad you are all safe, and with that in mind, I'm granting you all seven days additional – and compulsory – leave. You'll report back a week today for reassignment duties, hopefully feeling much better and back to your normal selves." He looked pale and tired but he smiled as he stood up.

There was an awkward silence as the words sank.

And then Phillip said, "Thank you, sir – I can see that this lot are definitely in need of the rest and I'm sure they're appreciative of the gesture."

Derek blinked and said, "Yes, of course, thank you sir," but his initial impulse to gratitude had been undermined by the nagging thought of the missing page in the file. Perhaps the raid had been authorised to deliberately thwart the normal process of surveillance. Perhaps Malone and his well-connected superiors didn't want anyone following this particular chain up the ladder to the roof…but he was too tired now to articulate it even to himself, and he was actually more than grateful for the leave. He knew he couldn't stay awake for much longer and would probably sleep for the whole week.

iv

And he did, pretty much, drifting, surfacing, smoking, drinking, sleeping, for the first 48 hours anyway. After that, it was still just a blur, but he was feeling physically a lot better when he finally reported for duty. He was still getting flashbacks but they were shorter. What he couldn't shake off, though, were his nagging concerns about the reasons for the raid, especially that flimsy file, the insistence the raid took

29

place – and that missing page, torn out of Gerry Hardcastle's notebook – and what had happened to Gerry? Where the fuck was he on his 'extended leave'?

Derek didn't know him except by sight, he was on a different team based on the floor below, but he did know he was a very experienced Investigating Officer. Derek had spent some hours during the week phoning colleagues to check up on him and no one had a bad word to say about him – and they were all surprised at his sudden disappearance – for that's what it was – no one seemed to know where he'd gone on his gardening leave. So he was glad to be back on duty, hoping to track back over the case with Ron and Bill.

But when he walked into the office, he quickly spotted that neither were there and before he could ask anyone, Phillip Manson came out of his office and shouted him in.

"Hello, Derek, welcome back, come in, sit down…coffee?"

Derek nodded, "Black please, no sugar."

"Two coffees please, one black no sugar, one black with two. Thanks. So, Derek, how are you feeling now? Managed to get some rest? You look a lot better than when we last met!"

Derek grinned. "Well, I guess I couldn't have been much worse. We were pretty shaken up – it was so fast, so close…" he paused as the secretary brought in the coffees and took a grateful gulp of his.

"Yes, it must have been. I've spoken to Bill and Ron separately this morning and each of them said the same. Not surprising really, not exactly every day we come that close to violence like that. And death. I've never once been shot at. In fact, worst I've had was that raid in Canning Town years ago – I think you were on that, weren't you?"

"Yes, it was my first field op for drugs – the MAD one? Up until now that was my worst as well, bit of a baptism of fire really. One or two dodgy moments but nothing like this – or that either."

MAD was the acronym for Mutual Aids Destruction. Derek was on his second case when he was called into the knock on another case, last minute, Phillip the field officer in charge. The target was a flat in one of the pre-war red brick blocks, entrance from walkways. They'd smashed open the door, and as they rushed into the hall, a primitive pulley system winched up a hinged plywood board flat against the hall wall., embedded with syringe needles sticking out like a deadly pine forest, needle after needle…all supposedly infected with HIV from addicts… hence 'mutual aids'.

He'd been nearly the last one in, and actually no one had been scratched…but the idea of it still made him shudder. They both paused, thinking back.

"Anyway," said Manson. "Let's not dwell on the good old days! Last week was bad and could have been worse. So as I've said to the other two, we're easing you back in, light duties for a few weeks, if that's OK with you."

Derek wasn't sure what to say. He trusted Phillip but something didn't feel right. "All separate? Doing what? I really wanted to get hold of the Hardcastle file and go through it again…"

"No, Derek, not possible I'm afraid…"

"Not possible? Why?"

"Well, for a start, it isn't there any more…Malone and a couple of spooks have removed it – actually, the spooks did – even Malone looked pissed off and confused. Whatever's going on, I honestly don't think he's involved this time."

"Spooks? Which ones?"

"No idea – MI5 or 6 I guess, not Met. Not Special Branch. So no point in even thinking about it. Gone."

"Christ…" Neither really knew what to say, but after another pause, Manson took a deep breath. "So, lighter duties. I know it all sounds odd but that bit has come from me. I honestly think you need more of a break than a week but I know you three wouldn't want to be just kicking your heels at home…"

"OK, thanks, sir. I'm not going to argue or pretend – I'm still shaken up by it all. So, what have you got in mind for me?"

"Well, we've got an obs on towards the end of the week, seems straightforward enough, low level – thought you might like it, it would mean a weekend back oop north for you. We think the mark is heading for a meeting in Manchester and it's looking like it will happen on Friday, so you could have a free weekend up there – what do you think?"

Derek realised he was still too tired to think properly but at first hearing it sounded great. He'd not been back to Manchester or Salford for…years. Kept meaning to but it just hadn't happened, there never seemed to be the time. Plain and simple inertia, in the absence of any compelling 'pull factor'. Most of his old mates had left now and there weren't any relatives still up there. But he could get in touch with the old friends who were still left, Pete in particular. Yes, it could be just what he needed to draw a line under East Ham.

"Who'd be on the team?"

"Ah, now 'team' is a bit grand – just two of you…with all the cuts we really can't justify more. It's not 100% intel, might be a dummy run…"

"Two? Who's the other one?"

"Val Henderson…do you know her?"

"Henderson, yes, seen her in the pub on Fridays a couple of times – works on the second floor, doesn't she? VAT teams? Christ, she's barely out of probation…has she done anything like this before? I'm not being funny but two might just be enough if we both know what we're doing but…"

"Come on, Derek, there has to be a first time for everyone."

"Yes but two doesn't leave any slack for mistakes – and me being walking wounded and her a complete novice, Christ it isn't fair – on her, I mean."

Phillip sighed. "I know, I know but we have to work with what we've got. Actually, I think it will be good for both of you – she's really bright, got a university background like you, not sure what she studied. But more to the point, her SOI really rates her. Quick learner, dedicated, enthusiastic – a bit like you a few years ago…you know what I mean, Derek. Might rekindle some of that enthusiasm again. For what it's worth, despite everything, I think you are still potentially one of our best field officers…and I think we can agree that you've lost your way a bit in the last few years – so perhaps this East Ham business can be a sort of watershed, red line, fresh start? What do you think?"

Derek was desperately trying to process it all – he knew it was true, he'd certainly lost his way and failed to 'fulfil his potential', as they say. But he hadn't articulated it as clearly as Phillip now had and the unexpectedly brutal clarity of it winded him. But what he did suddenly grasp immediately was that it was true something positive had to come out of East Ham, something had to change in response to the deep shock of it all. Here he was, nearly 40, and failing on just every aspect of his life. He'd been avoiding confronting it all, and now he could see it. Clearly. And the biggest thing he felt was whether he was in time to rescue anything at all from the last few years of drifting or whether he'd drifted far too far now from the safety of the shore…

"Yes. Yes, when did you say?"

"Well, at the moment it looks like coming Friday…I know that's not long to prepare…"

Derek was actually pleased by the short run in, as it also meant not too long to get anxious about it all but enough to brief himself and introduce himself to Val Henderson. "No, that's fine. Where's the file? Hopefully there is a file this time!"

Chapter 3

He was right that the short lead in was a good thing for him and for Val. Once he'd checked out the file, he realised it was a low level and pretty straightforward case and he'd arranged to meet Val. He'd knew who she was, a face in the swirling crowd of the packed Friday afternoon pub sessions in 'The Black Lion', where the Customs and Excise investigation teams used to mark the end of the week – 'poets day', piss off early tomorrow's Saturday. They never did piss off early as they didn't work regular hours anyway – and the sessions went on all afternoon sometimes – with Derek always one of the last to leave. It had all been really good fun when he first left university and started in the job but latterly as the years had worn on, he realised he was now staying late because he had nowhere else to go. Worse, he had started to dread going back to his empty flat, more often nowadays on his own. In the early days he'd always ended up with someone – from one of the teams or someone just out in the pub for the night but always someone. It had all been so easy, just a continuation of life at uni minus the drugs bit of course – but lots of sex and rock and roll. In the end, though, somewhere along the way, he'd gradually found it…stale, boring? Not quite the right words…tiresome, repetitive? He couldn't place exactly when he'd become aware, it was so gradual that he'd never really consciously thought about it, almost hadn't noticed it happening. He'd got bored with it all, and like everything, he now realised, he'd just drifted and drifted…

Still, perhaps there was time to turn it all around and everything that had happened at East Ham was surely a good place to start, a still point to stop, look back on it all, pause, assess – and turn it around, look forward and plan. Readjust, realign.

So, he'd taken the file down to the second floor and sat with her to go through the details and found out she'd already been through it, thoroughly. She seemed confident, asked all the right questions, a real eye for detail – and she listened carefully when he explained some of the techniques they might need to avoid being spotted. He could see why her SIO rated her, definitely a fast track candidate. He felt greatly reassured, and on top of that, she was charming and attractive, she had really bright eyes, though he had the uneasy feeling that there was a slight hint of amusement somewhere in that sparkle. All the same, he was beginning to feel more relaxed about Friday and the weekend back 'home'.

Derek was wrong about the sparkle. It wasn't amusement behind the brightness, it was a deep uneasiness. She found the briefing far from reassuring. She'd been excited to be selected for the assignment, her first drugs field operation, if you could call it an operation. And she'd been intrigued to find out it was Derek Brown who'd be leading it. The whole floor was buzzing after the shootings in East Ham but even before that he'd often been the subject of office tittle-tattle. Most of it seemed to relate to personal scandal and days when he'd been an enthusiastic firebrand taking on the management…and he'd had a certain charisma about him when she'd seen him across the pub on Friday sessions – funny enough, interesting on the odd occasion she'd heard him talking politics, just that hint still edginess, – but a bit … she wasn't sure of the right word – a bit tired? But her older teammates still told legendary tales about him, about his drinking, his womanising, his incisive wit and quick thinking as association rep, so much so they'd nicknamed him 'Red' Brown (of course) but also quieter stories of his kindness and sensitivity. So 'intriguing' was the best choice in the end. But today, he presented as distracted, dishevelled, jittery, the last qualities she needed on her first real outing. It wasn't because of what she'd heard had happened in East Ham, they all knew that wasn't his fault – but from what she had witnessed today, he just didn't look …

right…she wasn't an expert but she'd have said he wasn't ready at all for any sort of responsibility out in the field, so soon. The word 'unnerved' came to mind – her and him. She really needed this first op to go well, not just because she was ambitious but because she genuinely loved the job, wanted to learn it all and excel at it all – and if that brought promotion, well and good. So jury out on Derek Brown – though when she unpicked it looking at her notes later, she'd been impressed by some of the tips he'd gone through with her and a big part of his reputation was that he was a very good field officer. And there was no doubt that there was something …attractive …about him, perhaps even more so with the hints of vulnerability and world-weariness …intriguing.

FRIDAY MORNING.

He looked at Val and made himself relax a little, sensing how tense she must be, knowing that he must try not to show even a hint of nerves himself, and even less of the irritation he felt at being there at all. After all, it wasn't her fault that she'd been landed with him in this way, and it certainly wasn't her fault that on top of everything else, he had the mother of all hangovers. He must keep reminding himself that this was her first surveillance case, and although it was a fairly straightforward one, it was important that it went as smoothly as possible to give her the confidence that she'd need for future operations. Following someone while remaining unobserved is not at all the easy business they make it look on TV. It needed focus, a cool head and very quick thinking. In theory that was why he was there, as the mature, experienced, calming influence, though that was a bit of a joke really, because in fact he always felt anxious himself when doing this sort of job, even when it was all as clear-cut as this one appeared to be and even without everything that had happened to him. And after all, you needed some adrenal. He had learnt the first and most critical lesson of all, which was never be complacent, never underestimate the most straightforward of situations, they could turn into a dangerous fuck up in seconds without warning – and if he hadn't learnt it years ago he'd certainly had the lesson of a lifetime last week – fuck, only a week ago? Even on a job like this things could go wrong. And then there were the staffing cuts – just two officers didn't leave any margin for error. Also, he was uneasily aware that he was not one hundred per cent over the East Ham incident yet – the shock of the shooting, the sudden death, especially that young girl on the stairs – so close, so fast, so easy and all such a bloody waste – and not an ounce of *anything found in the house*. It all seemed like a classic set up, but for him it had resonated somewhere deep inside, stirred up something he still hadn't confronted let along got over. And for all the way we think about our inner selves as something more than blood and bone, well, he'd seen what there was inside, splattered all over the wall behind her head. Just blood and bone after all. And since, he'd felt twitchy, restless, a shakiness that wasn't quite explained by his increased drinking. He'd found himself developing what he felt was a distinctly unhealthy introspection, a kind of anxious brooding on the significance of events, in particular the events that had made up his existence, his life so far. In the past, he had been able to shrug most things off with little effort, and his crazy, hectic existence had left little time to contemplate anything at all. But he couldn't shrug this off, it hung around him like a cold damp mist, or as The Boss would have it like a brooding 'darkness of the edge of town'. He was trying to ignore it, weakly hoping it would go away, and now he was thinking that this trip back to Manchester, to the place where he had been young, different, nascent, might help him to let some light into the present impending darkness. Part of him half mockingly described his symptoms as the cliched bog standard mid-life crisis, but another knew that it was not just that, or if it was, it was far more serious than how the stereotypical crises were portrayed. Seeing that plod and the young girl, both zipped up in their body bags had forced into his consciousness the wretched truth that if it had been him, as it so easily could have been, lying there panting out his last gasp, what the fuck would his life have amounted to? No kids, no wife, nobody to even notice he'd been here, let alone miss him when he'd gone. It would have made not a scrap of difference to the universe if he'd never been born at all, not a scrap.

He looked at Val, young, enthusiastic Val and knew he had to get his mind out of it all, at least for the time being, or he could easily botch up even this operation, which would be a disaster for him after the East Ham debacle and do her no good at all. He knew he could distract himself by talking, it always worked. Anything would do to get his mind out of himself at least in the short term.

"How are you feeling?" he asked, trying to sound firm and confident, casual, friendly.

"Fine thanks." No lead into easy chat – clipped tones, but sounding in fact anything but the nervousness he'd expected.

"Well, that's good but it's natural enough to be a bit anxious, the adrenaline keeps you on your toes, it's better than being too laid back, especially with only the two of us, you need to keep your wits about you." He glanced around, keeping a studiedly casual eye on their target, ahead of them in the queue for the Manchester train, platform 12, Euston. "Before all the bloody cutbacks, there'd have been three or probably four of us on a job like this." He paused and in the split second of silence that followed, he realised that this was hardly the confidence-building inspiration he was supposed to be providing. He quickly added, "But I'm sure we'll cope – that's what they rely on when they make these cutbacks – the dedication of the officers on the ground – seriously, there's nothing to worry about."

"Well, that's just as well, Derek, because until now I wasn't worried about anything. Did you have a bad night on the town last night?"

So it did show – and not just the hangover, but that something was wrong with him. Well, anyway, she already seemed confident enough without his efforts, in fact he was a bit taken aback by the undertone of challenge in her voice. He was after all a full grade above her, and he couldn't make out that sparkle in her eyes again – was it mocking or dry humour or just sheer confidence? Kids these days, he smiled to himself. But she wasn't going to put him off a point he thought was important, even if she did make him feel a bit like an old schoolteacher. "Yes, well, I just get really pissed off – they go on in public about the campaign against drugs in those fine moral tones they like to use, but in practice, they're cutting back on our ability to effectively combat it – words are cheap, staffing isn't."

"We'll manage, Derek, if you keep your mind on the job."

"What? Oh yeah, sorry, I didn't mean to go on." He looked at her. Well, she certainly had something about her, this one – a sort of freshness that stopped short of being offensive or irritating, a vitality that somehow wrong-footed him and made him feel worn out and rather shabby, which was just about what he'd been thinking when he started the conversation.

He glanced again at their target, conspicuous enough with his black trench coat, and his white bald head. It is surprising how anonymous most of us are but there was something amateurish about this guy which reassured Derek – because experience should have taught him to accentuate the anonymity. Their instructions were to follow him to Manchester until he made a contact up there. The tip-off had said that there would definitely be a meet, but beyond that there were no details. Derek had double-checked the intel and there was no doubt it was good regarding a big importation of heroin within the last two weeks, and they knew that the importers would want rid of it as quickly as possible into the hands of the dealers and the pushers and into the needles of the junkies. Smack flowing one way, and big, big money swilling back the other. Big money like any other big money, whether it was drugs-money or 'legitimate', there wasn't much difference in the end- it was all dirty and corrupt when there were piles and stinking, steaming piles of it. Whenever there was money to be made, Derek thought, look for the poor sod at the wrong end of it, the poor bastard who is the source of all profit – the junkie, the sweatshop worker, the consumer, you and me.

Anyway, the tip-off was that someone was trying to arrange a sale up in Manchester, where Thatcher's creative unemployment had led to the development of a brand-new enterprise zone for drugs dealers. So their job at this stage was just to keep an eye on the courier. Derek had arranged to be met at Manchester by a local team with a car standing by just in case. Luckily, this was just a case involving C&E, no plods this time, and he was sure he could rely on his colleagues to have everything ready in Manchester. The only problem was that they wouldn't know who Derek and Val were, nor the target, and neither Derek nor Val would recognise any of the Manchester Division. And they could hardly advertise their presence. The only hope was radio contact.

Derek felt for the small transmit switch that projected into the palm of his right hand from the sleeve of his jacket. The radio itself was wrapped around his chest and connected to a tiny earpiece. Being kitted out like this was known in the job as being 'coverted', and it should have given Derek a sense of security, but it didn't. You can forget High Tech this and digital that. Communications in the field was still the most problematic element of most operations – it only all works on T.V. propaganda programmes designed to make would-be criminals feel uneasy. He looked at Val and decided to keep the conversation going, despite the rather cool tenor of the responses he'd been getting so far – apart from anything else it would look more natural. "I've got the radio fitted, by the way, so we should be able to make contact as soon as we get up to Manchester – assuming he stays on the train all the way up – it stops twice before then, I think."

"Oh well, that's reassuring – God, Derek, I've been on the team long enough to know what they say about the radios they give us – the one reliable thing about them is that they're not reliable. SNAFU's they call them. Don't they?"

"Yes, I'm sorry, of course, yes. Anyway, you never know, we might be OK." She really was alert, he thought, but why so sharp with me? Perhaps it's just the way nerves come out in her.

"Well, according to Bill Haggerty in the pub once," and here she put on a Scots accent, "it's as inescapable as death, my dear. It might not be today, but you can be sure that it'll happen one day, and there's never a good time for it."

"Yes, well he's right of course. It's incredible when you think they cost over £500 each – anyone with £150 quid in his pocket could do better down the High Street – but we're tied up with contracts with the yanks, that's life nowadays – no staff, but plenty of useless hardware casting a fortune."

"Not like it were in the good old days when you were a lad, eh?" she grinned and he found himself grinning back, though it was a remark that pricked him more than it once would have done – he was feeling altogether too vulnerable for his own comfort. It was lucky that her grin was so infectious and anyway, before he had time to think of a response, the queue began to shuffle forward towards the now open ticket gate. The main thing about following any target is to be as natural as possible, to get into a sort of role-playing – imagining that you really are just another traveller. Not only does this help to prevent you from looking guilty and drawing attention to yourself in some unconscious way, but it calms you down. Derek picked up his suitcase and moved forward, Val at his side. He looked at her again, and saw the tension in her tightly closed lips, betraying her anxiety to him, though no one else in the queue would have noticed. She was keeping herself well under control, certainly looking less flustered than he had probably felt on his first 'excursion'. As they neared the gate, he could feel the muscles of his stomach tighten, feel the acid and adrenaline flowing, reminding him that no matter how often you did this sort of thing, no matter how minor and straightforward the job, it was never something you could do without it taking hours or days off your life. And over the years that all added up, he thought wearily, a sort of war of attrition against yourself.

The target was only a couple of feet ahead of them now. In his left hand he carried a black executive case, and with his right he showed his ticket to the collector, and turned, just for a split second, to look over his shoulder. Derek only just managed to avoid direct eye contact. He looked at Val and, to avoid looking back up too soon, he said the first thing that came into his head, "Have you got the tickets?" He knew it was a stupid thing to say as soon as he'd said it, and it threw Val.

"What?" She stared at him, a confused look bordering on the early stages of panic flickering across her face. She was wary enough of Derek anyway, but he seemed to be losing it, behaving in a thoroughly bizarre way that she couldn't understand and it was making her nervous and a little bit impatient with him now. This was her first chance to prove herself in the field and even if he thought it was clever to be casual or cavalier about it, she bloody well wanted to get it right. She was beginning to think that he probably had the idea that it was somehow heroic or cool to throw away your career with Noel Coward nonchalance, but she was just starting out on hers and it really mattered. She knew that as a woman it was going to take more dedication and effort than it would have done for a man, post-feminism or not post feminism (and what a joke that was, as far as she could see from male banter on the teams, it was mostly definitely still pre rather than post for most people). It made her really angry and frustrated that for all his reputation for left wing politics, he didn't appear to have the same determination and commitment to his own career or more importantly any awareness and sensitivity to what this might mean to hers.

As calmly as possible, he replied, "Oh, nothing, it's alright, I've found them." He took them out of his pocket and risked a quick look up. The man had disappeared through the barrier and seconds later they were following him down the ramp to the platform, where Derek's sigh of relief was lost amongst the chaotic bustle, noise and urgency you find on the platforms of all large railway stations.

"It's like the storm before the calm." Derek gestured at the crowd bustling along the platform, quite pleased with the phrase. "When I was a kid, I used to think it was as if the train was a hoover, sucking in all the noise and colour and life off the platform and whisking it away leaving a complete vacuum

– no noise, no movement, complete stillness." He wasn't sure what he expected her to say. She said nothing, feeling more and more unsure of what she was dealing with.

The man was about a coach length ahead when he decided to get into the train, just after the restaurant car. Derek and Val moved to the same doorway and followed him into the compartment. The aisle was full of jostling people. Some, having found places, were trying to push their luggage into the racks, while others were still making increasingly frantic efforts to manoeuvre their way through to vacant seats. Derek couldn't see the target as he and Val edged forward through the melee. No matter, perhaps he'd just gone into the next carriage. Val said something which Derek couldn't quite hear above the noise and confusion in the carriage.

"What?" he asked, ducking to avoid a heavy suitcase being swung onto an overhead luggage rack. In reply, Val pointed towards the window and Derek turned to look. He stared for a moment, not quite taking in what he was seeing. The target was standing just by the window, outside on the platform.

"Oh Christ," he muttered. The man glanced in each direction and then began to walk down the platform, back towards the ticket barrier. Derek froze for a second, before Val brought him to his senses, pushing him gently towards the end of the compartment.

"These look OK," she said, pointing at two vacant seats with their backs to the engine.

"Yes. yes, they'll do fine." He pushed his case onto the rack above and reached down for hers.

"No, it's OK, I'll keep this by me," she said, putting the small overnight case behind the seat. She lowered her voice, "There's nothing we can do now is there?" She looked at him, sensing that, for all his experience, the events had caught him off balance.

"No, you're right, we might as well settle down and get comfy. You know, this is real text-book stuff. I'm afraid I've done exactly what I was warning against – been a bit complacent about him. I just never thought." Derek paused and shivered slightly with the sheer embarrassment he was feeling. He could have kicked himself, falling for such an obvious tactic. The question now, though, was what to do next. He sat down by the window, and Val sat beside him. He looked out at the now almost deserted platform.

"One of us should have hung around on the platform until we were sure," he said. "It's my fault." Val didn't know what to say – he was right, it really *was* his fault and she was pissed off about it, but she felt guilty as well, that he was obviously feeling so bad – and then she felt even more pissed off with herself for feeling guilty – why the hell should she feel guilty because the man who is supposed to be in charge of the operation had made a cock up that threatened the whole day's work if not the operation itself? Men were all too ready to feel sorry for themselves when their male pride was pierced to the quick, without women having to feel bad about it as well. She could imagine only too well what the reaction of her male colleagues would have been if it was her that had made a mistake. She'd have had to run the gauntlet of that humiliating mix of patronising sympathy and 'well what do you expect if you let women in to do a man's job' arrogance. But at the same time, she sensed that certain defenceless vulnerability about Derek that made her feel…sorry for him? …protective towards him? She wasn't sure, but it was certainly not what she had expected from herself or him, from what she'd heard about him. It was far easier dealing with the obvious 'lads' than someone who seemed so exposed and sensitive. She chose her next words carefully – she didn't want him to think that she was unaware of what had happened, but it had happened now and there was no point in harping on about it – and she didn't want to do anything to freak him out and jeopardise whatever might be left of the operation. What was necessary now was to make the most of the situation by weighing it up carefully to make the best decision for action, that was what a good officer would do, and she decided that she had to assert herself for the good of both of them and the operation.

"You're right about us waiting to see if he settled. He's really got us now. We can't follow him, it would be too obvious – he could be at the top of the ramp, just waiting to see if anyone else gets out."

"Yes, but even then, all's not lost – he might just get the next train up, so we can make contact with our lads up north, and watch the next few trains after ours arrives. But you never know, he might have got back on this one. It sometimes pays to look on the bright side." Derek grinned an embarrassed grin, feeling like a complete idiot but desperate to redeem the situation. She sensed that she had to push him a bit. She was well aware of his reputation – fast track graduate like her but gone wrong, radical union rep, well out of favour with the bosses, slightly dangerous to know too well, and so on. Well, when he was younger, perhaps. But this was a different case now, he just looked washed up and confused and the only danger in knowing him at the moment was that he was likely to screw up on her.

"Well, it would be better to look on the bright side after we've had a look on the train, don't you think? It should be going any second now," she snapped, trying to sound firm and in control but perhaps coming out more brusque than she had intended, and seeing a look she interpreted as one of hurt apprehension flicker across his face, she added quickly, "which means that the bar will be open. We might as well relax now, whatever he's done. Mine's a Gin and tonic." She grinned, realising that it would be better not to get wound up about all this. It could all have been a lot worse, after all. At least Derek didn't go in for all that boring macho posturing that was so common on the team and he hadn't tried to shrug off the blunder with some lame excuse. Perhaps that was what had made her feel whatever it was she was feeling about him – and anyway, she was sitting pretty really – whatever happened in the case, even if it went disastrously awry, there was no way they'd give her a black mark, not on her first trip out and especially not with Derek as the 'minder'. They'd only too pleased to have another stick to beat him with, because she also knew that senior management had long been wanting him out. She smiled at him and watched him visibly relax in response. He grinned back at her, though she could tell that he was still feeling foolish.

"Right, Gin and tonic it is. I'll do as you say, have a bit of a scout around, so don't worry if I'm not straight back."

With a slight, almost imperceptible jolt, the train began to snake smoothly out of the station.

Chapter 4

You just can't be too careful, George Miller thought as he stepped down onto the platform, smug beyond belief at how clever he was. Smooth George, clever bastard George. He was thoroughly enjoying himself. He'd never done anything like this before, and as they don't exactly publish manuals, he was combining common sense and 'knowledge' gleaned from all the detective and espionage films he'd ever seen- James Bond eat your heart out. They didn't come any cooler than George. There was some edginess, some adrenaline, but it was mostly just pure enjoyment- even if he was stopped, all he was carrying were some innocent-looking business documents and a couple of maps and coordinates and numbers- they meant nothing to him and they certainly weren't incriminating. Ignorance really is bliss- he was genuinely unaware of just how small a cog he really was or how big and dangerous a machine he was making himself a part of. The cover story was flimsy – that he was heading to a sports car exhibition at GMEX and a mate of a mate had asked him to take the documents – 'save me a journey, mate – I'll make it worth your while if they sign the contract'. He knew it was drugs, of course- he could only guess what but didn't go there. He vaguely assumed it was coke but truth to tell, through the dimness and genuine lack of imagination, he didn't want to know. It might spoil it all. He glanced along the platform, walking slowly towards the rear of the train. He passed the restaurant car and another carriage. The crowds had thinned now and he knew it could only be a minute, perhaps less, before the train started. The guard was beginning his journey along the platform, slamming the doors. Miller glanced back over his shoulder. No one had got out. Should he go now, or wait for the next one?

"You on or off, mate?" The guard had reached him, as he dawdled along. It made him jump, the harsh South London accent breaking into his meandering thought processes.

"Oh, on, yes," and he climbed back on board. Oh well, it had made up his mind for him, and after all, there was no really rational way to decide. If they were watching the station, they'd know he was waiting for the next train, and so it would make no difference. He'd actually read this in a detective story somewhere once, and it seemed to make sense to him. Finding the first vacant seat, he sat down, without acknowledging the people sitting opposite. He looked vacantly out of the window. Well, he'd done all he could. He began to relax as the train started. He was forty-two, bald and running to fat, but that was only how the mirror and the rest of the world saw him. In his own mind he was playing a role, the sophisticated playboy living in a dangerous and glamorous world – which in reality meant hanging around second rate sleazy nightclubs and membership of a third-rate golf club. He'd dabbled a little is some petty crime but today, this was different, at once it confirmed his fantasy existence and gave it external credibility- and it paid well. Greed was, of course, his other motive, real greed, the love of money for its own sake and that wasn't because he'd had a deprived childhood in a blighted inner-city slum or indeed ever experienced poverty in any form. Oh no, he'd never been without money, never known financial hardship. His background was suburban middle class, a minor private school designed to cheat kids through their exams. After school, because there wasn't enough money to cheat him into university, he'd left and dodged himself through a succession of more or less crooked entrepreneurial ventures (are there any other kind?) – making a fast buck and moving on. If he'd been even more sly and cunning in his dishonesty he'd have probably been on one of Thatcher's honours lists.

It never really entered his head in any tangible form that he could go to prison for what he was doing because, apart from the fact that he was convinced that there was nothing directly incriminating in what he was carrying, it never entered his head in any tangible form that what he was doing *was* a crime. There was never any sense at all in which for even the briefest of moments he felt that laws were there to regulate his behaviour. After all, prison was for real, actual criminals, which he obviously wasn't. He wasn't hurting anyone, threatening anyone, stealing, mugging, stabbing anyone, he didn't live on a council estate. All that he'd ever done was fiddle his taxes, rip off a few investors with a couple of failed investment schemes, and well, yes he did cocaine every now and then, but didn't everyone? It was all part of the game to him, high spirits they'd have called it at his school. The law was there to protect him from the muggers and the burglars and the blacks and the hippy convoys and gypsies and pickets and, well, from criminals, and he believed in enforcing that law with as much rigour and brutality as even the splenetic editor of a rag like the Daily Mail would have found hard to match.

But, on the other hand there was no doubt that there were such things as bad laws, of course, petty, bureaucratic, meddlesome laws emanating no doubt in the Socialist Republic of Brussels, that everyone knew were in fact just so much stuff and nonsense, all his chums at the Golf Club said so every Sunday, after the double G&T's and before the high speed drunken drive home. Even on his present assignment, which he strongly suspected involved class A's, he wasn't doing anything he considered criminal. He wasn't handling the stuff. He wouldn't ever see it. No, it was just straightforward venture capitalism, with the added zest of excitement, adding another sparkling facet to his champagne fantasies, life in the fast-lane underworld. His real life was so completely empty that he couldn't possibly face up to it – no real parties, no real friends, no real relationships and always, in the background, a sort of bubbling anger born in the darkness of failure and emptiness. So rather than going under into the desolation of reality, he'd created a different world and filled it with bright lights and excitement and now had crossed all the fantasy into actual reality. He really was being paid by the real underworld to work on a big deal... And anyway, the people he was avoiding were of course the baddies for God's sake, not even the police, just Government agents, taxmen, fuck it, the bloody Customs and Excise. State bureaucrats the lot, like in bloody Russia, even with that new drunken bastard in charge – was he still in charge? Anyway, they were killjoys, who'd be better employed tracking down the hordes of dole scroungers and illegal immigrants that are threatening the stability of the realm and undermining the British way of life. George was just a businessman trying to maximise his profits and occasionally make a quid or two on the side (well, rather a lot of quids this time, enough to run his shiny new second-hand open-top sports car. He wasn't harming anyone – and the junkies, well, they didn't have to buy the stuff, did they? He wasn't sticking a needle in their arm, was he? – Freedom of choice, that was what he was helping to provide and at least he wasn't a burden on the taxpayer, a scrounger expecting someone else to earn money for him while he lounged around in the betting shop. God! He looked at the people sat opposite him, wondering if they'd noticed him, he'd been getting so worked up inside. But they just looked back blank, nondescript, showing as little interest in him as he had in them. Time for a drink, he thought, that'll sharpen me up a bit.

ii

Derek worked his way towards the bar, eyes flitting from side to side as casually as he could. He had decided against wandering through all the carriages on the train, it would be too obvious and serve no real purpose. At Manchester they could get off smartly and watch everyone else through the barriers. If the guy wasn't there, well too bad. They could wait for the next couple of trains, and if he didn't show they'd assume he'd cancelled. So what! It didn't mean that he and

Val had made a balls up of it- well him, actually, Val really hadn't done anything wrong. The guy might never have meant to go up today- it could all have been an elaborate ploy- well not even elaborate really. You could never tell what they'd got in mind. Derek leant onto the bar and caught sight of himself in the mirror behind the rack of spirits. It gave him quite a shock – he looked so old and tired, almost haggard. It was so different from the image of himself that he had in his mind and from the one he'd become used to imposing on the mirror he used each day in his bathroom. He looked away and thought instead about the present situation. Poor Val, stuck on her first field trip with *him, wiped out, drained...* He'd make sure that his bosses knew that anything wrong was his fault when he wrote the report. Not that it would need him to tell them that. He was still only in the Special Team by the skin of his teeth, subject like all the others to the annual review, but in his case, it was a very thin skin. He worked well enough, and he got on with the others on the team well enough, but there had been so many years of sniping between him and some of his superiors, a sort of day in day out war of attrition, and he was losing even if they hadn't won yet and he was feeling totally worn down by it even before East Ham – they had the big battalions and staying power. Gradually it had begun to erode his belief in the job, and for some time he had been doing little more than just going through the motions, the energy and eagerness of his early days replaced by an enervating lethargy. He'd been a fast learner and a good officer but he'd also tangled with some senior officers, especially when he'd been elected Staff Association rep – he'd wounded some egos, embarrassed a few careerists, showing off, really, but he hadn't shaken the system one little bit, just posed on the barricades waving a very tiny flag. Still, it was a source of astonishment to him that they seemed both willing and able to sustain their institutional ill-will towards him. He lacked their vindictiveness and pettiness to ever keep something going as long as they did. And in the end, it was with cynicism rather than bitterness that he'd retreated into simple acceptance. But again he felt sorry for Val – she was just starting out and was apparently, on present showing, a conscientious and committed officer, and it wasn't fair for her to be tainted by his world-weariness. They'd have a field day with him if he cocked up a simple operation, and it would be awful if she got caught in the crossfire. Mind you, they'd have their work cut out making too much of a fuss about anything going wrong on this one, sending only the two of them. Even if the informant was an unknown, you had to take it seriously. Come to that, he couldn't remember who the source of this one was. He stopped to think for a moment, but couldn't remember. He made a mental note to check the file when he got back to London, and self-indulgently returned to his musings on the inequities of under-resourcing. Still, he thought, on a brighter note, at least it gave him the chance to get up to Manchester again after all these years.

"Yes sir?" the barman's young voice startled him out of his ponderous self-absorption.

"Oh, a gin and tonic, ice and lemon and a bottle of light ale…" and then, thinking that he could just enjoy one at the bar before taking them back, "er, make that two bottles of light."

"Two glasses?"

"Yes, thanks." It was crowded and smoky in the bar, and on the rationalising basis that he'd rather smoke his own than everyone else's, Derek lit up, only his second of the day. He *must* give up soon, he told himself yet again. He took a long drag, sucking hard, dragging the smoke back into his lungs, feeling that satisfying kick at the back of his throat. He took a gulp of his beer and began to think about the whole journey, the coming weekend and just as he was taking the second drag on his cigarette, he noticed something in the mirror behind the bar. It was sunlight glinting on… a bald head. He turned slightly to his left.

"A double brandy and soda, please," an exaggeratedly posh voice next to him, the sort of accent that had been going out of fashion until Thatcher's comical efforts at sounding more than just the shop keeper's daughter from Grantham, had given it a perverse boost. He risked a quick glance and yes, fucking hell, it was the target, standing right there beside him. He mustn't look again, he knew that, but he also knew that he mustn't make it obvious that he wasn't looking. Thank god there were so many people around. Derek gulped back the rest of the beer, picked up the remaining drinks, and set off back to Val.

Back at their seat, he gave Val her Gin and Tonic and took a sip of his second glass of beer. He smiled broadly.

"Well," she said, "you've found him, haven't you?"

He nodded, the smile breaking into a full grin, "Yep, we're back in business. Christ, that's a relief. And it means that he probably feels more secure than he did. He's knocking back a double brandy at the moment. He was standing right next to me at the bar, touching shoulders we were."

"Well, well, well, how exciting for you."

"Yes." He'd given up trying to make out her tone, but couldn't shake off his disappointment that he just couldn't read her – and his surprise that it was bothering him. Was she still pissed off about the carelessness on the platform – *his* carelessness? Or was she just a bit nervous still, perhaps? She seemed so composed, so sure of herself but her way of talking to him seemed brusque to the point almost of rudeness – and at the end of the day. He was the senior officer. God, what was he thinking? Was it just his poor old ego feeling a bit neglected? He felt suddenly awkward, didn't know what to say. He sat back and there was a silence. He glanced at her and then, looking out of the window, found himself thinking about her, her brown hair, hazel eyes, yes, she was physically attractive alright, but that wasn't what was on his mind. There was something else about her, something he hadn't registered before, in the short time she'd been working with the team. Whatever it was, she was making him feel more awkward and uncomfortable about himself than he had ever done. He felt tired again and was increasingly aware that whatever was happening to him, it was more than just a bad hangover.

He took another gulp of the gassy beer and tried again. "You can never tell what they're going to do, you know, targets. I remember a few years ago, we had *thirty* customs and police ready to knock a place in south London, Bermondsey, a huge operation. Anyway, the bloke just didn't turn up, we were there for hours before they stood us down. We thought he must have been tipped off – logical enough given how leaky the dibbles are –and we started an investigation – caused some really bad blood between us and the met, though nothing new there. Then, we eventually tracked the bloke down and took him in and when we were questioning him, I asked him about that morning and it turns out, straight up, he'd just overslept. Nothing else. No tip off's, nothing. He'd overslept and decided not to keep the appointment. Amazing." When he stopped, Derek wasn't actually sure what the point of the story was, or what kind of reaction it was meant to elicit, and he found himself wondering if he'd already told her on some previous office encounter – or in the pub one Friday. Val simply smiled, more it seemed to him out of politeness than amusement. There was another pause in the conversation. God, it's getting like one of Pinter's plays he thought, then she said,

"You're staying up in Manchester for the weekend, aren't you?" He was disconcerted to find her looking at him as if the answer actually mattered, as if she was really interested and not just making conversation which further unnerved him.

"Yes. I grew up there. It's a great city. Do you know it?"

"No, it's just one of those polluted northern Lowry cities to me. Always raining isn't it, and not a patch on St. Petersburg or something like that. That's the one isn't it?"

She looked perfectly serious, not a hint of a smile and she sounded straight enough for him to be unsure if she was teasing or not. He'd heard enough of the genuine South East ignorance and prejudice against the north to know that she might well mean every word of it and once upon a time he'd have risen to the bait, tease or not. Mind you, he'd lived long enough in the South and London to know that there was just as much ignorance and prejudice from the north to the south – the idea that London was cold and unfriendly was just bollocks, for a start – and in terms of beer, well, Youngs and Fullers would give any northern beer a run for their money.

But it wasn't an equal competition, London held all the high cards – but Manchester and Salford were always in there, punching above their weight in terms of culture and science and politics – and from everything he'd heard it was rising up from the austerity-kicking Thatcher had given the North West, picking itself up and dusting itself down like it always had. Anyway, he'd been away for a long time now, he'd repeated the arguments and praises so often, that he just couldn't be bothered anymore, not even in jest. He didn't even know if he believed it anymore, and he realised with something of a shock that even his fondness for the place had, like everything else about him, become just another hollow pose, just another sham to be trotted out at dinner parties, endlessly until even he was tired of it, like he seemed so tired of everything at the moment.

"Yes, that's the place. Still, it will be nice for me to see it again. Then I can feel how lucky I am to be living in London instead." He laid on the sarcasm but it didn't quite work and he moved quickly on, "I'm actually going back to see an old school friend of mine. There's a big demonstration on Saturday, and he's one of the main speakers at the rally afterwards. He's got parliamentary aspirations, hoping for a safe seat for the New Model Labour Party this next time. He was a councillor on the Greater Manchester Council until they abolished it." He didn't know why he was telling her all this – political activity wasn't something you broadcast in the service, as he had good reason to know only too well and anyway there was always the risk of boring the hell out of someone. When he'd been young, politics had been vibrant, tense, exciting. Now, well, what could anyone get excited about? John Smith, rising stars from public schools like Tony Blair?

"Wow, so it's all true what they say about you and politics, then? I heard you used to be the association rep. or something when there was a lot of trouble a few years back, is that right?"

"Or something." He felt uneasy and shifted in his seat. That was a time he didn't want to think about let alone talk to a virtual stranger about. But he was also acutely aware of another level of embarrassment – because, although he *had* once been active politically, a bit of a rebel, he really didn't do much anymore, except mouth off a lot when he was drunk. Ouch, another sting of self-realisation. The fact that she'd heard about all that even after such a short time in the team meant that somewhere his notoriety was still alive and kicking, but if only they knew the stale reality behind it now.

"Let's say I take a keen interest in the world around me. I used to be very active in the union when I first moved to London, but I don't actually *do* very much nowadays, I'm afraid. Well, I got a bit involved during the miner's strike – got a collection going, that sort of thing. But I'm very much on the side-lines."

She had this way of throwing him, wrong-footing him, making him confront things about himself. He found himself talking to her about things he'd spent years not even thinking about. Even though he lived alone, and theoretically had plenty of time for reflection, there were areas of his life that he'd rather not have to face up to. He tried to avoid too much introspection, though he was finding it harder and harder. And the truth was, he just wasn't *engaged with anything* anymore – nothing. He suddenly felt trapped, pricked by her questions and he decided, in a flow of aggressive defensiveness, to throw the question back at her, sounding more aggressive than he had intended "Why, are you *political*?" It sounded almost like a sneer, perfected in his days on the sixth form debating team.

"In some ways." She looked as if she was going to say something else but then didn't. She realised the conversation was going wrong, but couldn't make out why he was so touchy, so she decided to retreat from it, the safest course of action. She'd heard that on top of everything else, Derek could be a bit volatile and the last thing she wanted was to set him off. There was another, longer pause, even more awkward than before, until Derek took hold of the situation, determined to assert himself and get off what at the moment was the most sensitive of subjects – himself. After all, who was this anyway, and what the hell would she understand? Christ, he didn't understand himself. Anyway, the second beer had made him really sleepy now and he thought he'd better outline the plan for the Manchester end, before perhaps having a doze, the safest way out of any more conversation.

"Right, let's get back to work. The first stop is at Stoke on Trent, and then at Wilmslow, about twenty minutes out of Manchester. There isn't much there, it's just a sort of yuppie dormitory, but he could always pull another of his tricks and get off there or of course at Stoke, and then back on again, or stay off, whatever he likes. Again, though, there's not much we can do about it. We'd be best just sitting tight until Manchester. Then you get off as quickly as you can, ahead of him, hopefully. As you clear the barriers, you'll see opposite you an open-plan John Menzies – you can pretend to be browsing there while you watch for him coming through, and follow him. I'll try and get behind him on the platform and contact Manchester Division. How does that sound?"

"Fine. With any luck I'll be on my way back in no time."

"It's not really that bad up there, you know…"

"Well, I'll take your word for it. But it is Friday. It would be nice to be back home for the weekend."

He looked at her again and found himself wondering what, or who, it was she was looking forward to, and again found himself wanting to know more about her. He looked out of the window without replying and tried to turn his mind to the case but his eyelids sagged, tired with the alcohol and the movement of the train. As he drifted off to sleep, he felt vaguely uneasy about it all, or, more precisely, unsettled…

… Or at least now, looking back, he thought he could almost remember some such feeling, a hint of premonition, a shiver…but perhaps not. He was so confused. He knew that now he couldn't just close his eyes and fall softly asleep as he had done that day on the train, that he must stay awake, or that would be the end for him, knew that they would come, and soon, and he knew that there was no longer any chance of his escaping whether they came or not. The pain had gone,

but still there was the fear that even the slightest movement was liable to start it off again. And the bleeding had started again, he was sure, warm and sticky, though much less than before, just seeping now, weeping... But if he couldn't get away, he'd make sure that he didn't go quietly. The press and T.V. would all be out there by now, smelling the blood, sensing the kill. And sooner or later someone would start asking the right questions. That was all he could hope for now. But that day on the train, that was when all this had really started. And with a shock of disbelief, he suddenly realised that it was less than a month since that day in early May, when he'd looked at Val on the train and felt so confused by her.

iii

"Derek, Derek, wake up!"

He felt chilly and shivered. Where was he? Who was it? "Val? Val?" What the fuck was going on? And then he remembered, his head cleared again, like driving in and out of wind-driven mists on a dark, bending mountain road, out he came into a clear patch, a moment of breath-taking clarity, the stars shining above, a moment of pure stillness before the black road plunged ahead into the next cloud of shifting, swirling fog. And then he was back, back on the train, with just a consciousness of that moment, that still point with the stars. He picked up. He picked... "What is it?" he mumbled, and then snapped awake.

Val was smiling, with a certain warmth, he thought. "It's alright, it's just that we're getting close to Wilmslow, I thought you'd like to know."

"God, I thought I'd only dozed off for a minute. I'm really sorry, I've not been much company. God, I'm just bloody hopeless..." he tried to gather his thoughts and composure, but initially failed on both counts.

"Don't worry, I've been asleep some of the time myself. And it's more relaxing, not having to make conversation sometimes."

"Er, yes." If he'd been more alert, he'd have been even more thrown by her response than he was. The train began to slow down, and people were starting to pick up their belongings and make their way down the corridor to the exit.

"God, I missed Stoke altogether."

"Yes, well, I'm sure you didn't miss much… Seriously, I kept an eye on the platform and I didn't see him get off, but then I can't see an awful lot from here without looking too obvious."

OK, he really had to get a grip of himself here – he was the mature, experienced senior officer meant to be mentoring her – Christ, he had to salvage some dignity here and reassert his authority while there was any left. He put a firmer edge into his voice. After all, he was in charge, if not at the moment fully in control. "Right, well look, we've got about another twenty minutes to Manchester. You get off as soon as we get there, as we said. I'll hang around until he's gone past and try and contact the team."

"Right." She sighed, and for the first time since Euston she again showed subtle signs of real nerves. Her smile was tighter, her whole body just that little bit stiffer, her movement as she reached for her bag behind the seat, just a little bit too precise, like a drunk trying to cover up a slurred voice by talking too carefully. Derek only noticed because he recognised his own symptoms and he knew there was nothing he could say that would settle her. So he just gazed out of the window, trying to keep his body from giving away his own tension with its twitching and fidgeting, as the last few minutes of the journey made themselves felt. He fixed his mind on the passing of these last moments, thinking how strange it was, that hours can pass like minutes, and minutes seem like hours. Or actually *be* hours, these minutes *were* hours for him, as the train hissed across the immense Victorian valley-spanning viaduct at Stockport and began the approach to Manchester through the same urban drabness and dereliction that surrounds large railway stations everywhere, even, no doubt, St. Petersburg. Despite his long experience of moments like this, Derek still had no strategy for stopping the physical reactions to the anxiety, and he could feel his stomach tightening with every passing second, tighter and tighter and tighter. Then they were into the station, and the train jolted to a stop. He clenched his fists. "Right, off you go then. I'll see you later." Val was on her feet almost before he had finished speaking, gently easing herself into the jostle of people pushing along the corridor, retrieving her small case and moving along, quickly out of sight. Derek stayed where he was, watching the platform until he saw her clear the train, and then he too stood up. He hadn't noticed if the target had passed yet, but he doubted it. If the guy had any idea at all, he'd wait until nearly everyone else had gone, and see if someone like Derek was also lingering around.

The crowd in the carriage was thinning out now, but the platform was still fairly busy. The worst of the rush had passed, though, so Derek pulled his case down from the rack, and shuffled towards the exit door, keeping his eye on the window. Any longer delay would blow the whole thing. Yet still no sign. Then he was past the toilets and out onto the platform, and almost as soon as he stepped down, he saw the bald head flash past him- so he had waited. He did not follow, but knelt down and undid his right shoelace, and then slowly re-tied it. He smiled to himself, thinking if laces didn't exist, they would have had to be invented by surveillance teams – they were an ideally legitimate way of stopping still in a busy street without drawing attention to yourself. Still down on one knee, he glanced towards the ticket gate. There was quite a bottleneck there now, and he could see the target joining the queue. Val should have been well clear and waiting on the other side to pick him up, so now was the time pull in the Manchester team to take over the surveillance. There were a few people still straggling off the train, so he stepped behind one of the huge pillars which supported the vast Victorian roof, put his small overnight bag down beside him, and with one last look around, he checked that the tiny earpiece was properly in place, pressed the transmit switch and ... BANG! There was a piercing explosion in his ear, and he must have gasped out loud because several people passing by turned to peer at him. One even looked so concerned he thought she was going to come over and see if he was alright, but one manic glare from Derek was enough to convince her to think better of it. Derek dragged the earpiece out of his ear, still in pain.

"Shit, shit, shit!" He shook his head, trying to think quickly, but feeling dizzy and sick. He'd have to catch up with Val, that must be his priority. They'd have to contact the Manchester team some other way.

By the time he was through the ticket barrier, he was feeling better, though not for long. Straight ahead of him was the Newsagents stall, and standing there, browsing at the paperback stand, was Val. He hesitated and then walked towards her. Had she missed the target? By now he was only a couple of feet from her, but he knew he mustn't make any contact – if the coast were clear, that would be up to her. He walked up to the counter, from where he could get a better view of her.

"Guardian, please. Thanks." He took his change and the paper, and risked a glance toward where Val had been standing. He was surprised to see her looking straight back at him. No, not straight at him, slightly to his left. He followed the gaze, slowly, carefully. Black coat, bald head. The bastard was standing right next to him again, the second time in two hours. Shit. Derek's heart was pounding so loud that he was sure the whole bloody station could hear it and he felt as though he might just as well be wearing a great big flashing neon sign reading 'Customs and Excise Officer – I am following the man standing next to me'. Before he could react in any way, the man turned and walked past him, heading for the booking office area between the newsagent's and the exit. A second later, Val followed, and then Derek too joined the trail.

The booking hall was modern, open plan, with a low ceiling. Ahead was the exit, to the left the wall was occupied by the glass windows of the booking office itself, while on the right were the steamed-up floor-to-ceiling windows of the station cafeteria and it was into here that the target went, followed by Val. The adrenaline was making Derek feel really high now, almost giggly, a feeling he had known only too well and too often over the years. It made external reality seem so ridiculous, a kiddies' game acted out by adults, like in that Dennis Potter play he'd seen, what was it called? 'Blue Remembered Hills' or something like that. But in a sense he was ready for anything since East Ham and forced his mind to focus and weigh up all the alternatives. This was how it always was, one minute normal and calm, the next splintering out of control. He took a deep breath to head off any flashbacks from East Ham. One thing was certain, it would be altogether too crowded in the cafeteria if he went in as well. After being so close twice now, it would be better if the guy didn't see any more of Derek, so he sat down in the concourse, making sure that he had a clear view of the door. He knew that there was no other exit, as he'd used the café so many times when he was at university, once the romantic excitement of hitchhiking had been lost forever in the icy sleet at three a.m. on the slip road of the Watford Gap services and he went back to using the train. But he immediately dismissed the reminiscing, not yet, he had all weekend for that. He had to stay alert. He made himself glance at his newspaper, eyes flickering from the undeciphered black marks of the headlines to the blankness of the steamed-up cafe windows. Time again, stretching like the muscles of his stomach, seconds, hours, minutes slurring into each other, suspended in limbo, until, unsure how long had actually passed, he decided to risk having a look at what was going on. He felt calmer now, heavier, wearier, as the first surge of adrenaline began to work off. He hesitated for a moment and then decided that he had no choice – Val was confident and well trained, but even so, it was her first time in the field, and no amount of training can ever prepare you for all the possibilities or for the speed with which things happen. He gritted his teeth as just that single train of thought threw up a flash of the bleeding policemen on the hallway floor, dying. He shook the image away and carefully folded the paper, tucked it under his arm, and walked firmly but without any appearance of undue haste towards the door of the cafeteria. He pushed it open and joined the queue for hot drinks, and only then allowing himself a quick look around. And it *was* a quick look, for as he lifted his head he saw a rapid blur of movement to his left that resolved itself into three people leaving the cafe – a young, casually dressed young man, student looking, carrying an artwork folder under his right arm, followed by Val, followed by the man with the bald head. In that order. They weren't actually right behind one another, and others were coming and going, enough to make each departure from the busy room look unconnected to the others, but that was the order in which they left, and for a second he just couldn't believe it. He stood there, money in his hand, and mouth literally hanging open. And then he moved, quickly back out of the door and into the concourse. To his left he saw the target heading *back* towards the trains. A quick glance to the right caught Val going in the opposite direction, out of the station. And for the first time that day, he felt angry and frustrated, but also in command – not of these events, that much was clear, but of himself and the wider situation. He knew exactly what to do without thinking, which was just as well because conscious thought was out of the question now, no time. He decisively followed the target. That was their brief, and that was what they had to do. He walked briskly towards the platforms and immediately saw him through the crowds. He had joined the queue for the train back to London! A quick glance at the departure board told Derek that it would be at least thirty minutes before it left, so he decided to look for Val. He found her coming back into the station.

"What the hell do you think you're doing?" He held her arm, looking around as he realised people might be watching.

"Did you follow the target?" she asked firmly, calmly brushing off his hand.

"Yes, but…" His obvious anger and his snappy assertion of authority were met only by such cool confidence and assurance that he was at a loss for words.

"Good, I thought you'd be out there – I knew I could rely on you."

"Well, thanks a lot. But what the bloody hell do you think you were doing?" He again tried to sound as if he was in charge but he could feel himself just losing his temper, exasperated by the cool sense of competence she exuded.

"I saw the switch. In the cafe. As cool as you please. It was so fast that I didn't even realise what was happening at first. Did you see the guy I followed out? Well, he was already there when we went in, and our guy sits opposite him with his coffee. They didn't even look at each other. I sat a little way to the left, and saw our man take some papers out of his case and put them on the table as if he was reading them. That was all that happened – neither of them spoke. The other chap seemed to be reading as well, but I didn't pay much attention to him. And then suddenly, as he stood up, I saw him pick up the papers baldy had been reading, slip them into his folder, and head for the door. It was *so* smooth. I decided to see where he went, perhaps get a car number or something." She saw the look on Derek's face, and before he could say anything, added, "I know, we're not supposed to let anything distract us from the target, but don't forget, I knew that you'd be around out there somewhere. Anyway, I headed for the door and saw you coming in. That threw me a bit, and as I passed baldy, I saw him putting some papers away, and I thought, 'God, its non-stop action here', and kept going. And that's it. The art student didn't have a car nearby and I knew I shouldn't follow him too far anyway, so I just let him disappear into the crowd. Still, I can give a good description of him." Suddenly she exclaimed, "The target, God, where is he?"

"It's alright, he's queuing up for the return to London. It goes in about twenty minutes. It might be worth your while getting a later one if you think he'll recognise you."

"No, I'm sure he won't. Anyway, I rather fancy seeing if I can follow him in London, see where he goes if I can. It's really exciting, isn't it?" Her face was flushed, colour coming back after the pallor of stress.

"Yes, I suppose it is." His anger had cooled as quickly as it had flared up, dampened by the distant recollection of how exhilarating it could feel being involved in real action for the first time. But he also knew only too well that enthusiasm without discipline and structure could be disastrous and dangerous, for a case and for an officer. As they walked back towards the trains, he felt that he ought to say something reassuring to her, because for all her confidence, she was bound to feel worried later when she reviewed her actions for her case report. And he suddenly felt a sort of tenderness for her that confused him, though when he spoke it all came out sharper, more like an order than a show of concern. "Be careful, won't you?" Terribly stiff upper lip sort of stuff.

"Don't worry, sir, I won't mess up the operation." She smiled at him.

"No, I know you won't. That's not what I meant. Anyway, I'll leave you here. It's best now that he doesn't see us together, just in case. It's platform seven, by the way. And...I'm sorry I was so pissed off just now – you were right, rules are there to be broken. But don't hand in a report until we find some creative way to avoid mentioning exactly what did happen. We'll have to get together and sort out what we're going to put, so we don't contradict each other'. He looked up at her and saw that she was staring at him." She paused ever so slightly and then,

"Yes, I'd like that. That's very good of you."

He took out a pen and wrote down his telephone number for her on a strip of card he tore from his cigarette packet. "I'll be back sometime Sunday evening, so give me a ring, say after eight." He felt his voice tremble slightly, and he didn't know what to say next. They stood for a second, silent.

"Right." She turned to go and then turned back again. "Thanks – for worrying about me. I'll give you a ring on Sunday. I hope you enjoy your weekend." And then she was off towards the platform.

Derek stood for a moment, and watched her go, feeling a sort of emptiness that confused him – what did George Elliot say, 'Every parting is a reflection of death?' Or something like that. Great. But he knew what it meant and no doubt because of deeper memories of old goodbyes, he had neither the time nor the inclination at that moment to pursue any other explanations. He was impatient now to tie up the loose ends, and in particular knew that he had to try again to contact the Manchester team and let them know what had been happening. He turned decisively around and walked out of the station, into the warmth of the afternoon. He walked a short distance from the entrance, put the earpiece back in place, and, wincing at the memory of his previous attempt, pressed the transmit switch. It worked perfectly.

"Hello, Manchester Division, Delta tango. London, Delta Bravo here, come in."

"Delta Tango receiving you. Hello, Brown. About time, isn't it? Go to Enquiries, show them your warrant card and ask for the security rooms. See you in a minute. Out."

He followed the directions and was shown to the bare concrete stairs up to the security area. At the top of the stairs was a large man in his late twenties, beaming at him through a thick ginger beard. "Brown? Come on, you must see this. And smile man, you're on candid camera!" He ushered the increasingly disorientated Derek into a small, windowless room, where three other men were standing in front of a closed-circuit T. V. monitor. In the corner was a crate of French beer, and as soon as he'd been introduced to them all, they thrust a bottle into his hand. He didn't take in the names, but the one with the beard explained that they had been waiting for contact, watching the platform on the station's C. C. T. V. when one of them had recognised Val from a recent training course they'd both been on. Well, from then on, they'd tracked the whole thing, and recorded it all. So now they all watched the highlights again, with much laughter, and a good deal of drinking.

"Derek, it's a classic – the look on your face there…" – roars of laughter, Derek embarrassed and entertained in equal measure. And then,

"Cor, look at the body language there, pal…go on, give 'er a kiss…she's just waiting for it, looks like a scene from 'Brief Encounter, mate'."

He blushed and looked at the grainy images of him and Val both standing on the platform and thought they were right, they just looked…like a couple saying goodbye, all that was missing was an embrace, a kiss…

And an hour later, at five o'clock on that warm spring afternoon, Derek stepped drunkenly into the back of a taxi, back in Manchester, home after so long. But would there be a fatted calf?

***

On the London train at almost the same time, Val began to settle down into her seat – she felt she could really relax now – the job was officially over, and she didn't have to worry about Derek. She'd made sure the target was on the train, so there was nothing more she could do – following him back might provide some additional intel, but if she lost him, in one sense it didn't matter at all as it wasn't part of the formal schedule anyway. She looked out of the window and felt sleepy in a satisfying way. The densely packed red brick terraces of Stockport were beginning to fray and untangle into the soft green spaces of the Derbyshire Cheshire borders and she felt a deep, subconscious release, as if her breathing were lighter and easier, as the train slipped further away from the tightness of the city.

She'd done it. Her first field operation with the drugs team. And not only had she done it successfully, but she'd done it despite the difficult conditions, with only two of them on the job and one of them not firing on all cylinders – in fact, even worse, he was firing on all the wrong cylinders. It had needed her cool professionalism to hold it all together. She didn't know what to make of it all, especially Derek – she felt frustration, impatience, almost anger on the one hand, yet she still couldn't suppress other feelings surfacing about him that confused her and even irritated her. It was a massive achievement for her to have made her way in the male-dominated (in every way) world of the Customs and Excise undercover teams – and none more so than the drugs division. OK, it wasn't The Sweeney or the toxic ethos of the Met but it still felt more like the 1950s than 1991. So she'd had to bite her lip, take the jokes, join in the banter – but here she was at a moment of personal triumph feeling…sorry?…for her male senior officer who had been almost useless to the point of screwing it all up. She should have been feeling only the frustration and anger but she couldn't. And to be fair, Derek had never actually been one of the dinosaurs in the pub on a Friday, there had always been something different about him…but why the hell was she thinking about him at all. She forced herself to focus on her achievement and suddenly found herself transported back to the last time she could remember feeling quite as exhilarated with an achievement as this – her first day at university, Christ! Ten years ago. She sat up, drowsiness gone, eyes alert but not taking in the blurred scenery rushing past. First day, but not the minute by minute details of administration, rather the stunning, heavy distillation of the euphoria she felt at being away, of being free… She found herself almost sniffing as if she were savouring a Damascus perfume or a deep fine wine… freedom, escape, a light-headed thrill of… liberty. She wasn't getting away from anything dreadful in her family or anything like that, in fact, quite the opposite, she'd had a lovely life at home. No, it was the getting away to a new place, a new life, where no one knew her, where she could do anything, be anyone. and it brought with it a sense of space and independence that was intoxicating- not the getting away *from* anything, but the getting *to* something brilliant. And she'd made the most of it, the sex, the drugs, the rock and roll and even the studying – she loved learning, loved experiencing – it was all learning and trying and enjoying. Now, having isolated the memory, as the rush of it softened, at the same time she felt an uncomfortable ambiguity towards it, tinged at the edges with the reality, ten years on, of the way her life had gone, with all its apparently inevitable compromises. She knew the adrenalin was wearing off and she was feeling tired, and it was taking the edge off her triumph and dragging her down. Christ, in a sense it put a real downer on everything – fancy getting so worked up about something so mundane. That memory from ten years ago when everything was possible and whittled down to this – and now, well, she still had her independence, in the physical sense that she was not in any 'full time' relationship, but even that was beginning to feel more like loneliness than achievement. And then she found herself thinking of Derek again. There was something about him that she really liked, but she found herself unwilling to pursue what or why – somehow it seemed tied up with those memories and she didn't feel she had the energy to face up to analysing all that now – but it was too late, she couldn't stop herself. None of her career had been easy once she'd left university, especially getting herself onto the almost exclusively male special team, it was her inner strength that had sustained her through times when the necessary effort and commitment seemed almost too much. Perhaps that was a reason why she felt a resentful ambiguity towards Derek. S*he was* attracted by him, she had to face up to that, but the laid-back attitude he seemed to have to his career, according to things she'd heard about him – state school, top university, great things expected but apparently deliberately unfulfilled. It all seemed to her to be a decadent luxury that a woman making her way in a male-dominated culture could ill afford, and it really pissed her off. But she also knew that it was an irritation more because there was something about him which resonated deep inside her, which she related to, or felt she would if she could identify it more clearly – it was certainly more than just fancying him, though with some unease she had to admit to herself now that she did. But if only that were all there was to it, there would have been no problem. She could easily have seduced him and moved on as she'd happily done many times with many men before. No, perhaps that was why she had started to think of that first day at university. She suddenly realised that if anything started with him, it would be more complicated and threaten what sense of independence she still had left, though she wasn't sure anymore that 'threaten' was the right word. She looked out at the passing countryside and smiled again. Had all that business with the phone number been just him shooting a line? She decided that there was at very least something…

intriguing...that was the word that kept coming back, about him and her reaction to him, and that she'd keep an open mind. But she probably wouldn't phone him, she'd wait to see him at work – there'd be plenty of time to sort out the report...and then she drifted off to into an untroubled sleep. Anyone passing by casually would have seen on her face an apparently peaceful beauty. A closer observer may have also noticed a certain sadness.

Chapter 5

Derek glanced around the hotel room. Not a bad size, well-appointed in a rather cold, modern sort of a way, but best of all, it was on expenses. He'd been feeling excited by the prospect of the weekend ahead, but now he was here there was something inherently sad about having to stay in a hotel in the city where you grew up, and he felt an underlying gloom. He sat down on the bed and lit a cigarette, feeling exhausted by the events of the day and the drinking that had rounded them off. Outside, through the double glazing, he could hear the bustle of the city soothingly distant, floating up from Piccadilly Gardens, grimy with the comings and goings of the buses and trams. He knew what it was like down there, or would be soon, as the night filtered in. First the theatre-goers and restaurant eaters, happy and frivolous, and then, in the vacuum of colour as the night deepened, the drunks and prostitutes, the down and outs. And rising above, rising up from it like a mushroom from the dung heap, was this luxury hotel – it was like one of those microcosmic illustrations of the nature of society that the Bolsheviks and Anarchists circulated in pre-Revolutionary Russia – the king at the top, then the next layer the aristocrats and priests so on – 'we rule you, then we fool you,' and so on down the widening tiers. And here it was in this one building – top layer, the idle rich in the hotel, the next layer the bourgeoisie in their shops below and then down to the streets, everybody else, scrabbling for the crumbs. It was an entertaining conceit, and once upon a time he would have made a note of it for some future writing he had once had in mind – poem or novel or political tract, but now he just smiled at it and let it go. At least he had the honesty to recognise that he would now never write it, whatever it might have been.

Instead, he gazed out of the window and reflected on the fact that he now knew only one person in this great metropolis. His parents had moved out, his friends had moved away, most of them to find work in the South, long before Tebbitt's cycling advice, long before the tabloids had discovered the North – South divide as if it was something new. He'd grown up with that divide and it wasn't just a matter of economic deprivation – class divisions and poverty, after all, are not limited to the North of England, they can be found anywhere, more widespread now after twenty years of Thatcherism. And he knew from personal experience the scale of poverty in London – but it wasn't about a race to the bottom, not even about culture, whatever that means – it's about power. It's the total domination and at the same time neglect of the North, West, or East by the South, or more precisely by London and the South East. And the further from the political centre you go, the worse it gets – out of sight, out of mind. God alone knows why the Scots have put up with it for so long.

But he didn't share the knee jerk, deeply ingrained view of London itself. He'd started working there straight from university and soon found that the stereotypes just weren't true – people were friendly enough, the beer was great if you could get hold of Fullers or Youngs – and it all worked, millions of people of different backgrounds somehow managed to rub along together. It never ceased to amaze and impress him. True, it was big and dirty and dangerous and stressful but he'd loved the edginess when he'd first arrived in the mid-70s and into the 80s– with punk as the soundtrack to the street politics of the Anti-Nazi League, Grunwicks, Wapping.

What he had quickly realised that outsiders just don't get is that it isn't one place – it isn't defined by the City or the West End which tourists flock to – but by fiercely defined local areas – North or South of the river, Bermondsey or East

Ham, West Ham or Forest Gate or Finchley, Leystonstone, Walfomstow, New Eltham and so on. And it was just such a mix of people from the regions and the world who all felt one thing common once they'd been there long enough – that they were all in some way Landerners. In fact, more of his Manchester friends now lived in London than in the North West, and on his team of six, one was from Yorkshire, one from Liverpool, one was a Scot, and one from the West Country. All of them, of course, retained their accents and pride in their region but if pushed all of them would have admitted a love of London. He suspected it must, along with Manchester, of course, be one of the greatest cities in the world.

Still, here he was, back for the weekend. Picking up the phone, he dialled Peter, the one friend who had remained in Manchester, or Salford to be more precise, but the number was engaged. He could have stayed with Peter, of course, but it would have meant sleeping on the settee, and as Peter was unmarried, and still lived with his parents and brother and sister, their grim council flat was overcrowded in the first place. No, it was much better this way and it left him much more of a free agent – and anyway, he'd grown used to indulging in some of life's little luxuries over the years, the compensations perhaps for the family life enjoyed by his colleagues – though judging by their accounts of family life, enjoyed was the wrong word to use- endured was more like it. He definitely had the best of it according to them, though deep down inside, he was beginning to suspect it wasn't the case. On the other hand, staying with Peter would have restricted him, and above all else at the moment, he needed time on his own, time to face up to things, to try to sort out answers about himself, rather than the endless avoidance strategies of talk talk talk. It was, after all, a sort of pilgrimage, and for that he would need time to himself. The truth was that he was more than a little anxious at the prospect of seeing all his old haunts again. When he had decided to make a weekend of it, it had seemed like a good idea, take stock of his life, remind himself of his youth, and he had known all along that it must be more than a harmless indulgence in nostalgia. Yet now that he was here, it all seemed more menacing than he had anticipated. He'd underestimated the impact of the shootings, he realised that now but he also realised that what East Ham had done was force him to take a very long hard look at his life. The events of that night would have been deeply disturbing for anyone, but for him the timing couldn't have been worse. He'd been forced to focus on himself and his life and hadn't liked what he'd seen – just desolation stretching around him and ahead – empty, hollow, shallow, no spark, no belief, no enthusiasm – but he had not always been like this. What *had* he been like, back in the days of his youth? And when had he changed, what were the waypoints when things could have been different? He'd been happy in this city, he'd put so much energy into his life here, the energy and exuberance that go with being young and active and happy anywhere, when you still feel vital and optimistic, when you have no past, only a future that sparkles like a vast field of snow beneath a blue sky, clear and clean. Everything now was staler and duller and greyer and more tired. And to complicate it all, the city had changed, no doubt, as all organic things change. He had changed, and things out there had changed, and having been away, he'd be able to see those changes clearly, see things that those who had stayed behind would not have noticed, happening as gradually as they did. But that brought the real fear that they'd see the changes in him, ones he wasn't aware of and might well not like. He lit another cigarette, walked over to the fridge in the corner of the room, and took out a bottle of cold beer. He poured it and took a long, deep drink. Perhaps all this was after all what he had dismissed so readily as not being a serious reality - just the standard mid-life crisis – if he'd been married, perhaps the cure would have been one of those ridiculous affairs that people have to reassure themselves that everything is alright and to catch up on all the things they imagined they'd missed out on in their adolescence – no, he knew there was nothing to miss out on, that's all he'd ever been doing for years and years, having a series of affairs, and that was what wasn't enough anymore. Perhaps it was as simple as that. Perhaps that's why he had been so thrown by Val, because he was restless and he saw in her something deeper than he'd been used to, though why her? Because it was now? Because in a strange way he saw something of himself in her? – that startled him for a moment. Because she was there? Because he was drinking…No, this was a complete distraction, he was going round and round in circles. After years, perhaps a lifetime, completely lacking in introspection, he was suddenly making up for lost time. He'd have to think about her more when the weekend was over, if at all. It was most likely nothing, just still shaken up and exhausted – his old cheerful self would just have shrugged it all off and said, "Come on, let's just forget all this, have a drink, screw Val, go out to a party." He laughed to his drunken self – did he mean 'screw' her actually or screw her meaning dismiss her. HE searched for an alternative 'fuck Val' – same ambiguity – curious…But he was too tired to even shrug. Anyway, perhaps the weekend would give him some kind of clearer picture of himself, perhaps a sense of direction that for so long he had been lacking, though quite how it would do all this he wasn't sure. But he had to do something to get himself out of all the darkness because he knew it wasn't going to go away on its own, and if he didn't get out of it soon, he would be in real trouble.

At worst, of course, he knew the visit could act as a sort of measure of him against which to throw into relief his total failure, his complete inadequacies, a milestone, breaking up the blurred years into examinable units. More than ten years had gone by since he was last in Manchester, over twenty since he had been young there, day by day, hour by hour, minute by minute and now he would be forced to ask of himself where it had gone, what he had done with it. How could all those millions on millions on millions of seconds have just gone, evaporated, frothed away like the bubbles in a fizzy drink, taking all the promise and zest with them, leaving just a glass of flat, tepid liquid behind? And at the edge of these thoughts, he knew there was a dark, dangerous fear prowling, ready to pounce, claws cutting deep. Fear of the waste, fear of getting older, fear of all those things that he'd not done, fear broaching on terror at how fast it was all going. He could feel it gathering momentum, faster and faster and faster. There was a time when a month was an eternity, and now a year went by like an hour. And worst of all was that *you* didn't seem to change. He could remember old ladies at family parties when he was little, talking about getting older. "It seems to go so fast", "It was just like yesterday", "But I don't feel any different", and he'd laughed because surely, they'd always been old, just as he would always be young. Yet now, as he approached forty, he realised that he was losing his footing on the slippery slope into the deep, dark chasm, could feel the hint of a breeze through his receding hair, as the slope steepened and his descent accelerated, and one day, WHOOSH, his feet would go from under him, and … he wouldn't be there. He would simply not be there. And all his thoughts, all his hopes and dreams and ideas and perceptions and feelings and experiences would just not be there either, might just as well never have existed in the first place. If he'd never lived, never worried, never felt, never thought, the result for the world would be exactly the same. He'd made no difference to anything. He'd contributed nothing. He felt no commitment to anything. It was all so worn-out, his job, his politics and even his social life. The endless easy, casual sex that had been so exciting, the constant parties and meals out and evenings in pubs, the exhilaration of the job. It had been such a heady whirl of pleasure when he'd first come down from university to work in London, almost just a continuation of student days with the added edginess of the work. Now it was all just tedious repetition, manic and desperate – and perhaps just a little bit pathetic… or god forbid, even comical in someone his age.

He finished his beer and opened another. He tried to force a smile, but his body gave an involuntary shiver instead. No bad thing though, he thought, to get a strong whiff of your own mortality every now and then. He picked up the phone and dialled again. This time it rang.

Next morning, Saturday, he woke just after seven and had a shower. He felt refreshed and relaxed now, excited rather than nervous. He had all morning to do a tour of his old haunts before he met up with Pete, who was apparently speaking at a march and rally in the afternoon. As that didn't start until three, and would probably be over by about half five at the latest, he still had three or four hours to himself and even on the newly deregulated buses he'd have plenty of time to get where he wanted.

By the time he'd finished the shower he was feeling quite elated. It was a beautiful morning, and he'd had a very pleasant evening in the end, getting to bed early after a good meal and a decent bottle of Cotes du Rhone to himself. And he'd slept right through, best sleep for days. Now he was feeling refreshed and looking forward to a cooked breakfast. He was going to enjoy himself and why not? Forget everything, relax, reminisce, get pissed with Pete, recharge his political batteries on the march – then get even more pissed. Great! – just like being back in the sixth form but without the grass and acid.

He walked to the window and pulled back the net curtain, letting in the bracing sunshine. He felt so good that he wanted a cigarette, which he knew would make him feel worse, but what the hell!

He certainly felt a great deal worse as he sat upstairs on the double-decker bus rolling along Eccles New Road, which ran west out of Manchester towards Liverpool, parallel to the great Manchester Ship canal, but it wasn't because of his smoking. It was because of what he could see out of the windows. It was like a journey into the Inferno, but no poetry here, no colour, and this was a spring day, with sun and blue sky. Bleak, open, demolished remains of old streets, just brick-strewn spaces, with an occasional row of terraces left standing. Then, near what used to be the docks, the grey barracks of the rehousing project which would soon replace the old slums. Meet the new slums, same as the old slums...

These, the first completed phase, couldn't have been more than a couple of years old, but already they looked tattered and torn like cardboard boxes. And beyond them, he could just make out the new private housing project that had replaced the docks, Salford Quays, a fortified island of prosperity in a sea of darkest poverty. And after that came what seemed like miles of thirties tenements. They looked solid enough but half of them were boarded up, and pity the poor sods who still lived in the others – ripe for selling off to be done up at a huge profit for someone, though certainly not for the people who were short of money and short of somewhere to live. Just bad housing replacing bad housing – and somewhere a 'landlord must have been laughing till he wet his pants' as Lou Reed so caustically put it on 'Dirty Blvd'. The journey took just over twenty minutes, and he felt he'd been travelling through a cross between a Beirut war zone and a recreation of Dickensian London. He felt pale, drained and angry that anyone should have to live like this, especially in a country awash with money. Angry that this scene was only one of so many, in this city, in all our cities. And all the time *they* were spending so much money on defence, and big houses and locking the rest of us out. What on earth were they defending? The people living here needed defending from *them*. And what was worse was that the poor housing and unemployment weren't just an accidental by-product of the Thatcher years, but the essential prerequisite of them. The vast wealth owned by the smaller and smaller number of people at the top hadn't been earned, it had been stolen and these people were the real collateral damage, the walking wounded hidden away in the new ghettos of the new underclass. Out of sight, disappeared, sleight of hand, magic...but darkest black magic. And the rest of us, we suspended disbelief and let the magicians work their darkest arts. We were happy with the crumbs, too busy earning our share to lift up our eyes and see. And who did the poor and oppressed now have as their leader, the champion of the Labour Party – for the first time ever, a bloody smarmy faced public schoolboy. God help them, he thought, god help us.

He'll probably win the next election and then…well, don't hold your breath. Just be more of the same with a nicer smile.

He got off the bus at Eccles Cross, surprised just how worked up he was – he hadn't felt so emotional about anything for years, and at least he felt alive, tingling to all his nerve ends. He glanced around. All the old main routes to Liverpool passed through here since the middle ages – in fact the world's first commercial railway line from Liverpool to Manchester was still in use and on the inaugural opening day in 1830, there had been a tragic reminder that progress can bring benefits and unforeseen dangerous consequences. Huskisson, President of the Board of Trade, was fatally injured and carried to Eccles Vicarage, where he died. But it was also world-famous for its cakes and licentious wakes that had needed their own act of parliament to control. And there had been a connection with the inventor of Arkwright's Mule or Compton's something or other. He couldn't remember the details, but he could remember how the place had all looked when he'd been a child here, when it had still been called 'The Village'. There had been narrow streets and small shops when he was young, as well as the bombsites, the ubiquitous reminders, in his own lifetime, that civilised Europeans had engaged in a savage war to destroy each other's cities and peoples. But that had gone when they built the motorway through the middle of the place. That was the beginning of the end. The next stage was bulldozing all the houses near the centre, and then the old, walled bowling green near the 'Cross Keys', where he'd played on the beautifully kept crown green with his dad years before. In its place now was a vast car park to service the office blocks that had replaced the houses. Pretty standard 1970s' municipal vandalism.

He began to walk uphill along Church Street, past the recently built and already run-down shopping centre, and the office blocks, most of which still looked empty. He walked on, past the old 12th. Century church which had, no doubt miraculously, survived more or less intact, and up towards the railway station, from where he had waited to set off on many a happy holiday on those giant, platform – shaking steam trains. In his mind he could still see the well-tended flower beds on the platforms, still sense the happy atmosphere as crowds of festive northerners waited with anticipation and humour in those days before anyone he knew had a car. It came as no surprise to find that even that was no longer there. There was no sign of its grand, weather-boarded facade or of the old shops that had snuggled up alongside it. Its friendly but dignified design must have been an effrontery to the people who'd built the office blocks, its very existence an exposure of their bankrupt imaginations. So they had obliterated it. Completely. But that was not enough for them. Oh no, they had to grind out its very memory and then spit on its grave – so on the spot where the station had been there was now a plastic ticket office cubicle, like the ones they have at car parks. He nearly burst out laughing in disbelief. Perhaps it was just that he was getting older. Since time began, people had been moaning about things changing for the worse, you could hear them at any bus stop, in any pub at any time, in any country in any age.

"Kids these days, they've no bloody manners."

"Aye, and they never do owt but fight. A spell in th' army ud sort 'em out."

"God, when we were young, we'd some *respect*…"

There must have been old men and women sitting around in ancient Greece having that same conversation. Their parents had said it – and theirs and theirs … And he could see now that much of it was just the way our perceptions and needs change as we get older – we have some sort of convenient amnesia about what we were like when we were young and what the world was like. Worse than amnesia – people didn't forget, they simply distorted. But that wasn't what he meant. No, in a tangible and objective way, things *were* getting worse, there was no doubt about it, though not, of course for everyone at the same time, that was the key, not even for the likes of him, materially. Only for those groups of people that you might as well call working-class, though politicians of every party seemed anxious to reassure us (and themselves) that no such group any longer exist. "Class is dead," he'd heard smart-arsed Blair apologist friends at dinner parties argue, the working class no longer exists, cleverly tying you up with the difficulties of defining terms – as they desperately searched for some way of justifying their support for the new non-Labour Party, and for a rationale to justify what in the end was their own moral cowardice. But you knew class when you saw it, and he saw it here. He remembered an evening one winter long, long ago, safe and warm in front of the coal fire, sitting watching television with his Gran. They were sat quietly watching 'The Good Old Days' on the B.B.C., the fire crackling and spitting, when his Gran suddenly leaned forward and said, "It's not true, you know. They weren't the good old days. They were terrible times, terrible, cruel and hard. Never believe them if they tell you they were the good old days." It was one of those moments that stick in your mind, somewhere in there, forever, though it was a long time since he'd thought of it. For her, though, and for his mum and dad, the post-war reforms had brought at least the promise of something better to come, a glimpse through the fence into the rich man's garden. He'd been brought up amidst optimism that everything was automatically improving for everyone, and he'd believed it. Free medical treatment, Grammar School places for lads like him, that thrill of hearing regional accents for the first time on the radio, as those cheerful, clever young Liverpudlian rock singers gave the run around to the Establishment while the sparklingly optimistic sixties washed over us like in a wave of freshness and light. The problem was, everyone had underestimated the downright unease and resentment felt by the Establishment at even the limited share out of wealth and power and culture that the welfare state represented. And as soon as a time came when they thought it had all gone too far, guess who had to tighten their belts? Guess who had to pay the price while the rich bastards sat around their clubs buying and selling futures, (people's futures)? Guess who it was whose hospitals they were closing, whose schools were being pulled down?

He took a long drag on his cigarette and sang in a whisper,

"It's the rich what gets the pleasure, and the poor what gets the blame."

Then he walked quickly back down Church Street, shoulders hunched as if against a cold wind, though it was still a warm, spring morning. There was nothing else here for him. It offered him nothing really new that he hadn't already known and it highlighted with depressing clarity that he could no longer offer it anything back – except impotent rhetoric when he'd had a few drinks.

iii

By the time he got back into town and made his way to the Mark Addy, he'd pushed most it out of mind, like he'd done with so many things for so many years. He was getting really very good at doing it, dropping things into little boxes marked 'for urgent attention – LATER' He'd avoided confronting unpleasant things for so long now. And anyway, he would just overheat and meltdown if he carried on the way he was doing. And he had learned something of crucial importance about himself, that he did still have the capacity to care, that his beliefs were still there, that he did still *feel*. Deep down inside there was a reassurance that something positive would come out of all this, once when he had time to sit down and open up some of the boxes.

And so it was a more light-hearted Derek who was now looking forward to seeing Peter after so long and determined to enjoy himself. They'd kept in touch, the odd letter, the occasional phone call, but it was over six years since they'd last met, and that had only been for an hour or two on a march in London. 'The Mark Addy' was a modern pub on the Salford side of the River Irwell – the darkness on the edge of town. It was named after some bloke who used to throw himself into the Irwell every now and then to save other people who had somehow fallen in, whether they wanted saving or not. It was built right on the side of the river, made of an all-glass construction so that you could admire the view. Architects just love glass and it doesn't always work, but in this case it certainly did, looking sleek and shiny and modern. It was a far-sighted venture, because one day, no doubt, it would be a view worth admiring if plans to clean up the river ever came to fruition. At the moment, though, it was a reeking, stinking slow-moving sludge of a river, with crumbling disused warehouses lining the far bank. Still, they'd obviously gone to town on the decor – lots of good solid wood, and brass fittings, and most important of all, good beer. Boddington's Best, before Interbrew got hold of it and still brewed right next to Strangeways Prison, planning which was no doubt the deliberate result of the Victorians' twisted sense of sadistic morality. As if it wasn't enough to be shut up inside one of the most intimidating prisons in England, you had to look out on one of the best breweries. No wonder they'd had riots!

He was quite early but, after all that self- punishment he deserved and needed a drink – and he could get something to eat while he was waiting, line his stomach as a safety measure to help him survive the onslaught of a drinking session with Pete. He might have slowed down, of course, but Derek doubted if anyone changed *that* much. He took his pint of Boddies, and a huge slice of Pate and wholemeal bread over to a table near the window. The river was as filthy as ever, as thick as Guinness, with patches of froth here and there. An old Coca-Cola can slid slowly past, not so much floating as glued into the sticky, glutinous water. They used to say that if you fell in you'd poison before you drowned. The idea of walking on water had never seemed particularly miraculous in Manchester. One look at the River Irwell, and who could doubt that it was possible? God knows what that Mark Addy had thought he was playing at.

"Hello, Derek." He felt a firm hand on his shoulder making him jump and he looked up to see Pete standing behind him, grinning. Derek stood up and faced him and there was a moment's awkwardness. "What are you drinking?" Peter asked. "Blimey, you're not wasting time eating, are you?"

"I'll have another pint, I'm one up on you already." He couldn't help the adolescent need to establish his lead. "And there's more than enough of this for two – ask for another plate."

"Right." Peter turned and walked to the bar. Derek sat down and watched him. God, he looked older. He'd always been rather corpulent, too heavy for his height, but now he was downright fat, and it was the sloppy, wobbly fat of far too much beer far too often. Derek could at least take comfort from the fact that he wasn't overweight, the stress of the job saw to that. But otherwise, he thought he was probably doing OK, he certainly hadn't noticed any ageing when he looked in the mirror. He finished his first pint with a gulp, just in time for Pete's return with the second.

"Cheers."

"Cheers."

Another moment of self-conscious unease as they took their first gulp of beer, but only for a second.

"Christ you're looking older Derek. You look worn out. What have they been doing to you down south?"

"Oh cheers, mate, thanks for that, just what I needed – fuck you!" he grinned. "Seriously, how've you been keeping? Still on the council?"

"No, they abolished it – I was on the G. M. C., not the city council."

"Yes, I know, but I thought you'd have been running Salford by now. Ah, the fortunes of the class war. How's the rest of the family?"

"Dad's still not so good, but the rest of them are all right. Bill's still not got a job, but that's how things are."

"Yes. There are parts of London getting it bad now, but you don't notice it as much down there, somehow." Derek realised as soon as he'd said it how facile that sounded.

"I'm sure you notice it if you've not got a job up here or down there. Anyway, how's things otherwise. Caught any good smugglers recently?"

"Not enough. There's more of them than there are of us, and I think they work more sociable hours."

"Well, they've probably got a better union."

"That's true all right, it's called the Bullingdon Old Bullies Club. Otherwise, everything's about the same as ever. What about you? Have you seen any of our old crowd?" He noticed that Pete had nearly finished his beer already, so he took a deep swig to catch up. The alcohol was beginning to work its beguiling magic as the first pint began to warm through his veins and reach his brain.

"No, I haven't seen anyone, not even heard from anyone for a long time. Except for John, his wife's just had a baby, a little girl. They live up Bolton way now, he's the managing director of a place producing glue. Doing very nicely for himself, rolling in money."

"Glue? Fucking hell, Pete, I've really missed my way somewhere. There seems to be so much money around, all this success, and it seems to be passing me by. We must be doing something wrong."

"Can't say it bothers me. I've never had ambitions in that direction, though I must say a bit of extra cash would come in at the moment. I'm the only earner in our house now." He was one of those people who'd always been middle-aged, even in his youth. He'd never bothered about anything except beer and politics. Derek had never seen him with a girl, though he probably wasn't gay either. Derek had never really figured it out, but it cheered him up a bit. He had at least had a good time with his years. Sod the bloody careerists. As long as he had enough money to enjoy himself, that'd do him. Why not? Stuff all this self-pitying rubbish. "There's always someone worse off than yourself," and here he was, sitting with more proof. And as an old prof at university had said to him once, "There's only one philosophy that actually works when it comes down to it – just get on and enjoy it until you can't any more as long as it's not at anyone else's expense. Hedonism rules, OK."

'Come on Derek, that's the point isn't it? It's always at someone else's expense. Look at your London flat, all mod cons, security camera, fitted dishwasher, cooker, all made by some poor exploited sod so you can live in the lap of luxury'

Derek laughed – 'Spot on, never been averse to a bit of champagne socialism, mate. And don't forget, the rich have always had labour saving devices. They call them servants…'

And they both laughed, but for Derek there was a deeper resonance. The life he'd been living was all hedonism and materialism and there was simply no happiness in it anymore. He'd reached a point now where he couldn't do it anymore, it was empty, bleak and as Peter said –always at someone else's expense, isn't that the rub? But in this case it was now even at his own expense.

Derek took the glass from him. "Same again?" He didn't wait for an answer. He needed another pint. He eased his way through the now crowded pub, realising that there were still many questions, but that he *was* on the way to some answers, he had a direction now, something that he had not had for years.

All that, all that and the journey to Manchester and Val and that fucking job, they were all somehow there in that pub, all swilling around in the smoke and the chatter and the laughter. And now he knew all the answers, knew with a terrible certainty everything there is to know – at the precise moment in his life when it no longer mattered and he no longer cared. There were no more grey areas now, no more questions where he was now. This was where he was, where everything had been leading, to this dirty little room, with the coldness seeping clammily into him where the blood had almost finished seeping stickily out. That weekend, seeing the desolation, another of the signposts on the road that had led him here. And seeing how they'd treated anyone who protested. Yes, the demo… that was what came next

Chapter 6

Four pints later and Derek was feeling properly relaxed now, that comfortable, tranquil feeling of warmth towards the world and everyone in it which good brewers instil in their beers, and he could easily have made an afternoon of it. But somewhere inside his brain, little warning bells were ringing about this triumph of expansive bonhomie over capacity, and he suddenly remembered the demonstration.

"Hey, are you going to be alright for speaking this afternoon? We'd better get going hadn't we?" Derek asked, though there was little conviction in his voice, which reflected a genuine lack of concern in his mind, which was now reverting to his natural state of being a lotus eater. He'd have been more than happy if Peter had said, 'Oh sod it, there's plenty more demos, let's leave it and have another pint,' but he knew it wouldn't happen.

"Yeah, right, we'd better get a move on – but I'll get a couple of cans to top up with on the way. Christ, it'd be a disaster if I was to get up and speak sober – I never have before, mind you, so I don't actually know what it'd be like." A genuinely reflective look flickered for a second across his face as if he was actively pursuing that line of thought and he looked as if he was about to add something profound, but instead he just burped.

"Oh Christ, come on then," said Derek, taking the initiative.

The march was due to start at three, but they both knew from experience that it would be much later before it set off, especially if it was as big as was expected. The weather was marvellous, which boded well for a good turnout, and it was only a short route, from the Cathedral to the Free Trade Hall, where the Rally was to be held, so there was no sense of urgency as they set off from the pub. Blue sky, warm sunshine, alcohol, fresh air – or at least as fresh as it gets in a city. It felt fresh anyway. He gazed around with a slight smile playing across his lips for anyone who cared to look carefully enough and lit another cigarette. He suddenly felt so happy about the world, about his world, himself, his… yes, for the first time in ages he could actually allow the word to pass his lips, his *future*.

"Who else is speaking, by the way?" He couldn't have cared less, but it opened a conversation as they made their way along a maze of narrow Victorian side streets.

"I don't know exactly, I've not been involved with organising this one. Benn and Skinner, definitely and a whole queue of support acts like me."

"Benn – great stuff, I've not heard him for ages. Back in the eighties, you know when the Deputy Leadership push was on, I heard him in Ilford – bloody good, that ability to give a closely reasoned speech and yet make it so accessible, so inspiring. No wonder they were frightened by him, especially the dead wood on our side… Hey, listen… they must have set off on time." They were cutting through the back streets towards Deansgate and in the distance could hear chants and shouts mingling with the brass band.

"Probably the police have insisted, they're getting to be a real pain on sticking to precise arrangements nowadays. Let's cut down here, we'll be able to see some of it go by. As long as I'm at the Hall by about four it'll be alright. We don't need to march at the head or anything."

"Time for another pint then. God, I'm dying for a piss already."

"Sounds good to me. And would you believe it…" They were right outside Mulligan's.

The noise was getting louder and louder as they downed their pints and headed out towards the noise, then they turned a final corner and were suddenly out into a great burst of noise and colour on Deansgate, wide, fashionable and lined with great, solid, not quite elegant Victorian buildings. Derek began to feel quite giddy, as if he was being washed away by the great flood of sound and sensation, – bright clothes, red banners, the glinting gold of the brass band instruments. His senses were swamped, overwhelmed, but not drowned- no they were stimulated, heightened, tingling from fingertip to toe with emotion, so that he would have found it difficult to speak, had the need arisen. Old and young, men and women, a chanting, smiling, laughing, jeering, joking, shouting, cheering carnival of humour and colour and noise. The sheer variety of people was an entertainment in itself, as punks and pensioners marched arm in arm, the whole demonstration a vivid and immediate celebration of the vibrancy of radical, alternative dissent. No wonder the Government wanted to stamp them out and Blair's bunch of wets were desperately uncomfortable about them – the politics of the street, public demonstrations. They were such a visual and unignorable affirmation of a world beyond the Editorial Offices and television studios, existing, no, *thriving* in glorious, defiant challenge to Westminster and the village media. This was the radical left, with all its humour and colour and music and diversity and complete divergence from the stereotypes trotted out by the centre parties.

"Tories out…"

"Tories out."

"Tories, Tories, Tories."

"Out, out OUT."

"It's marvellous," Derek shouted above the din, "I'd forgotten what it feels like. Come on, let's join in." He caught hold of Peter's arm, and stepped out, off the bank and into the river, to be swirled along in the bubbling, frothing torrent of good will. He could feel the sheer energy flowing through him and round him, felt the power of people so much greater than the sum of each puny individual there. He gazed at it and he saw that it was *good*.

"Glorious," he laughed, "Absolutely bloody marvellous."

Pete was smiling. "Has it been that long, Derek? We'll have to find a fatted calf for you – can't you remember, it's always this good. And a great day for it. I'll tell you what, it looks bigger than they were expecting. This lot'll never fit in the Free Trade Hall. I wonder what they'll do. Rig up a P. A. system outside, I suppose."

Derek couldn't have cared less even if he'd heard. He was high with the sensations, he felt better than he'd felt for ages. It wasn't that a march like this on it would have a direct effect on government policy but it was just so good for the morale of all those people who day in and day out campaigned for change, everyone on it would go back to the fight reinvigorated.

"THE WORKERS UNITED…"
"WILL NEVER BE DEFEATED…"
"THE WORKERS…"

"It just does you good to know there are still ordinary people like this out there."

"Yeah, especially as our lot have left them in the lurch. It wouldn't take much for me to leave the party, except I don't know where to go." Derek was stunned. Peter had joined the Labour Party at sixteen, had always defended it, come what may, particularly from those to the Left of it, and his reward was to see them proved right. Perhaps Blair was not that different to before. Under Wilson the party had been truly to the left and willing to introduce radical legislation that really made a difference – in four years. 66 to 70 they'd legalised homosexuality and abortion, introduced an equal pay act, anti-race discrimination acts, created the open university, comprehensive education – and refused to send troops to support the US in Vietnam. Blimey, Derek thought – and we youngsters heckled him for being too moderate. But since, the party had just got blander and blander and Blair was just the inevitable consequence. But it felt different – now it seemed the way into power was to sell out before you got there –was that just honesty or despair? But Derek wasn't going to get on a downer. They could talk about details later.

"God, there must be somewhere to go, look at all this." He swept his arm around, banging into a woman behind.

And on they marched, past the posh department stores and the northern presses of the National Papers, arm in arm under the warm spring sun, towards Peter Street and the Free Trade Hall, this vast host of bubbling, colourful humanity, ringed in by the uniforms and sombre grey faces of the forces of darkness and reaction, like a black -gloved hand trying to snuff out the light.

They were about fifty yards behind the head of the march, with the bulk of the demonstration still behind them. Derek saw the leading banners ahead, turning left into Peter's Street. It was only yards from there that the Peterloo massacre had taken place, in an age not so very different from this one. Derek looked at the people around him, the oldish lady he'd knocked, a young woman with her two young children holding balloons, two solid looking middle-aged men, raincoats over their arms, cloth caps over their eyes, both smiling. And it was then that he became aware of something wrong. His nerves jangling, his senses aroused, his heightened state of awareness reminded him of taking acid in the sixth form, tilting crazily from ecstasy to damnation, he just knew that something awful had happened or was about to happen and he shivered, cold, in the sunshine. He realised with complete clarity cutting through the alcohol, that a Chief Constable like Anderson couldn't possibly allow an exhibition of pure sensory delight like this to continue – it would be a defeat in itself. Up ahead it had gone deadly quiet, and the silence rippled back like cold water washing through the crowd. The bunching up near the corner told him that the head of the march had come to a standstill somewhere around the bend. From the police helicopter hovering above like an angry wasp, the march would now have been L shaped, with Derek and Peter almost at the right angle, just unable to see around the corner.

Then people began talking in what sounded like subdued voices after the exuberance of just a few minutes earlier. There was a cold stillness now, and Derek sensed the chill uneasiness, though unsure if he was just imposing his own increasing jitteriness on the crowd. Peter glanced at Derek and saw the tension on his face, knowing of old that Derek was unhappy in large crowds. "It's probably not, Derek, they'll have reached the Hall by now. It'll be a slow process getting people in. If it takes too long, we can nip out and take a short cut. I'll make sure you get a grandstand seat." Peter seemed calm enough, but Derek could detect a slight uneasiness even in his eyes. All around him the energy and exuberance was transforming into the sparky electricity of group tension. He felt himself getting really nervous, the alcohol and excitement tipping him from high to low. He had seen the way the collective mood of a crowd could swing wildly and he could sense his own mood shifting irreversibly now, unable to control it, watching himself like a helpless bystander witnessing an accident. Impulsively, he thought about getting out, onto the pavement. The invigorating swirl of earlier was now a cold and stagnant pool, sucking him down. He could hardly suppress a surge of panic welling up from his stomach, East Ham again. And worse, it was compounded by the scenes he'd witnessed at Wapping back in '87 when the police had cut off the crowd and methodically attacked them, smashing ambulance windows, taking out the TV cameras, buttoning everyone, women, children – and him caught up in the rush and the panic. Talk, that might help – or he'd have to bolt for the pavement – he'd always had this fear of crowds since he was a kid going to Old Trafford. But sometimes, the alcohol and talking could distract him just enough.

"Right. Listen, if we get separated, when you make your speech, where shall we meet? I might not hang around if it's too crowded, what with my claustrophobia and all." He forced himself to smile, hoping that the act itself would help him to recapture the fast fading feelings of just moments before.

"Or if you've heard all the speeches before, do you mean? Well, what about Thomas's Chop House on Cross Street? A decent pint of Bass in there. Real lunatic broth. Good place to start."

"Right, As soon as they open, then… that is, if I don't stay to the end, of course."

"Yes, of course," he paused. "The claustrophobia, no better, then?"

Derek didn't answer. "I'd forgotten – three men and a dog and you'd be getting panicky. You shouldn't feel so bad about it, though – God, after Hillsborough, I should think everyone gets uneasy in a big crowd. Hey – do you remember David Hall at school? He used to have the same sort of problem with flying you know, a real phobia. He went on some kind of course to get over it."

"Yes, I remember him. Did it work?" Derek was warming to the conversation – talk, talk, talk, the secret weapon in the war to distract him from his own reactions.

"Oh yes, cured him completely, though it took a long time and a lot of effort. It wasn't easy."

"Good for him – I keep promising myself I'll do something about this, but I never do – it doesn't really interfere with much nowadays, though I try to avoid using the tube, and I get a bit uneasy when the traffic's slow in the Blackwall Tunnel in rush hour – but you'd have to be a lump of wood not to. Anyway, what's David up to nowadays? Do you still see him?"

"Not exactly, no – he was killed it that plane crash at Malaga last year."

"What?"

"Only joking, Derek – relax."

"Christ, you bastard, you really had me going there."

Just then a young man in a green anorak came around the corner with a megaphone.

"... WILL BE A SLIGHT DELAY, COMRADES. THERE IS NOTHING TO WORRY ABOUT."

"I recognise that bloke, he's from our ward..." Peter stepped through the line of police onto the pavement, Derek at his shoulder. "Hey, Billy."

The young man turned. "Peter! They're looking for you up at the front, they're trying to get all the speakers together. There's going to be real trouble soon. The police are trying to cancel the whole meeting because of the numbers that will be left outside."

"Oh, Christ! Come on, Derek, let's get up there and see what's going on."

Derek felt numb. 'Up there' was the last place he wanted to be but he found himself following despite himself, legs weak now. As they rounded the corner, having now to push their way through the thickening crowd, they both stopped for a moment and stared.

"Good God!" It was Derek who spoke for both of them.

Peter's Street is about 150 yards long, with the Free Trade Hall on the right about halfway up the gently sloping hill. It had seen many political meetings in its long history – it was here the young Pankhursts had been arrested heckling Churchill – and it was home to the world's first permanent orchestra, the Halle, as well as venue to all the big groups in the late 60s and seventies. In fact it was where Dylan on tour had been booed for using an electric guitar. Just beyond it, the street opened up in Peters Square with the magnificent Public Library building on one side and the grand Midland Hotel on the other. Just below the hall was the head of the march, banners fluttering in the breeze, now facing rows of police several ranks deep. That wasn't what made them stop and stare, though – they had expected to see large numbers of police on any march nowadays. No, it was the sheer scale of it that made them gape. The whole of the upper half of the street beyond the hall was a solid mass of blue-black uniforms. The sunlight sparkled on long shields and polished helmets, drawn up in rank on rank. Across every side street was a cordon of men with round shields, truncheons already drawn. Behind them, horses, flank to flank, the hard, gaunt faces of their riders just visible behind their visors. In the distance, surrounding the Library itself, he could just make out row on row of transit vans and green buses. The crowd was really tense now, he could tell it wasn't just in his mind, but there still seemed to be some good humour around, in a nervous, more restrained way.

Peter and Derek made their way through without much difficulty, though as they got nearer to the steps of the Free Trade Hall the crush was greater. The steps ran the whole length of the building, and two rows of police cordoned them off from the marchers. Pete pushed his way to the front line. At the top of the steps, beyond the police, stood a group of six or seven people and three obviously senior police officers, weighed down with the silver pips on their shoulders, like comic opera generalissimos. Pete recognised one of the group. "JOHN," he yelled, above the bustle of the crowd, "IT'S ME, PETER FURNESS." The man he was evidently shouting at, short and stocky, pointed towards them and came down the steps with one of the policemen.

"Hello, Pete."

The policeman spoke to the constables directly in front of them, and the line parted. "There's two of us," Pete gasped, as the pressure of the crowd forced them through the narrow gap, which immediately closed up again behind them. "This is Derek Brown, an old friend of mine. Derek, this is John Nicholson, T&G."

John nodded, but there were obviously more pressing things on his mind than introductions. The three of them walked up the stairs to the group at the top where there was an almighty row going on. Derek could only half concentrate, feeling relief at being out of the crowd, but from his new vantage point, more keenly aware that trouble was inevitable now if the pressure on the front rows of police was not relieved. And you couldn't just ask ten thousand people to all take two steps backwards in an orderly fashion. He was dazed by all this and tried to turn his full attention to the argument going on around him. The faces of the participants were grey, drawn, anxious and he recognised Chief Constable Anderson from T.V. pictures, with his old testament black beard and wild eyes. He was talking with studied restraint, an infuriatingly supercilious half-grin playing across his face. It made Derek want to slap him.

"... and I repeat, it is my duty to enforce the law, and if you cannot guarantee freedom of movement for the ordinary citizens of this city, then I'm afraid I must use the powers invested in me and inform you that I am not allowing this demonstration to continue. You must ask your followers to disperse immediately." He reminded Derek of Mussolini, swaggering around like a clown, ostensibly comic but ultimately lethal. One of the march organisers pushed past Derek.

"What do you want us to do, eh? Just wave a fucking wand and make them all disappear, or what, eh?"

"There's no need to use foul language, now, Mr Ashton…"

"Oh, for Christ's sake, man, don't you realise what you're doing?" Something told Derek that Anderson knew exactly what he was doing and that any argument was just a waste of breath, but before anyone could say anything else, there was a great roar from the crowd, echoing hard off the cold stone facings of the buildings. Derek turned to see what was happening and there, where the crowd met the police lines, where light met darkness, where there were no shades of grey, the trouble had started, and it happened fast.

Derek felt his stomach tighten as he saw a helmet go flying and fists smack into faces with the sickening noise of reality that no amount of violent television actually prepares you for in real life. The speed of events, the fact that the outcome isn't known, the fact that it isn't limited to the screen but all around, with no soothing voice-overs, no one to shout 'Cut' and edit the evidence for safe public consumption, and no chance of just changing channel if it all got too much, no way out, nowhere to go, nowhere to hide. Yet at least he wasn't actually in it, thank God, standing and staring with the vicarious fascination of the bystander, shocked by the sheer, sharp-edged reality of it all.

"You bastard, look what you've done," Ashton yelled, grabbing Anderson by the lapels of his toy soldier uniform, pushing into Derek. Anderson stumbled back, and several constables dragged Ashton off. Recovering his posture, smoothing down his jacket, Anderson sneered imperiously, "Take him away," and Ashton was dragged struggling down the steps and up towards the top of the street. The remaining march organisers raised no protest, not through fear of suffering the same fate, but because they were simply overwhelmed by the events unfolding around them. Anderson turned to them, and gestured towards the crowd with his cane. "Now, gentlemen, I must be about my business." He and his other officers strode off in the same direction they'd taken Ashton, leaving five impotent figures standing dejectedly on the steps. Even if they'd wanted to, they couldn't have reached the crowd now, as more and more rows of police had wedged along the bottom of the steps, completely cutting off access to the building. It was inescapably becoming more and more obvious that this, like Wapping, was a carefully planned operation, and all they could do was stand and watch.

The noise was deafening now but Derek could make out clear individual visual details, like truncheons being jabbed into stomachs or raised, glistening, whacking down with that slap of a sound they make, horribly audible even above the shouting and screaming.

In fact, the whole thing couldn't have lasted more than about five minutes, Ashton being bundled off, the parting of the police lines to let through the riot squads, with their short shields and no numbers, arms flailing into the defenceless crowd. A few in the crowd tried to fight back, fists against shields and helmets, but they were soon beaten to the ground, to be kicked and trampled by the black boots of the officers of law and order, and no doubt later to be pilloried on the evening news as the 'rent-a-mob' cause of the violence. But most were intent only on escaping from this barbaric madness, prevented from doing so by the crush from behind, itself made worse by the horse police who were now pressing in from the streets on either side of the march, narrowing down the path of escape, trapping hundreds in the bottleneck they were deliberately creating. Derek could see terror, absolute fear, in the faces of those now trapped between the two lines of police. Then, suddenly, the cavalry widened the escape gap allowing the terrified crowd to spill out down the road, gushing out like fizz from a shaken-up coke bottle, a mass of running, stumbling individuals, bewildered and disorganised. As they broke and ran back down towards Deansgate, the foot police gave chase, harassing, harrying, kicking those who fell.

And then, quite suddenly, the crowd was gone, leaving a vacuum of colour and sound. The street was strewn with the crumpled-up bodies of injured marchers, scattered like litter after a carnival parade. Groups of riot police were making their way back up the road, two of them half carrying an injured colleague. The remaining ranks of police remained in formation, still, grey-faced and silent.

Derek found himself facing the backs of the police cordon and in the eerie silence heard himself give vent to the increasing awareness of what he had just witnessed. He wiped tears from his cheeks and muttered, "You bastards," and then louder and then again louder still, "You FUCKING BASTARDS," only vaguely aware of the attention he was beginning to attract from the officers directly in front of him. It was as if for an instant, time had stopped and there was just his voice echoing in an empty universe, "You fucking bastards."

And then the instant was gone, and noise and vision rushed in on him like a wave of cold surf. Two policemen had grabbed him, one to each arm, pushing him forward with pressure on his elbows, rushing him across the road, his feet hardly touching the ground. He felt a vicious stab in his kidneys as a third officer jabbed him hard with the end of his truncheon and then, before he could draw a breath to even cry out, he was banged against the side of a green arresting bus. As he bounced back, he felt someone grab his hair, pull so tight that he gasped, and then his face was smashed into the side of the bus. He felt his right cheek split, felt his upper lip gash open, felt blood, hot on his chin, felt the most absolute panic that he had ever felt. And then he was being dragged again and bundled into the bus, pushed along the aisle and forced into a seat near the back. His hands were dragged forward and he was handcuffed to the seat in front, forced forward into a mockery of pious prayer. Then the pace seemed to slow down and he looked up at the two who had arrested him, one pushing onto the seat next to him. "I'll do 'im."

"Right, the fucking little shit." The one standing, looking down, breathing heavily, truncheon still in his hand – "You, you little shit bag, I'm talking to you." He lifted Derek's face toward him by forcing the truncheon under his chin "You scum." And he spat, the gob hitting Derek just below the left eye. The two policemen laughed, their laughter sounding hollow and metallic on the otherwise empty bus.

There had been relatively few arrests and those that had been made had already been driven off to police stations around the city – not because they couldn't have been accommodated at one or two central stations, but so that it was difficult to trace their whereabouts very quickly, giving time for cuts to be dressed and stories sorted out before the nuisance of interfering solicitors could arrive. But as is so often the case, after just two hours in a filthy cell on his own, Derek was released without charge. He was no stranger to police stations, or police behaviour in them – he'd been in enough of them on the other side of the desk with his job. And if he'd not been worn out and in pain, he'd have been amused at the puzzlement on their faces, the raised eyebrows when they saw his warrant card during their search, heard the muttered expletives and he knew then it was unlikely that he would be charged. Even so, he had prepared himself for longer than two hours, though Christ knows, two hours in that dirty, stinking, cold dark oubliette was more than enough. As they returned his belongings to him at the desk, he could sense that there was some embarrassment on the part of the desk sergeant, not remorse for the arrest, but a sort of shifty sullen resentment at having been caught out doing something they normally get away with – Derek's right eye was now so swollen that it was hardly open at all, just visible above the dressing on the cut in his cheek. His upper lip was a mess, looked like he'd been in a bare-knuckle fight, which in a way he had. He felt like he should say something, insult them, make a formal complaint, threaten action of some sort, even just cast a defiant sneer at them but at the same time he felt too awful, too dirty, too degraded too worn out and…and, yes, still too frightened to say anything. He felt vulnerable, fragile and defeated. He knew he would more easily start crying at the sheer humiliation of the experience than be able to brazen it out with some show of macho bravado. So he just put his things in his pockets and shuffled out, relieved to be free of that dreadful place. He knew more or less where he was, just past the university complex on Oxford Road, and he dragged himself a little way along towards the city centre, back towards Peter Square, aware that he must look a complete mess, confirmed by sideways glances from people he passed. Above all, he felt he was going under – so much seemed to have been happening to him or around him that it was hard to see it all as just coincidental – yet he had no mental framework for seeing it any other way. Nonetheless, the roller coaster ride of physical and emotional ups and downs was taking its toll on his mind. He was developing a distinct feeling of being got at, of unfairness, of events ganging up on him, towering ominously, darkly over him and a sense that as soon as he seemed to sort himself out over one thing, there were more and more just piling up, waiting to have a kick at him. "Infamy infamy, they've all got it in for me," he muttered to himself and almost managed a smile but it wasn't even vaguely funny because that's exactly how it felt. He needed time to sort himself out once and for all but there never was the time, never was the space and it was all getting too fucking much. But he had other more immediate priorities now – he had to contact Peter and get somewhere he felt safe. Probably should get checked out for concussion but definitely needed a drink. He gazed vacantly at the traffic, the whole world going on just as normal. Something momentous and terrible had happened in the city and to him, but life was going on everywhere just as before despite the events of the afternoon – that's one of the ways they got away with outrages like this – it was out of sight and out of mind for most of the people most of the time.

Across the bleak and busy Oxford Road he noticed a pub – looked like an old run-down house, and he wouldn't ordinarily have gone anywhere near it, but needs must, he needed a phone and he couldn't see any boxes anywhere –and in the absence of anywhere else in sight, it acquired an almost siren like attraction. He walked in, only vaguely aware that his entry was immediately eliciting interest from the few customers scattered at tables in the large, red-carpeted bar room.

"Been at the match, mate?" the barman smiled, but his tone managed to convey both concern and suspicion as well as a landlord's light heartedness. Derek looked dishevelled, down and out and could mean trouble.

An old man seated further along the bar laughed. "Been at it? Looks like he was in it – that Robson's got a great right hook," Derek tried to smile, but stopped as his swollen lips began to crack open again. He turned to the barman. "Double Southern Comfort, please." The barman poured a large measure straight from the bottle, didn't bother with the optic.

"Ice?"

"No, thanks."

"Seriously, the ice would be good mate. For the lip. You look pretty grim, you know." Derek's voice and bearing had immediately reassured the wary instincts of the publican and it was now definitely concern rather than suspicion which dominated.

"No, I'll be fine, honestly. Thanks." Derek took a drink, wincing as the spirit seared into his cut lips. "Do you have a phone I could use?"

"Yeah, help yourself." And he pointed to the dirty payphone on the wall at the end of the bar. And then, feeling sorry for Derek, he took his private avocado phone off the shelf behind him and placed it on the bar. And then walked away to chat to customers – there was only so much concern you could show to strangers and he really didn't want to eavesdrop on anything he might regret hearing.

Derek assumed that Peter would have gone to the Chop House as arranged, so he got the number from Directory Enquiries and dialled. Luckily the barman there was very helpful and managed to identify Peter and within half an hour, he had got a taxi over, picked Derek up.

"Jesus Derek, what the fuck?" as he walked into the bar – and then to the barman, "Two of whatever he's on, I'll get them. Cheers."

"Police. Bastards," muttered Derek as he downed the second drink.

Peter did the same. "I've got a taxi on the meter outside so let's get going." Derek half shuffled towards the door, leaning slightly on Peter, until they reached the black cab.

"Hope Hospital or the Labour Club?" Peter asked him as he helped him into the back seat.

Derek almost laughed but it hurt and any it obviously wasn't meant as a joke even with dry Manc wit.

"Salford West Labour Club – Seedley Park," Peter said to the taxi driver – "Do you know it?"

"Yes pal – but I'd keep Hope Hospital in mind by the looks of your mate!"

This time Derek did smile and it did hurt, but he felt safe now.

Finally, they made it to the club and stumbled inside and into one of the committee rooms off the main hall of the club, which looked bare and unwelcoming in its afternoon emptiness.

"Derek, Are you sure you don't want to get checked out at Hope? It's almost walking distance…"

They both laughed. "If I could walk it, I wouldn't need it, would I?"

"I'm thinking concussion…they don't recommend sleeping or drinking…"

They both paused.

Then Derek smiled. "Fuck it, get me a beer and brandy chaser. I'll risk it."

As Peter headed out to the bar, an old guy came in who Derek recognised as a councillor from back in the day, but he couldn't remember the name.

"Hello, Derek, long time no see, no fuck, don't get up – you look like you should be in A&E…bastards."

He sat down and offered his cigs and they both lit up. "Come on then, what happened exactly. I've heard the outline?" and Derek started to try and go through it all, with the old guy shaking his head every now and then and tutting. "Always the bloody same, always the bloody same." Derek tried to structure the story into some semblance of a timeline but–through the haze of alcohol and tobacco smoke and pain and shock, one question kept emerging – how on earth were people ever going to get anywhere if they didn't face the fact that sooner or later real change was going to lead to physical conflict. Democratic dissent would only be allowed for as long as it had no effect, but as soon as it began to bite and was perceived as a threat, Democratic Governments would react with the same violence as any tin pot dictatorship because essentially they don't like Democracy when it gives them the wrong answers. That was what he had seen during his years in London, from Grunwicks to the miners' strike, during the poll tax campaign, Wapping and now this afternoon. Always the police, their violence prevailing over the essentially decent people who opposed them, whose instincts were always to behave, to obey, to be peaceful. Never were they ruthless enough to push home the advantage of their numbers. "We are many, they are few," okay but we never ever use it.

As soon as Derek had finished his brief account, they had another drink and then another and a constant stream of cigarettes, as the alcohol relaxed away the pain and the nicotine revived him from the bewilderment that had numbed him since his release from the cells. "But how many beatings will people take before they do something about it? Its nearly two hundred years since Peterloo, for Christ sake. And it's still fucking happening." He knew he needed to get this out his system, knew he was in the right place for it.

"Right, so what do we do? If I got you the guns tomorrow, how many would there be with you at the barricades? Revolutions don't happen out of the blue you know. Actually, mass uprisings tend not to happen at all – Russia was a small number of people in two cities to start with and it was touch and go. And we can't even elect a labour government. Three elections on the trot we've lost. There's more to overthrowing a system than having an emotional spasm after seeing a bit of police brutality, Derek."

"Feeling it, Peter, feeling it, not just bloody seeing it."

"OK, mate, it's shit but we're all on the same side."

"Yes, OK, but there must be something we can do. They've been having it their own way for so bloody long. And all the Labour Party does is make it easier for them, channels their anger, *our* anger, into ballot boxes and the promise of something better to come in some vague and very misty future, like riches in heaven – God, Kinnock wasn't even making promises any more, just boring everyone into a coma. And who else have we got? Smith? Even worse, Blair in the wings???"

"Oh, Right on, Derek, right on – but what are *you* doing? It's alright being shocked, but righteous indignation and getting punched isn't a substitute for hard work and building an organised movement. And I happen to think we might as well use a readymade movement if we can. You say we should try to do something well, like what? armed struggle? General Strike? It wouldn't even amount to a gesture. Times have changed, Derek. They knocked the wind out of us with the miners, and then look how they kicked them when they were down – Christ, we're buying in coal from Poland and closing our own pits just to neuter their power. And then the printers…and now it's all a question of who's next in this Tory wonderland of fear and austerity. And the party seems helpless. Kinnock fucked up his chance to get Thatcher out over Westmoreland. We lost the challenges to their authority and the ruthless bastards have made sure we can't do that again for a long time. You can't mount momentous strikes like that every week, you know. And when you lose, the losers pay the price. You and me cheering them on from the touchline, we still have our jobs and homes to go back to. What we need to do now is to get the Tories out, and rebuild, regroup and it might take a generation. I agree about Blair – his idea is to get Labour in by not being Labour but I think Smith understands the party. Even so, we might have to find somewhere else but where? The trots are insignificant, amateurish, tiny. Look at the militant mess – I don't think they should have been kicked them out but they weren't a credible alternative. And the CP is still a force in some of the unions but it no longer has the numbers and has never been really... progressive." Pete took another swig of beer, on a roll now. "And we keep talking about the working class as if it's one solid mass and something to protect and aspire to – we idealise it and fair enough, you and me, we are part of it or were when we grew up – but don't forget what you're gran said to us when we joined the party – do you remember? I do – socialism isn't about speaking with a bluff northern accent and bragging about being working class – it's not about worshipping the workers it's about abolishing class all together.' Half the working class don't give a toss, don't even vote, course they don't. They're not any more stupid or ignorant than any other class but they're not any better either – just poorer. We don't protect them and advance their condition by somehow spinning a myth about how wonderful they all are because they're not, and the labour party will forever fail until it recognises that – and she left school at twelve and worked all her life in the mills, Derek, as you should never forget."

Derek held up his hands in an act of surrender, suddenly tired deep inside, the stresses of the day draining his inner energies away like blood seeping out of his split lip, salty. He gripped the edge of the table, feeling suddenly dizzy. "OK, OK, fair point. I just feel so fucking pissed off that the bloody 'powers that be' seem to get it all their own way all of the time. They just keep winning. They're more ruthless than we are. And so bloody cocky they feel unassailable – have you seen some of those arrogant crooks justifying their bloody huge salaries – they just couldn't give a damn. I know individual terrorism is never a substitute for a mass movement and all that, and that killing a few of them wouldn't bring about a revolution or even any significant change, but fuck, it would be nice to think of some of them getting their comeuppance once in a while. I see more than you do of the 'Ruling Class' or whatever you like to call them, and they really are a bunch of smug crooks, Pete. Do you remember all those shitty little playground bullies at school? Well, they don't go away when they grow up, they just join the Conservative Party and become M.P.'s or top businessmen. Just the same trash but with power, Peter, power. I just can't help feeling that when all else fails, they shouldn't be allowed to get away with treating people like shit all the time. Perhaps they should be made to live in fear so that they can never take their money for granted, so they know that someone somewhere is going to get them for all their exploitation and bullying..."

"Christ, Derek. Have another drink and calm down. I thought you'd given up politics. Mind you, I'm not sure all that wild-eyed stuff counts as politics... Remember, we're an electoral party, not a fucking pressure group or a bunch of poseur revolutionaries – an electoral party and that means our only raison d'etre is to win elections to win power to change lives. Atlee transformed the country and set up the NHS – Wilson legalised abortion, legalised homosexuality, passed equal pay legislation, passed the first anti race discrimination legislation, created the open university, abolished the death penalty, reformed the divorce laws, refused to send troops to Vietnam and on and on. You have to win elections to change life for the better. And we've just lost three elections and you can't just blame the press. Wilson won four times on a left programme despite the media"

"Well, alright, alright, can't disagree. But what happens if we win and don't do anything with it all, that's my worry. I'm just so utterly frustrated by it all... oh fuck it' He looked down at his hands '...I think I've just about stopped shaking. I'll have another pint – and a chaser. Do you think it's true that you start to feel better just before the end? Here, it's my round..."

The main hall of the club was quite large, with a stage at one end for the Saturday Night Cabaret. The bar ran along half the length of the room, well-stocked with fizzy beer and even fizzier lager. There must have been sixty tables in the room, all with red Formica tops, each with six red plastic chairs and it was beginning to fill up for the Saturday night 'do'.

In the side room, Derek finished another brandy and began to sip at yet another pint. He was still feeling badly shaken. But as the evening wore on, he leaned back in his chair and raised his glass in a toast

"What a fucking weekend! Last time I'm bloody coming up here for a pint with you, mate." They laughed, and despite everything, he felt *alive* again. The Great Rollercoaster was on an up. He had felt real conviction when he'd been arguing, not just alcohol-induced posturing and now he realised that he was actually looking forward to getting back to London, getting back to some sort of normality, sorting out his day to day life, not the fucking world.

Peter took a sip from another pint to avoid spilling it on his way back from the bar. He glanced across the now quite crowded hall to where Derek was sitting and for a second, noticed a strange smile play across Derek's lips and saw that he was apparently muttering to himself. Though he was too drunk to follow it through, he registered a concern that had surfaced a couple of times during the day, that all was not at all well with his old friend.

Next morning, Derek felt barely alive. He couldn't remember getting back to the hotel at all but judging by his surroundings, that was where he was. He managed to get out of bed, and stagger into the shower, while fragmented images of the night flickered through his mind – the laughter and shouting and smoke and drinking and more drinking, all at the Labour Club. He had a vague recollection of the brash cabaret, of being sick, of a taxi, door gaping wide open, black like a gothic hearse.

Drying himself, he winced seeing the bruised swelling around his eye. Christ he really did look a mess and felt a mess. Astonishingly, through the aches and pains of his beating and the alcohol-scrambled disaster that was his brain that morning, he actually remembered his final 'resolution' – to turn it all around, get something real back into his life, stop the drift and all the clever arse gesture politics at work, get on track for some meaning in terms of real life. And he found himself thinking about Val – would she phone? And could that be part of his new world?

And then his next thought was one familiar to every drunk after every party – How many grovelingly sheepish apologies did he need to make? He thought of phoning Pete to see if he'd made too much of a bloody fool of himself, but he knew he wouldn't – too much of a coward, he wanted to isolate the weekend now, seal it until he could fully absorb it, sit down sober, rested and sort it all out. But it could be sorted, he had no doubt about that now and perhaps that was why despite everything, despite the physical injuries, despite the drinking, the smoking, the dreadful hangover. He smiled through his cracked and swollen lips and mouthed 'everything gonna be alright' – the case, his life, yes, even the F word – his Future. He really was going to be alright.

Chapter 7

The trek back to London was a nightmare. The train jolted and jerked its way along from one set of Sunday engineering works to the next, sometimes a burst of speed and then, before the journey could take on any restful sense of rhythm, a complete stop. It took nearly five hours to get to Euston, by which time he was in a state of shock: stale, numb, nauseous, dizzy. And still there was the long haul on the central line, out beyond the slums of the East End to the bland suburbs where he had the small but expensive bachelor pad he never quite thought of as 'home'. It was a pale and haggard Derek who climbed the stairs at seven that evening, all the emotions and physical upheavals of the weekend catching up on him. He felt like he needed a complete break from everything, felt as if he needed to plunge his hot brain into ice-cold water.

He took a bottle of Muscadet from the fridge and opened it, taking off his jacket and laying down on the settee. He gulped a long drink straight from the bottle, his eyes stinging as his eyelids sagged slowly shut...

... into a deep, dark, warm dream, which suddenly took a turn for the worse, with bright lights and ringing bells, ringing bells, ringing... dragging him up into a cold splash of sudden consciousness, as the blur of sound snapped into harsh reality of his telephone ringing. He jerked himself across the room and into the hall.

"Hello, 534 4384." What the fuck was the time?

"Derek? Its Val, can you get into the office straight away?"

He rubbed his face, trying to wake up, "What time is it?" Well, she'd called but this was ridiculous.

"It's about half two – in the morning – I'm sorry it's so late but it really is important."

"Well, yes, it must be," thinking *it had fucking better be* but he managed, god knows how, to sound more pleasant than anyone could ever possibly be feeling at half past two in the morning. "So what's the rush?"

"Well, really it was Bill's idea to phone you. There's been a development on our case, they're out investigating now and he actually said you *ought* to be here and that you'd absolutely, without any doubt whatsoever, want to be involved."

"Well, not a clue what he's on about but not like him to exaggerate. Anyway, glad he gave you the job of calling me, I'd much rather be talking to you in the middle of the night than Bill." A bit forward, he was moving into automatic mode and somewhere deep inside he knew it wasn't going to wash with this one. There was a slight pause and then,

"Anyway, I can't give you all the details over the phone. I'll bring you up to date when you get here." Not a flicker, she wasn't playing his game. Well perhaps no bad thing.

"OK, give me an hour to get dressed and I'll be there. See you then."

"You mean you're standing there talking to me with nothing on?" Deadpan, it threw him completely.

And then she laughed that slight, knowing laugh of hers. She wasn't playing his games, she'd cleverly taken the lead and left him on the backfoot, not knowing what to say, how to respond, what was she playing at. And then, softly, warm

"Bye. See you in an hour." And click.

He put the phone down and fumbled for the cigarettes in his jacket, which was hanging by the phone. He felt a lot better once he'd lit up and made himself a coffee and the drive to office at Holborn was actually quite enjoyable. As the dark empty streets blurred by, he felt warm and safe, cocooned in the womb of his car, Sibelius' fifth on the stereo. It actually took him less than the hour to drive through the East End and into the City so it was about quarter past three when he walked into the brightly lit foyer of 'Victory Mansions'. He showed his pass to the security man and climbed two flights of dingy stairs – the lifts were out of order again – and then along the green-tiled echoing corridor and into the office, that bare office with the ghastly headache-brightness of the throbbing neon lights instantly tormenting him. Val was sitting behind one of the desks, typing into one of the new computers, black screen, green font. "Hello, Val. What's all this about then?"

She glanced up and then caught sight of his injured face.

"My God, what on earth happened to you? I'm sorry its none of..."

"No, don't worry, just a typical good time out in Salford! I'll tell you all about it later, but what's this about first, it's got to be something special?"

She paused just for a second and he thought he saw something more than just concern on her face, a hint of caring...

"Well, there's been a lot happening since you went up to Manchester."

"Yes, there was a lot happening up there as well."

"I can see that!"

He became aware again of that strange feeling he'd had on the train with her, of being relaxed yet feeling awkward, of distance and intimacy at the same time. Trying to look cool and at ease, he sat casually on the corner of her desk.

She continued, "Well, we think we're really onto something big."

"Yes, that's the impression the lads in Manchester had. I was going to put it into my report tomorrow – well, today now." He turned to look at her. "By the way, did you ring earlier – I was back later than I thought and I wondered if you'd rung..." He couldn't help asking, checking if perhaps she'd tried earlier, a more social call. He was watching how she would react, but she didn't, not in any discernible way. He shifted self-consciously on the edge of the desk and winced slightly as he tried to smile through his swollen lips.

"No, no I've been working on this job since we got the lead. Since *I* got the lead." She looked tired out, but her eyes were sparkling again and she made him feel distinctly jaded.

"Well, I'm waiting. Come on, spill the beans, I'm losing the will here?"

And then she grinned at him. "You're very ratty tonight! Still, I'm not going to let that put me off. And it is late – I'll forgive you." And then she pouted ever so slightly at him and, quite un self-consciously gave a slight giggle and he suddenly felt a surge of emotion towards her but before he could say anything, she carried on and the moment had passed, leaving him once more confused about his own emotions. Was he sensing some reciprocation, or was it just wishful thinking, his own ego on overtime?

"I followed our Manchester target back from Euston to a posh house in one of those nice squares near the Institute. Russell Square, just near, you know? Anyway, that was when we had our lucky break. He went up the steps, rang the bell, left the case on the doorstep and came back down again. I carried on following him and I was walking past when I noticed a bloke getting out of a car. I don't know why he caught my eye, but I risked a quick glance back at him and I was sure that I'd seen his face somewhere before. I kept walking and glanced round again, just in time to see this new bloke going into the same house, picking up the case as he went."

"Brilliant. Well done you – but they'll crucify you, you were putting yourself in real danger, on your own like that…"

"Derek, you sound as if you really care?"

Again, she completely threw him.

"Well, of course…" But before he could finish, she carried on,

"So, I found the nearest phone box and had the office send a photographer down fast. I managed to speak to Bill and he got clearance to set up a quick stake out and this is what we came up with…" She handed him a large black and white photograph. He took it, thinking what a good officer she was, straight from the textbook. Cool and collected. His eyes flickered over the grainy images and then sharpened.

"Bloody hell! That's Salter!" He stood up, overwhelmed not just by this sudden burst of emotion, but by the distinct, hairs on the back of his neck sensation that something of great significance was happening to him in his life. And now, this, after two days of mayhem in Manchester, up pops Salter. It was the bloody Wizard of Oz, black and white suddenly bursting into colour. And Salter, as neat as a missing piece in a jigsaw puzzle, Salter, his icon for all that he hated about the establishment, everything. The timing was perfect, this would be his revenge for the beating he'd had. He'd nail the fucking bastard this time. He felt his fists tightening as he confirmed the identity to be absolutely sure there was no mistake. "It *is* Salter isn't it?"

"Yes, it is. And that's where the real luck came in because it was the Salter case Bill used as an example when he was showing me how to use the filing system. He was so worked up about it as he told me about you and him and the case, that the face in the file must have just stuck in my mind. Anyway, tonight we sent the garbage crew around on the off chance, and they're on their way back this very minute. He said you'd need to be in on it."

It wasn't the flame of enthusiasm that Salter's name kindled in Derek, it was a blow torch of hatred. "Too right. Christ, if we could get that bastard, I'd die a happy man." The whirling confusions in Derek's mind suddenly seemed to be clearing. The job, the way he was feeling about Val, the vivid images of the weekend. It was as if he was waking up inside after years of sleepwalking. "Who's this other bloke coming out of the house with him? I'm sure I recognise him too from somewhere."

"No one knows, but Bill thought he'd seen him before as well. He arrived about an hour after Salter. We didn't have enough officers to follow them, so we're focussing on the house – we didn't know Salter had a place there – it's registered to some company of other." The second of the two men looked nervous and shifty, but then these black and white candid camera shots made everyone look like that, even passers-by. He stared at Harry Salter and felt a great loathing in his stomach, the same loathing that he'd felt when he'd interviewed the man.

"I still don't know how he managed to get away with it. God, the judge said he was granting bail because it was 'only a financial offence'. It was only the biggest V.A.T. fraud we'd ever got to court. Can you imagine a judge saying that to some poor sod caught fiddling his dole? I'm taking a lenient view of this case, because it's only a financial offence."

"So what happened then?"

"We did absolutely everything we could. We were even leaking the story to 'Private Eye', to keep the profile high but in the end the word came down from above. National Interest intervention. Drop it! Just like that. I don't know where it came from, Spooks, MI5 and 6? god knows who, but that was the end of that. Just like that. But you must have heard all this before from Bill."

"But didn't you follow it through?"

"Yes, as far as we could, but we just came up against the stone wall. We were told to withdraw from the case because it wasn't in the National Interest and there were problems with our evidence. It was the first big case I worked on when I moved to London, but it still leaves a foul taste in my mouth –"

"As the actress said to the bishop." Val laughed, again taking him completely by surprise.

"God, where do you get your energy at this time of the day…night…morning? Anyway, when I interviewed him. I was new to the team, like I said. The rest had put nearly two years work into it. It just happened that I was on duty when they picked him up, and they let me do the first interview, for the experience. Bill was with me, of course, and the amazing thing I remember once was that this fat obnoxious slob we'd picked was looking at us as if we were scum, sneering at us. It simply did not occur to him that that he was subject to the same rules and regulations and laws as everybody else – or that he would ever be held responsible for his actions, certainly not in this way. There was not one single sign of fear or wariness, just outrage that he had been brought in. He actually said, 'Why've you brought me here? You're treating me like some criminal.'"

"I said, 'Well, Mr Salter, that's exactly what we suspect you are. You've been stealing money from the Government – from everyone, if you like.' And he just laughs, 'Grow up. I'm not a criminal, I'm a businessman. And now he's into Heroin!' The bastard, we'll get him this time."

"Well, you know, all in all, that doesn't sound too terrible, it's about par for the course isn't it? I mean you're not all that naive, are you? I thought you were at one of those Universities they all go to? Shouldn't have been a surprise – Bullingdon Bullies and all that?"

"Ouch! Well, you're sort of right, but even at Uni they mix in their own circles. Christ, I didn't have enough money to mingle with that lot, though you'd come across them from time to time obviously – but I never thought it would carry on after. I know, I know, the old school tie etc. but honestly, I thought it was probably mostly a bit of a myth – that's how they get away with it – the rest of us really don't think it's actually true when it's probably even worse than the worse conspiracy theorists come up with."

"Come on Derek – Look at that Baring's business – that guy was desperate to get to England because he knew we've got the weakest punishments for financial 'impropriety' in the world. I can't see why this one's got you all so worked up."

"No, no you're right, objectively it doesn't seem bad enough, does it? But it's hard to explain, he was just such a *shit*. Two years of hard work, all sewn up and the way it fell through. It all just got under our skin, he was that sort of git anyway, he'd have got us feeling pissed off at the best of times. You'd have to have been there, just have to take my word for it."

"Yes, I can see that. Anyway, it's all jolly exciting," putting on a comic upper-class accent. "And talking of exciting, what did happen to you up in… Manchester?"

"Oh something and nothing." She caught him off guard again and again. "It'd take a long time to explain. Listen, let me take you out for a meal and I'll tell you all about it." He blushed, but there, it was done, when even he least expected it. She hesitated, just slightly, looked down at her desk for a second and then, looking straight at him carried on in the same light tone he'd adopted. "Yes, OK But it had better be worth hearing."

"Well, if it's not, I'll make something up that is."

She laughed, "Well, I like stories, but I don't want a lecture."

Ouch again, "Right, point taken" – chastened but with no time to gather his thoughts, as a clattering sound outside announced the imminent arrival of the garbage gang.

"Ring me tomorrow night. And don't mention it to anyone in the office. I don't like mixing work with my social life. I'm making quite an exception for you."

And before he could say anything except 'Of course not', three men burst into the room, two carrying a metal dustbin between them. They were wearing grey one-piece nylon overalls and rubber gloves and were laughing raucously.

"Hello, Derek," said the tallest of them, a large, well-built man in his late twenties, with thick dark hair, a wiry beard and a grin as broad as his West Country accent.

"Hello, John, I see you've found your true vocation in life, eh? Shovelling shit. Or rather getting other people to shovel it for you."

"Ah yes, now that's the real secret of success, getting other people to do it for you, though you know you've really got to the top when people are grateful to you for letting them shovel it for you. Christ, I need something to swill away the taste of all that, where's the mouthwash?"

"Christ," said Derek. "You've not let him eat any of it, have you, Bill?"

Laughing, Bill rummaged inside his overalls and produced a bottle of scotch. "Now, if it's not being too sexist, might I suggest Ladies First." Val accepted the bottle and took a deep gulp from it before handing it to Derek. The other two came over, pulling off their gloves. Bill and Ron McCartney, looking better for their rest after East Ham.

"Christ Derek – I thought we were on gardening duties – Day of the Triffids in your garden was it? Someone's husband take a pop at you again?"

116

Derek didn't know what to say, but he glanced up to see that Val was looking straight at him.

"Leave it, Bill, just leave it – and no it wasn't anything like that - plenty of time to tell you all about it – but this, this is brilliant – toast to Val, I believe?"

"Absolutely, without question. Cheers."

He didn't turn to look at her but…but he felt a slight touch on his hand and heard her say 'thanks' to the group. It felt wonderful.

Bill wiped his face, spitting into his hands. That sour and sickly-sweet stink of rotting refuse was beginning to saturate the room. "When you've finished with that, Derek, if there's any left I'd appreciate another wee drop." His voice carried a gritty air of natural authority, which just as well as head of the team at this field level. Derek passed him the bottle. "Do you think the bin's worth it? Salter's a wily bastard and they seem to have organised everything very carefully so far – the lads up in Manchester got everything that happened up there on video – they've given me a copy The switch was very well done. I mean, if he is into heroin, he must know that his powerful friends won't find it easy to help him this time if he gets caught."

"Well not as easily, that's for sure," said Bill.

"Right, come on lads, less of the chit chat, we'd better get down to it," said Ron, taking a last swig of the whisky. "Of course the bins are always worth a shot, you know that, Derek."

Val looked across at the bin. "Won't he be suspicious when he finds it gone?"

"Not likely – we swapped his for one three doors down. He'll never notice." laughed Bill. "Come on, you two as well, we've got spare pairs of gloves." Derek noticed a smile from Val, not for him but for being included as just another member of the team – looked like she was on the move, exactly where she wanted to be, no questions asked, no hint of being an outsider – the whiskey, the bin, just automatic inclusion. It was a smile of pride in her achievement.

Derek looked at the bin and prayed that there would be something, anything, that they could start a case on. He wanted to get Salter more than ever now. He thought back to the conversation he'd had with Peter about the futility of individual acts. Well, it might be ultimately futile, but it would feel good to nail one of them. If there was anything here to make a case out of, he'd get him this time. He lit another cigarette and handed the packet round – "A quick drag before we start, after all, you lot don't seem to have any private lives to go back to."

"I thought you'd be raring to go," said Ron, "with it being Salter and all."

Bill looked up. "Yes, I've been thinking about that – we'd better all be careful of our feelings about this one. We mustn't rush it or cock up the evidence. I know we didn't cock it up last time but we've got to be extra careful of any pitfalls. We'll take it very steady, piece by piece and really make it stick. Don't forget, Philip will probably back us, but if anything goes wrong, we'll have that sod Maloney down on us." Maloney again – you really couldn't trust him, with his city-slicker style, despite the fact that he'd seemed genuinely concerned about the three of them after the East Ham incident. The truth was, he was too distant from them in every sense. They seldom saw him, he was hardly ever involved in the day to day business of their cases, except for the final stages of the more prestigious and successful ones. In these cases, it would be Maloney on the 10 o'clock news for the interviews. He moved in very different circles to them and they suspected his motives and ultimately his loyalty to their causes. He was a political figure, mixing with the very sort they were often investigating, drinking in their clubs, dining in their homes. If the team wanted to get Salter, they were going to have to have a completely cast-iron case and the dustbin was the start. But none of them was in any immediate hurry – it was full and it really did stink.

Chapter 8

Ron had been right, of course, always worth a shot. Even in this nascent age of electronic surveillance, with sophisticated technology developing on both sides of the law, it was still invariably the small human failings that continued to give criminals away. And so it was in this case, because the bin did have some secrets to reveal – or one, anyway. It wasn't much to go on, but it was a start, and it was hard copy and it might even be of some use as evidence if it could be traced back to the typewriter on which it had been written – and it was obviously typewritten and not word-processed. But most importantly, it gave them something to go on, a place to start. It was a crumpled sheet, torn almost in two and on it was typed the following:

C.W. 12.5.?
F.C.
M.C.16.5
C.W.
A.R.

Derek sat in front of one of the new computers that had just been installed in the Holborn office. There had been no dramatic progress in the four days since they'd discovered the paper, at least not on the job front. On the Val front, things were looking up, however. He'd phoned her of course and it had been a little edgy again, but they'd made the final arrangements for a meal on the coming Saturday and ever since, he'd been struggling to fight off the distraction of daydreaming about that.

He typed in his personal access code, followed by that of his team and then turned to Bill, who was looking over his shoulder at the copied-out version of the paper they'd found in the bin. "Well, here goes. I still find it incredible how people can think that if they throw something away, it ceases to exist."

"Well, thank goodness they do. Anyway, we don't know if this is going to do us any good. Even if these *are* sets of initials, the computer will probably throw up thousands of names for each one. It won't make the processing any easier."

"Yes, I know all that," Derek replied, "but it's worth the try. I'm sure we're onto something and this is our only lead. None of the initials rang any bells with us, so let's see if we can stumble onto anything this way."

"Another thing – they might not be real names anyway – they could just be codes. Salter's initials are not there, for example. You'd expect them to be, wouldn't you?"

"Not necessarily. If he was making notes, he wouldn't need to put himself down there. Anyway, most of it probably doesn't involve him. He's hardly likely to put himself into the front line, is he? No, what worries me is that it seems such a careless thing for him to have done, throwing this away. It crossed my mind that he could have done it deliberately, to lead us astray, set us up in some way, on the off chance that we're onto him."

Bill stared at Derek, and then grinned. "No, they'd have made it easier for us than this, if they were wanting to put us onto a false trail of some sort."

"Ah, but if it was too easy, we might not take the bait!" Derek grinned.

"ARGH! You fucking intellectuals. Overthinking everything all the time" Bill held his hands to his head. "We'll disappear up our own arses in a minute – you've been watching too much telly. Just get on with it. Just treat them as straight initials and see what you come up with. We'll assume the numbers are dates, and it's the 2nd now, so we'll put a full obs and tail op. on Salter from now until the 12th and then on to the 16th. if necessary. That gives us two weeks – we'll know by then if we're pissing up the wrong tree. Those dates must be the important thing."

"If indeed they are dates, of course," said Derek, ducking as Bill tried to grab his throat.

"If you don't come up with something by lunch time, I really will throttle you."

"Well, if all else fails, I'll come up with the price of a pint."

"Right, well I'll leave you to it. By the way, we've got the tap on Salter, but it took a lot of doing. Maloney said that he didn't want to know anything about it, but that nothing had better go wrong."

"The bloody sod! That man should be sacked. So Philip and the rest of us have to carry the can if it all goes wrong."

"Yeah, and Malone'll be the one on the box if it comes off. Such is life, Derek. See you later."

Derek punched the keys and, after a slight pause, names began to appear on the screen. The heroin connection had narrowed down the field and he scrolled through the thirty-four records thrown up by the initials C.W., though there was nothing obvious that seemed to tie in with Salter in any way. He looked at the clock, hardly able to believe that only three quarters of an hour had passed since he had begun staring at the green text on the black screen. And another two hours to go until lunch. He typed in the next set of initials. Only one more day to go before the weekend and the date with Val. It had been a long time since he had taken any real interest beyond sexual attraction in anyone and never as strongly as he was doing now.

ii

Harry Salter wasn't slaving over a hot computer. He was sitting back in a plush armchair feeling pleased as punch with himself. Smug, even. His face broke into a wide grin. Yes, he was feeling smug and enjoying every minute of it. Sipping his coffee, holding the small cup awkwardly in his podgy fingers, he looked round the room. Everything there, in the dining room of his London home, had cost a great deal of money. Not his money, of course, not exactly, but it was his house nonetheless. For Harry of course, money and taste were exactly the same thing. He didn't really understand taste or care one jot about it but he loved money and knowing how much everything cost as he looked around him made everything look…tasteful, sumptuous. Anyone else looking at the lashings of gilt borders and red velvet wallpaper would have immediately thought of a Berni Steakhouse or an East End Pub. He sat back and lit a cigar, rolling it between his thumb and fore finger, puffing out the smoke like an American gangster. He was a rich and successful man. Soon he would make even more money and he really relished the idea. His was a story of riches to even more riches and he was proud of it. He didn't stop to wonder why he was so excited about making even more money than he could ever spend, and if he had he would have proudly owned up – he was just plain greedy. Same thing with paying (or more precisely avoiding paying) his taxes – he paid an army of accountants more to avoid them than he'd have paid the Exchequer if he'd been honest. Because he could. His grandad had started with a small garage which he'd left to his son, Harry's father, who gradually expanded to a local chain and importing company based originally on bringing in spare car parts. Then a couple of small electrical shops and a car insurance brokers, all of which he left in turn to his only son, Harry. Harry had been given everything his dad and grandad had never had – they'd made money, more or less honestly but had essentially remained just two Ilford lads. Then the decision was made to spend on Harry's education, to break out and up. A good private prep, then minor public school and finally scraping into University – not Oxbridge, not enough money for that, but it was all enough to represent a step-change. His parents had made the physical break out into the depths of Epping Forest but with Harry, the break had been more profound, a complete change of class. And he'd made it all worthwhile, made the most of it – always sensed the people to keep close to, the ones who might help him in the future, the ones like him who were now successful and well established, who were rich and powerful – for as his wealth had increased so had his circle of 'friends'. Soon after university, he'd added two small independent supermarkets, and a chain of three estate agents, to the family portfolio – and then sold them at an enormous profit, all legitimate businesses, more or less. And he'd used the money wisely, helping out people who were then literally in his debt – not street loans, important people. He'd joined the Tory Party, become a donor; joined the masons; been invited to the members bar for drinks, been able to help all sorts of little problems out for people – and by the rules of the game they were duty-bound to help him should the need arise. And even if they weren't inclined to that by their sense of duty and kindness of heart, they realised when called upon that it was in their deepest interest to help him because of what he knew about them and the web of intrigue and dishonesty that wove them all together. One for all and all for one but bound by the most base of human values not the highest.

Yet always he wanted even more and he was willing to take risks to get it. In fact, the easier the money came in the more he realised there was another side to him – the enjoyment of the risk, within limits. He wasn't courageous or even fool hearty in courting risk – he would never have bet everything on a horse for the hell of it – but just enough to add a little spice, a sense of excitement that was sometimes lacking from his other enterprises. He'd never really been interested in sex – he paid for women when he needed relief, but he knew they loathed him instinctively, not just the ones he paid but the whole gender, on sight. No decent woman would want anything to do with him and any that did would invoke the Groucho Marks syndrome – he wouldn't have been seen dead with any woman who wanted to be seen with him.

He was so good at making money that he had come to expect success and was never disappointed. He was a good businessman, he planned carefully and in precise details so that often there was simply no room for failure. But with his little forays into the illegal, there were unknown variables and it was here that he saw the challenge. It was all more like a game than real life, just a sophisticated version of Monopoly or perhaps the sublimated titillation his subconscious craved. He took another deep drag on his cigar. True, he'd very nearly burnt his fingers once – 'Go straight to jail'. Ah, but he had his own community chest card at the ready to spring him from trouble. Yes, he could handle little upsets like that – but that business with the bloody excise men had shaken him. That was different from anything before, they were different from the police and they'd damn nearly had him. He'd learnt a lot from that little affair. He learnt just how important his money was and he'd had to call in quite a few favours to get away with that one. It was too bloody close for comfort and he'd made sure he had surrounded himself with a good many more guardian angels from then on. The ones who had helped him last time, they were none too pleased about it, but they'd had no choice. They'd supped at his table and he'd compromised them in a variety of ways. And once in, they couldn't get out – they'd always underestimated him, that was their problem, and so they found themselves suddenly well and truly compromised. And once they'd helped him at all, even in some minor way, they were sucked even deeper into his mire. But he knew he was pushing his luck this time. A financial affair was one thing but this, class A drugs in huge quantities…he probably didn't have that much clout, they weren't *that* important, these people …no, he'd had to ensure his safety in other ways with this one. The sheer amount of profit he stood to make had gone to his head, tempted him beyond his ability to say 'no'. So this time he'd decided to take a different approach, keep the operation tight and directly under his control, go for care and quality, not quantity in terms of who was involved. He knew that if he was caught, there was nothing anyone could do for him this time, so all efforts had to be concentrated on not getting caught. And the only way he could get caught would be through human error – people were always the weak link, he knew that. The more involved, the weaker the chain. So he had kept the operation small. There were only four people at the London end that knew about any of it, three apart from himself. Two of those were potentially a problem because they were not reliable and could link him to the operation. They were low level couriers, taking information up to Manchester on two separate trips. Neither of them had any idea of the final plan – he'd split the information between them, so that even if they had looked at it, it wouldn't have made any sense on its own. Neither of the couriers even knew for sure what drugs were involved, and certainly not how much or when or where. But they could tie him to a deal of some sort and that was bad news – for them. He shivered at his own cleverness and shifted in his seat.

He went through them in his mind, one by one – George, that ridiculously weak prat that Salter knew from his 'local' nightclub. The offer of the job had flattered George, pretentious sod. Salter sensed the excitement, the bravado, the underlying self-doubt and lack of confidence. They shared some background, private school and so on, though George hadn't gone on to university, or anything else, a failure but blinded by his own egotistical fantasies.

The second was a petty crook. Salter knew little about him at all, not even his name. He'd been hired by the third accomplice – the third man who Harry was now waiting for, the man who would sort out the two loose ends for him and ensure his safety. It was another dangerous meeting, dangerous but unavoidable. And there was a fairly credible cover story if anyone should see them together – that the man was coming to advise him on crime prevention and home security – how to protect his various premises most effectively. And it was very much in the interests of his guest to be discreet – he was, after all, a serving police officer – a Detective Inspector, no less.

The front doorbell rang. Salter sat back and waited for it to be answered. Then came the knock on the dining room door.

"Come in."

"There's a gentleman to see you, sir."

"Thank you, show him in."

The use of a butler was deliberately flamboyant, but the ostentation had a practical side to it, for it left many of his visitors feeling nervous and intimidated. It certainly had that effect on Charlie Whitcombe – D. I. Whitcombe of the C.I.D. This was the master stroke of Harry's insurance policy – only three other people knowing about the plans and one of them a policeman, in a position to monitor any investigation and every reason to do so – as he was up to his neck in debt and culpability. You can keep the corridors of power, thought Harry, this cheap little bent copper was worth all the rest put together.

"Come in, Charlie, come in. Is there anything I can get you? A brandy perhaps?" The servant closed the door, leaving the two of them together, Harry confident, enjoying himself, unable to keep a sneer out of his voice; Whitcombe nervous, shifty. He took the offered drink and sat down on the edge of a leather upholstered chair. He leaned forward, his hands fidgeting with the glass and suddenly spoke, his voice higher than expected and louder. "This had better be important. I hope everything's been worked out." What he imagined was a confident tone of authority, adopted to sound both assertive and at ease, succeeded merely in emphasising the weakness of his position and his own his insecurity.

"Yes, yes, yes, of course, Charlie, of course. You know I wouldn't have brought you here if it wasn't necessary. All the arrangements have now been made. There's one loose end, but I'll tell you about that later. Now, I'll go through this in one go. You listen and see if you can spot any flaws. OK? Right. And don't forget, it sounds much more complicated in the telling than it actually is. Try to get a picture of what's actually going on. The main thing behind it all is safety and security, theirs as well as ours."

"Good. The safer they feel the better. It will make things easier all round because there has to be an element of 'trust' in the final analysis. If they can see you've thought about them as well as us, they'll be more at ease." The brandy was beginning to loosen Charlie up, though it wasn't relaxing him.

"Yes, thank you, Charlie. Now try not to interrupt again until I've finished, there's a good chap. It's easier to go through it all in one go."

Charlie took another sip of his drink, settling back in the chair.

"Right. The Manchester people will come down on the 16th., by road. They'll have radio contact with us on the pre-arranged band and they'll park wherever they like within range. We won't know where they are, and they won't contact us at this point. Instead, one of them will make his way to Euston Station, wearing a red flower in his lapel." Charlie looked up and Harry chuckled.

"Style, Charlie, that's what I've got. Anyway, you'll hang around the bar at Euston until he shows and you'll make contact with him. You'll say 'That's a nice flower'."

Harry grinned as he watched Whitcombe flinch, but paused only long enough for the phrase to sink in. "And he will reply 'Yes, red like a good wine.' Nice that, don't you think? So then you take him to the van I'll provide you with and he'll go in the back, blindfolded. Take him to the warehouse in Wapping. Make sure the blindfold stays on until you're in the yard and the gates are closed and make absolutely sure you're not followed. We don't want them trying to get the goods without paying, do we?"

"OK. Then you let the bloke check out the goods and when he's happy, let him radio his mates and tell them everything's fine and to expect me, driving a black Jag. He then has to tell you where they are, and you'll radio me with the information. I'll drive out to them and you can meanwhile start loading up the van. When you've finished, radio the gang and let them know. Their man with you will have to confirm it for them and I should have finished checking the money by then. Don't forget, I'll be in their car by then, and they won't be letting me go anywhere until that call comes through. Then you release the van and go with him to wherever they are and we'll meet up there later."

There was a pause. Charlie looked up from his now empty glass. "Have you finished?"

Harry nodded.

"Well, I know that in all probability they're no more interested in double-crossing us than we are in pulling a fast one on them, but there does seem to be one point at which we're all vulnerable."

Harry smiled indulgently. He knew what was coming. If Charlie hadn't spotted it, he'd have been furious with him. But he was right to say that no one was really interested in the double-cross. It was more trouble than it was worth for anyone. The Manchester boys were getting a bargain anyway. It was costing them a cool five million, but they'd make twice that or more on the street. A double-cross might make for more complications than they already had. So there might just as well be honour among thieves as not. Harry raised his eyebrows questioningly.

"Well, suppose when you get there, they just stick a gun to your head and tell you to tell me that the money's all there when it isn't? And I could do the same thing to the Manchester guy. Force him to OK the goods but not release them to him."

"Right. So I'll work out some code words that I'll use in any such eventuality, something simple that I can add to anything I say that will negate any messages we send. I'm sure they'll do the same, if they've got any sense. Well done, Charlie. You've passed with flying colours. Another drink." Charlie at last began to look, and on one level did actually feel, more relaxed, but he knew that this was just the physical effect of the alcohol and that he couldn't, mustn't really unwind. He knew there was more to the visit than an outline of the plans – less risky ways could have been found to communicate that. He knew something big was coming and he didn't want to be caught off guard, because he was already so vulnerable and he could sense something inherently dangerous about Salter. He knew that he was being played with, but there was nothing he could do about it. He was in too deep now, they both knew that. There was nothing for it but to grit his teeth and wait for the money. And it was a lot of money.

"You know, Charlie, after all this is over, you're going to be a very rich man. I don't know what you have in mind, but if I was you, I'd hang around for a while, a year perhaps, keep up your job, begin to show an interest in early retirement schemes, perhaps develop an illness for disability pension, anything that wouldn't attract attention, and then… you'll be able to buy yourself a whole new world."

"Yes, I know…" *Here it comes,* he thought.

"But money like that doesn't come cheap, Charlie. We have the two loose ends, I mentioned earlier. I think you know who I mean, Miller and… what's the other guy called?"

"Frank Carter."

"Yes, Carter. They are the only weak links in our chain and I want them out of the way completely. One of them knows me and the other knows you. Neither of them knows that I'm actually running the whole thing but even so. They are the only ones who can tie us both into it all, so I want you to arrange for Carter to get rid of Miller and then you must get rid of Carter. And very soon."

Charlie didn't say anything for a moment. He took another sip of his drink, unsure whether Salter had finished. When the silence carried on, he realised it was his turn to speak, and he was about to say 'Yes, OK I'll arrange it' when the full meaning of the words began to sharpen in his brain. He had been vaguely thinking in bent cop terms, fitting them up, sending them down or something like that, but as the real meaning became sharp he felt the colour draining from his already pale cheeks. His mouth opened, but he couldn't think of anything to say. His brain felt giddy with confusion. Salter was watching him very carefully, gauging the reaction. He continued in a matter of fact tone, "Yes, by the 16th. – I want it all finished well before then, in fact, which gives you less than a fortnight, doesn't it? I'll leave all the details to you, but ideally I'd like everything out of the way by Sunday 12th. I know it might take a little longer, but I don't want it running over into the 16th. under any circumstances. Is that clear?"

"I don't know about Carter," Charlie found himself saying. Carter was one of his narks, passing on information in exchange for money or favours. Charlie had used him in this job to arrange the contact with the Manchester crew, because in his own way, he was reliable. And Charlie had enough on him to put him away for years if the worse came to the worse.

But murder? Was there enough of a lever? He'd need a bloody big carrot as well as a stick. By forcing himself to go quickly through the practicalities, he began to regain something of his composure. "I'd need quite a bit of cash up front to be sure of him."

"Yes, of course, Charlie. Of course. That's no problem. It will, after all, only be a short-term investment, though with huge dividends – I hope."

And what about himself? Could he then kill – murder – Carter? He really hadn't counted on anything like this, but the risks weren't actually any higher than he was already taking. The prison sentence for murder wouldn't be any more than for the combination of all the other offences he was committing. But even so, but, but, but… the big truth that he kept coming back to was that he had no choice. It was like patrolling one of those sprawling housing estates, round and round and always ending up in the same dead end.

"And no problem from your point of view, Charlie? I suppose half a million pounds buys off an awful lot of conscience, doesn't it? It's like your own jackpot on the lottery, Charlie."

Charlie felt the colour rising back into his cheeks. He knew that Salter was taunting him, relishing every minute of the encounter, in the profound knowledge that he was absolutely right. And anyway, Salter had him caught as helplessly as a trout with the hook in its throat. In fact, he'd stuffed the hook eagerly down his own throat and now he was being played by a sadistic angler. He was hooked and choking, being reeled in to be gutted. But half a million pounds *was* a lot of money. He was sick and tired of the pettiness of his life, the sordid and the sleazy and the second rate, and he was sick of himself for having become sordid and sleazy and second rate. For years and years, as long as he could remember, he'd been on the take, – nothing too dreadful, nothing out of the ordinary, nothing that wasn't pretty standard for the Met. He wasn't a young idealistic cop caught up in a web of deceit and corruption. He was just a standard C.I.D. officer, worn out by years of late-night drinking in low life bars with the low life crooks he was supposed to be putting away – it was a dirty, sleazy little life and now he had a way out of it once and for all. Salter had been a shrewd judge of character when he'd picked Charlie.

"No," he replied, "No problem at all."

***

In a modern office behind the faded elegance of a late Victorian facade just beyond Westminster Square, were three men who looked like sales executives for a multinational, the popular look of the Thatcherite Eighties, smooth suits and even smoother hairstyles. This was the look that had permeated every walk of life where people wanted to be seen as go ahead and efficient, but who generally achieved merely an appearance of comical middle-aged tackiness. In this case, it was two officers of MI5 and one senior Home Office civil servant. The civil servant, Henry Thomson, was deeply worried and looked it, as he always did in meetings like this, never comfortable. Aged fifty-one, he had faithfully, some might say slavishly, served the Government since leaving Oxford and he had every right to expect the knighthood he had for some time anticipated. But nothing was ever certain until it happened, he knew that better than most, and being involved in this sort of affair was the last thing he wanted – he knew that if it worked out well, there would be precious little in the way of thanks, and if it went wrong, he'd be finished, totally and completely. Yet it had to be done, and someone had to do it and it wasn't the first time it had been him. He picked up the dossier from the desk, feeling awkward with all three of them standing. He didn't know what rank they were and he didn't know whose office it was, so there was no obvious protocol to follow, no hierarchy to find refuge in. He wasn't even completely sure that they were MI5… He supposed that he was seen as being their superior, but he had no actual rank or formal authority within their structure. He took out the documents that he had already read and turned to the other two.

When he spoke, his voice sounded artificial to him, as if it was being relayed through a sound system. "We are pleased that you have brought the matter to our attention and we applaud your vigilance. I, we, that is my superiors and I are not exactly sure how to proceed or what you want from us – you do realise, I'm sure, that we are totally unable to offer any official advice or help whatsoever. All I can say is that there is a potential here for grave embarrassment to the national interest." He paused, put off for a second by the cynical smirks of the two officers which they made no effort to suppress or disguise. "Well, alright, the Government's interest or at least in the interests of people close to the government, especially with that... er... 'bent' – is that the current term? – policeman involved. And that such embarrassment may well be exploited by the sort of people that we all – you and my people, abhor. We, I'm sorry, I mean they, I'm of course completely non-political – they are, after all, the party of law and order and with an election sometime next year, well, I don't need to tell you that we, they, can do without any scandals."

He glanced at the two men, who just stood there and said nothing. He looked down at his feet and continued, the avoidance of eye contact making him look and feel shifty. "I mean, we're bound to get the odd one or two scandals, but we can handle most of them, God knows, if we can't with a press as craven as ours, we shouldn't be here. But let's not forget how it all plays out if it goes wrong and we lose control – we lost a generation of politicians after the Keeler case. In fact there hasn't been a public-school prime minister since, though there might be one again soon if Blair continues his rise through the ranks" He smiled but again the other two remained stony faced and silent for a moment but then also smiled, smiles that made him shiver and he rushed on. "OK, let's just get on with it, shall we? As far as we are concerned, the position is this – Salter is a revolting little shit, but he's become a well-connected revolting little shit, more well connected than perhaps he realises and any scandal involving him in serious trouble just might, in the wrong hands, lead to a few questions about sensitive acquaintances. All we need is some bloody Duncan Campbell to get hold of any of this and God alone knows where some of the contacts might lead, and we, they, the Country can do without any more embarrassments right now." He felt that the word 'embarrassment' was almost a joke – surely all the sleaze and sex scandals this government was sloshing around in, went far beyond embarrassment. It was more like the last days of Rome and on one level it revolted him. He saw himself as belonging to the patrician class, a civil servant with the highest ideals to serve the nation, as long as the people he was serving shared his view of how that nation should be governed. And the only reason he was still loyal to this present bunch of common, self-seeking, grasping small businessmen philistines was that they were a lot better than the bunch of wets in the Labour Party, circling like vultures. John Major didn't have a clue what he was doing but he was holding the fort. He knew that the real danger to him wasn't actually John Smith's Labour Party, it was that truly unpleasant gang of right wing old Etonian Eurosceptics who were desperately trying to get us out of Europe so they could take back power for the 'people', by which they meant themselves. But they didn't care less about the country or even their own party and he seriously feared they would bring Major down and let Labour in. And then what?

"Right." The taller of the two Kafkaesque agents spoke so suddenly that Thomson almost jumped – and the voice was much coarser than he had expected, though he couldn't identify the accent. "So you want us to make sure that he doesn't get into trouble with the drugs side of things? Let him get rid and then warn him off any future involvement, but keep the Customs boys off his back, is that right?"

There was just the hint of a sneer in the voice that threw Henry Thomson, unnerved him a little. "Yes, I suppose that just about sums it up."

"We thought that after he's sold it, we'd sort of tax his profits as lesson to him – there's plenty of things we could use the money for, you know, doing a Laurel and Hardy."

"A what?"

Now it was the turn of the two agents to be genuinely amused – they grinned broadly and the talker explained, "You know, Stan Laurel, Laurel and Hardy – Oliver Hardy – Oliver North – using illicit money to finance illicit schemes."

There was a pause. Thomson looked at the faces of the men opposite him, the last traces of their grins still distorting their normally implacably stern faces. Mention of Irangate, even if in jest, was no laughing matter for him. "Well, I can't possibly offer any sanction for such a course of action…"

"No, of course not, Sir. But then you are not categorically forbidding us to take such action?"

"Well, look, it's all rather academic, isn't it? I mean, you don't need my permission to do something that we all know nothing about and which we know, if anything comes to light, will be totally denied – I'll deny you, and if a connection is made between us, my superiors will deny me. There's not much point in asking permission is there?"

"No sir, just so long as we all understand each other. And this one may get just that little bit awkward, it always is with the bloody Customs. They tend to be really straight, not like the plods – but it's even worse in this case. The team who are onto Salter were involved last time, when we got him off and I'm sure that they're raring to have a go at him this time. Even worse, one of them's a fucking political. We've got a file on him from his student days, nothing special for 60s and 70s and we thought he'd have gone the way of all flesh, getting older, settling down, slippers and pipe…but look at this." Henry realised that one of the men had not spoken at all and this one now opened the attaché case he was holding with a flourish, like a magician's assistant, though hardly as glamorous. From it he produced a single sheet of A4 paper which he handed to Thomsom, who read it quickly and looked up for an explanation.

This time it was the quiet one who spoke, in a soft, better-educated voice than the smaller one. "We had officers covering the demo on Saturday in Manchester, as you'd expect. One of them came across this arrest – the local bill were quite embarrassed when they saw his warrant card – they'd given him a bit of a punching during the arrest. Anyway, our chap picked up on it and sent it in as part of his report. The point is that Brown is on the team looking into Salter, so we'll keep a special eye out for him. He's not married, so there may be some weakness there, some leverage. Whatever, we'll go carefully and you can toddle back and reassure your superiors that they can sleep well in their beds tonight." Thomson nodded and thought, *Mind you, if that was all they bloody well did in bed, his job would be one hell of a lot easier.*

He smiled what he hoped was a grateful smile, but he still felt uneasy. Why the hell couldn't things ever be straightforward? But then if they were, he'd be out of work and on the dole. You can't have it every which way.

Chapter 9

Derek stared at the screen, eyes stinging. Friday morning and still nothing. That was the thing about all these new computers. You expected them to be able to do everything for you – you know the scenario of a thousand T.V. films – the policeman taps a few keys, something seemingly deep in the heart of the machine whirs, the printer jerks into action and hey presto the crime is as near as damn it solved – deus ex computer. Well, this one wasn't working. A gust of wind hurled rain against the window of the empty office with a bleakness that made him shiver. He stood up, walked over to the misted-up glass and wiped away some of the condensation with his hand. The coldness felt good, a relief from the suffocating heat of the office central heating system. Outside it was grey and wet and depressing. There can be few places as drab as London in the rain. He looked at his watch – eight o'clock – the first time in years that he'd been into the office earlier than he had to be. Once again, he was struck by the effect this case seemed to be having on him. It was like waking up from suspended animation, so many things suddenly coming together for him – the march reaffirming his political commitment, the case reinvigorating his professional life and Val. And the most important of these was Val, without any doubt at all. Somehow, he felt that if something did develop with her, everything else would fall into place. He kept repeating them like a mantra, the three key elements in the dawning of his new age, as if by articulating them he was somehow making them more real. So that was how Derek was feeling as he touched the cold glass in the hot suffocating office on that dreary Friday morning in Holborn.

He jumped at the sound of the outer door opening and turned to see Val breezing in.

There was a moment's awkwardness, just the two of them there, but the pause had a pleasantness about it, the quiet intimacy of it.

She smiled and the moment passed. "Has anything come up...Hey, what time is it? I must be late if I'm in after you."

"Ho ho ho. And no, nothing. Is everything all right for tomorrow tonight?"

"Yes, of course, I'll be there on time." There was an irritated edge to her voice

"Right, good." Another awkwardness, but this one his fault and with no pleasantness. He knew he shouldn't have raised the date at work and mentally gave himself a kick. "Changing the subject, where did we get the original tip for this job?"

"I'm not sure. It was one of Bill Haggart's informers, I think. Why?"

"That's right, I remember now. It's just that I keep coming up with a name that rings a bell, but there's nothing on him on the police computer – yet we've got him down – not for much, mind, but he *is* there. Look – he's just here on a cross-reference for these other two jobs, but there are no details. I'll have to go down and check the references in the filing room."

"Yes – it'll be a good day when all the records are on the computer."

"I don't know about that – there's got to be a catch somewhere, but I suppose you're right. Where's our phone book? I'll see if I can get Bill – he's on obs shift, but not 'til eleven. Right, here it is."

He began dialling as Val handed him a cup of coffee. "Thanks... Oh, hello, Mrs Haggart, is Bill still there, please...oh good, thanks... ... morning, Bill, how's life?"

"Could be better. Is that you Derek? No, no it can't be, the sun's not over the yard arm yet."

"Right, Bill, that's cost you a pint. Now listen, what's the name of your informer, the one who gave us the tip on this Salter case?"

There was a pause. "How important is it, Derek?" His Scots accent seemed suddenly heavier, his tone more serious.

"I don't know."

"OK Look, I'll come on in and talk to you about it. I should have time. I'm due to relieve Ron on obs. Could you contact him and tell him I might be a few minutes late? I'll see you in about an hour." Something was wrong, something Derek sensed in the tone of the conversation.

"He's coming in. He sounded a bit put out. Perhaps I am on to something, but what does he know that I don't? Look, would you do me a big favour, Val? I need to carry on checking this list. Could you go down to Filing and see if there's any details on this character here – Frank Carter he's called. And see if the photos from yesterday's obs have been done – apparently our friend Salter had a visitor in the afternoon, could be something or nothing. God knows, we need to have a straw to clutch at before the briefing this afternoon. Philip needs to have something to keep Maloney happy."

"Yes I know. I'll pop down now and see what I can find. See you."

***

Bill arrived within the hour, his short, wiry frame bursting energetically into the office. "By God, it's like the Marie Celeste in here. Where is everyone, Derek?"

"All out on obs. Just me and Val, she's downstairs in Filing. So what's the big drama, Bill?"

Bill looked hard at Derek, pausing for a second. "Come off it, laddie, you know by now not to ask for the names of informers unless someone's life depends on it – and never, ever over the telephone!"

Derek stared at Bill. He'd never seen him so serious and edgy.

Derek was embarrassed and shocked in equal measure. He thanked god that Val wasn't there to hear him being ticked off. There was nothing he could say because in theory Bill was right, so he just sat there like a naughty schoolboy feeling small and naive while Bill continued,

"Now what is it you want to know?"

"Just his name."

"Why?"

"Well, it might be nothing at all, but I keep coming up with some cross references to a character called Carter, Frank Carter – you remember that one set of initials on the paper was F.C. We had him down on sus. for a couple of small jobs, but nothing certain. You were case officer for both cases and I thought the name rang a bell. Anyway, I cross checked with the Oscars and…"

"…nothing at all. Yes, I know. But no, he wasn't my source, though there is obviously a connection between them in some way. This guy moves in the shadows on the edge of things as you can guess from the files, same sort of circles as my snout, all snouts come to that. It's a safe bet they know of each other, though there's nothing to suggest they know each other well or even know the other is a snout. So if he's not one of ours, he probably informs for someone in the met. He's too petty for me to have bothered about him, but now that you mention him, I do remember that I checked up on him after that Jones case a couple of years ago – his name came up somewhere in the shadows and like you drew a blank. As I say, I've never been too worried, he's such a small fish it's not been worth it – until now, by the sounds of it. By the way, the reason I didn't want to say anything on the phone was in case it's being tapped. I'm getting paranoid in my old age, and it wouldn't be fair on the likes of my source if the wrong people knew he was a snout."

"God, I didn't even think… but who? Surely not…"

"It doesn't matter who, it could be organised crime, it could be the drug squad – same difference – it could, of course be no one at all, or both but I didn't want to risk anything in the middle of this job. You know how things went last time and the sort of people involved. I've got a feeling about this case, I really think we're onto a chance here. And you're not the only one who wants Salter. You know, Derek, I could kick myself – we should have gone back to basics and checked on sources from the start – but, as they said in Watergate somewhere – 'no one asked me!' Anyway, let's just move on it now and see if it's going to be any use to us – it's still pretty tenuous after all – I mean, what have we got? The fact that the snout who gave us this job has previously given us jobs which have somehow also involved Carter, though never directly? Which means there's a chance that Carter is one of the people on the list. FC, Frank Carter, it's got to be more than a coincidence? And definitely worth a shot It's not a lot, though and we can't exactly risk going back and asking for any more info, can we? –we don't want to arouse suspicions anywhere."

"No, but it sounds as if there's a chance that Carter has a loose tongue and loud mouth, that's how your snout has picked up so much from him. Let me get this straight in my mind – in the past, Carter could well have been the source for *your* source, the chap your snout overheard in the pub or whatever. And that it could be the same this time – is that what you're thinking?"

"Yes, laddie. But I smell rotten apples in the rotten barrel, here…this Carter should have a list of petties the length of your arm…"

"But he hasn't got anything recent at all. So a routine check against the police records wouldn't pull him in if there was a fishing exercise."

"And that's why we'd better tread very, very carefully on this one, Derek. I don't want to end up looking stupid and I don't want to end up dead." He paused. Derek had never seen him so serious. This sort of melodramatic tone should have been the cue for deflating mockery, but it was so out of character that Derek was gripped by it, swirled along with the dramatic tension of it, his disbelief well and truly suspended. Bill broke the silence, lowering his voice conspiratorially, and still without the slightest trace of irony that would normally have been his trademark. "Don't mention any of this at the briefing – it's being minuted for Maloney and I want all this watertight before he gets a whiff of it. See everyone individually and let them know – I'll tell Ron when I relieve him. We'll probably not have too much trouble tracking him down, this Carter so let's do that and put a tail on him for a couple of days, whether the files throw up anything or not. I mean, we've got absolutely nothing to lose, have we? Let's go for him and see what happens. We'll need someone good, though. He mustn't suspect anything. Put Val in charge of it. She's put a lot into this already you know, and she's a very capable lassie, that one."

"Right." Derek was trying to work out all the permutations, develop a narrative from which to spin, an operational hypothesis. The dark chill of the previous moments had passed with the renewed excitement and vigour of grasping that this might just be the breakthrough they needed to get Salter. "You'd better be off on obs, hadn't you, Bill? Are you going to be able to get back for the briefing?"

"Oh aye, I've arranged for Willy and young Andrew to take over for a couple of hours, it'll be good experience for them and they can contact me if there's anything crops up – I wouldn't miss this briefing for anything."

"Why, what's so special? I'm always missing out on the subtleties of office politics. I mean, I know that if it all goes wrong, Maloney will have us hanging by the balls for a day or two, but there's nothing new in that is there?"

Bill looked quickly round the still empty office. "Well, Philip is pretty pissed off with Maloney this time – all that crap about 'on our heads be it'. I mean, if Maloney isn't being paid to take responsibility, what is he being paid for? He does sod all else except appear on the box every now and then, taking the credit for the successes we have. Philip thinks he should stick by us when things go wrong – after all, he's cocked enough cases up himself, when he's interfered…"

"Yes, yes, I know all that. But we live with that. What's so special this time?" This case seemed to be so special for everyone, in different ways.

"Well, I just think Philip has had enough. I know Malone was good with us after the shooting, give him credit for that, but you'd bloody – well expect to be able to take that for granted, wouldn't you? The fact that it surprised us says it all

141

and I think David has just reached the point where he could afford to go for early retirement if it all comes to a big clash. This case has brought everything to a head for him. Maloney is looking for any chance to drop it rather than take a risk and back us. And after all, if anything does go wrong with someone like Salter for a second time, the shit really will hit the fan. But Maloney isn't concerned for the department – it's his own prospects that are concentrating his mind, which won't be any surprise to you. The department's successes are always *his* successes, its failures are always someone else's fault."

"But failure with Salter would mean more problems than usual."

"Absolutely – there's no doubt they share common friends, he and Salter, friends in high places – they might even know each other. I don't mean Malone would ever be bent, he's not corrupt in that way at all – but he's not loyal to us and he's ambitious as hell. Salter's a vulgar little bastard as you know only too well, but he's a wealthy, vulgar, well connected masonic little bastard and it's the rich bit which makes all the difference – I don't need to tell you that money really is the golden key to lots of gilded gates – where the hell is that a quote from – that's the problem with these O.U. units, you know, I pick up a lot but I never know where I'm up to. Anyway," he looked a little sheepish as he remembered that Derek had a degree in English and was looking as if he was about to enlighten him, so he ploughed on, "where was I? well, you know from last time how immune Salter is. I mean, wealth is the only qualification you need for anything under this government – yes, alright, I know I'm preaching to the converted. Anyway, let's wait and see. Don't forget to spread the word about Carter. If I was you, I'd get Val out straight away if we can come up with an address. Send one of the young lads with her, so that she's the senior officer, it'll do her good. I'll see you later. Oh – Derek – don't forget at the briefing – not too many details about the Carter business, but the case has to look as if it's going somewhere – otherwise…"

He drew a finger across his throat "... no case! Bye now." And then he'd gone.

Derek sat staring at the empty room, simply absorbing the silence until, a few minutes later, Val returned.

"We've got something anyway – an address and a photo, but not much else. The pictures are done of the obs yesterday – and something is obviously going down – the visitor is that same shady character that was there when our Manchester target reported in."

"Great, so we can give them something at the briefing – but you won't be there I'm afraid. Bill's just been in and we think you should take charge of an obs on this Carter character. We've got nothing else to go on and the clock's ticking away, so we might as well have a gamble on this connection – it's sort of all or nothing now. You'll need to work with one of the juniors – you take your pick, and you'll need to organise shift relief for tomorrow night."

"Yes, well, you'll have to do that for me, won't you – I'll be out on obs won't I?" she grinned. Always grinning or smiling, always cheerful. Ordinarily he'd have found it irritating, but with her it just wasn't.

"Right. By the way, where does this Carter live?"

"Well, the last address we have for him is in E14. I looked it up and it's just off the Commercial Rd. beyond Limehouse toward the Blackwall Tunnel – near the Isle of Dogs."

"Yes, I sort of know a couple of decent boozers out that way."

"That's a surprise, Derek."

"Anyway, you'd better start doing your planning. This could be key to the whole operation. What Bill told me amounted to this – Carter isn't his snout but there's a good chance that the snout got his info from Carter – they seem to mix in the same circles and there's been one or two other cases from Bill's guy which have also involved Carter – or almost involved him. Be very careful not to be seen..."

"I'm not stupid!"

"Christ no, I'm sorry, I didn't ..."

"No, it's OK," she said, but the smile was gone.

"What I meant was, well, there might be a police connection with Carter – Bill was very vague, I'm not sure to be honest that he's told me everything, but one thing's for sure, this Carter's living a charmed existence. He hardly exists on the records, which …"

"Makes him immune…"

"Makes him dangerous. That's what I meant about being careful."

"I'm not sure that isn't worse – patronising sod." But the smile was back again.

***

It was the smile he would remember for ever – though for ever wasn't going to be such a long time now. His eyelids were heavy and sagging, but at the same time he felt curiously lightheaded. He must stay awake… think, think, think, what came next?

***

The office was acrid with cigarette smoke by the time Derek arrived for the briefing, and the waste bins were full of beer cans – it was Friday afternoon and normally the team celebrated the coming weekend in the pub across the road. But there had been a great deal of work to do today, getting last minute details sorted out, scribbling down obs reports ready for the briefing, comparing notes. Derek had spent much of the time button-holing key people and letting them in on the details of the possible Carter connection, all of which helped to fuel the air of excitement and expectation that was building up around the case – and the briefing in particular.

Bill came in with Manson, both looking serious as they sat behind the most central desk. Conversation petered out and Derek looked round, counting the team – seven, eight including himself; two out with Carter; and Bill – eleven. All present and correct.

Bill stood up. "Well, if you're all sitting comfortably, we'll begin. We'll start by discussing the state of play – Derek will give us a run down on developments in the office; then we'll brainstorm on actions, see if we can come up with a coherent strategy – though judging by the number of empties I can see, some of you probably can't even say 'coherent'." There was some laughter, but less than there would normally have been. Everyone was tense, waiting to see what would happen, unsure of the appropriate tone, unsettled.

"By the way, you'll notice me taking notes – that's not just an attempt to impress my superiors… the meeting is, from now on, to be formally minuted at the express wish of our Assistant Chief Investigator, may the lord protect and preserve him," – there were some hisses – "and I would ask you all to bear that in mind. Finally, when we've sorted everything out, Philip would like a word with you all. Now, Derek…"

Bill sat down and ostentatiously shuffled some sheets of blank A4 paper, flourishing a pen.

Derek felt that sudden rush of blood pounding in his head that he always felt when he had to speak formally to groups of people, even though it was a fairly regular occurrence during briefings.

"Well, the situation now is that we are sure we are onto *something* – well, fairly sure – but developments are mostly circumstantial so far. What I'll do is go through everything up to the present time, and then you can add anything or clarify something you're not sure of. After that, we can look at what we're going to do over the next few days. Right:

"We know that a large amount of heroin has been imported recently and we know that a deal is being set up between someone here in London and some known drug dealers in Manchester. We're pretty sure from the intel that this is for that heroin.

"We also know that the courier for the Manchester connection went back to Salter's London home – so we can tie in Salter. We think we know the dates on which certain stages in the transaction will take place, but we can't be sure of those. And now we think that we may be able to tie down one of the sets of initials from the list of dates that we have – though I can't go into too much detail on that as we're still working on it – I'll let you know individually as soon as we get anything definite. Val Henderson is working on it at the moment and we hope to have some confirmation very quickly. Let's remember as well that it is only because of Val's 'beyond the call of duty' activities last weekend that we've uncovered any of this – so she's definitely now on the team and taking a leading role in the investigation – and she'll expect full cooperation from everyone' There was a ripple of applause. He paused and took a sip of water from the glass on his desk.

"Further, but again circumstantial, we have the photos from the obs on Salter's place – I'll give each of you a copy later – and they show that he had a visit from the same man who was in the original picture with the Manchester courier. So if we are right about all this, the flurry of activity might indeed suggest that something is imminent, which would fit in with the dates. It's the third now and so we have nine days before the first of the dates crops up. It gives us time to follow up the leads we have so far but it will mean some pretty strenuous hours over the next week. You'll be earning your extra hours allowance, that's for sure. That's just about it. Any questions?"

There was a pause, but no one said anything. Philip stood up.

"OK then. So as far as we're concerned, we'll carry on with the same procedures as at the moment – just solid observation work until something happens. If we don't have anything by the 16th., the last date on the slip of paper, we'll just have to call it a day. I'll leave it to Bill and you lot to work out your obs rotas, and we'll have 24-hour reports back to me here, through Bill so that we can sift through *everything* with the proverbial fine-tooth comb. And now I'd like a final word – off the record, Bill, if you don't mind – thanks. Well, I know that Derek, quite rightly, kept stressing the fact that we might have nothing at all here, but I'm sure all of you feel as I do

146

that we might equally have something very big indeed, with the icing on the cake being the fact that it involves Salter. You ought to know that if the operation is a success, our Assistant Chief Investigations Officer will probably clinch a place in the next Honours List – he's well in the running, especially since the Thames Estuary job – yes, I know he opposed the operation and nearly wound it up just before the breakthrough, but he did a wonderful job on the telly when we brought in the haul, and the situation is the same now – if this is a success, he'll get an O.B.E. If it isn't, he'll deny us. He's made it quite clear that if there are any sustainable complaints against us from Salter, he'll throw us to the wolves in order to save his own skin." he paused. "I've never spoken to you like this before – in the normal order of things I wouldn't regard it as professional – but I'm afraid that the situation is far from normal. It's as serious as this – if things go wrong I doubt if any of you will be in Special Investigations branch by July – you'll be back to whichever branch you came from, with a pay cut to match that will play havoc with your inflated mortgages. So watch out. Do the best job you've ever done, but be careful, in every sense. If it's any consolation, I'm more sure about going ahead with this one than I've been with any job for a long time. Now, when Bill's finished sorting out the rotas, I'll get the first round in over the road. Good luck."

He sat down and smiled at Bill. No one moved. Philip was highly regarded by all the team, but he was usually quiet, even a little reserved – *'professional'* was the word he had used in his talk, and it was the description of him which most readily came to mind. He was one of those people who feel somehow reassuring just to be with, who make you feel secure and safe, and even though they had all been expecting something like this, it still came as a shock to actually hear him saying it. Bill stood up. "Right then. Now if anyone has any special requests for the rota – times they just can't make and so on, could they see me now, and then I can get all this sorted out." He had broken the silence, but not the spell. Chattering broke out like small arms fire, but the mood was sober, sombre. No one laughed; no one was cracking any jokes. And that's how it was going to be on this case. The stakes were too high for everyone; they were all somehow too seriously involved, Derek thought and shivered.

He would have shivered all the more if he had heard the tape recorder being switched off in the small Whitehall office and seen the tired duty officer log the time of the recording. The talk of Honours Lists had made him prick up his ears and he picked up a pen to write a memo to accompany the tape to his superiors:

"Feel we may be onto something. Advise i. Should go ahead with phone tap on all members of the team ii. Derek Brown – bearing in mind his political background, suggest intense surveillance, 24 hrs. He's probably unaware just how much potential there is here to embarrass the government, not being privy to our intelligence! but if he finds anything out he would want to exploit it and he must be considered a risk if he gets close to anything."

Chapter 10

It was a lovely evening, even in the overheated oven that is London in the summer, though normally Derek would hardly have noticed anything about it except for the temperature. But tonight, filtering down from the softening sky, was the makings of a real Waterloo sunset. Spring really was in the air, and his senses were alert, sharpened by an almost adolescent nervousness that took him by surprise. It was seven thirty on this silky evening, and there he was, standing outside Charring Cross station waiting for Val, pacing up and down the pavement. The air heavy with the spicey brew of spring and diesel exhaust; redolent with romance; memories of being young –

"Boo!"

He nearly jumped out of his skin, whirling round to see Val, her eyes bright with laughter and looking…so different from in work.

"You're early," she said, still laughing, but with that sharp edge to her voice, so it came out more like an accusation than an observation.

"Better than being late. But you're early as well," he replied, sounding slightly more defensive than he intended. Before he had time to worry, though, Val gently, firmly took hold of his arm and smiled, calm, reassuring, and as he felt her touching him, his nerves and worries were disappeared in a wave of excitement and enjoyment that lifted him up and out of himself, like a rush of cocaine, like a whiteout, exhilarating and calming at the same time.

"Yes, well let's make the most of it – it's a beautiful evening isn't it?" she said, "What have you got planned for us?"

"Well, I thought we could have a drink and then head into Soho – I know an Indonesian Restaurant near there, just beyond Leicester Square – if I can find it."

"You mean you're not taking me to an exotic casino or something?"

"What? I …" He'd agonised over where to take her and finally decided on the restaurant as the most neutral of things to do. Once upon a time he would have flirted with her, teased her and not worried one jot about where to go, they'd just have gone, to a pub, to night club, whatever. But now he was taking it all so seriously he was overthinking and trying to second guess what was right and what was wrong and ending up at a complete loss.

She held up her hands in mock surrender. "Only joking, honest. The restaurant sounds great. What about that drink – I thought it was all pretty awful around here."

"All human life is here…Come on, let's get across while the lights are with us…I know a fairly ok place just up here."

***

Under the same soft spring sky, not five miles east of Leicester Square, Frank Carter was also preparing for a night out. In a dark street of terraced houses in Limehouse, he drew back the curtain of his upstairs bedsit and looked out. Still no taxi. He peered along the street from the bay window, hardly noticing how shabby it all looked, the litter, the grimy pavements splattered with dog shit, peeling paint on all the window frames. London 1991. Rundown, menacing, exactly what twelve years of Tory austerity looks like.

Still no taxi. Letting the curtain fall, he turned back to his joyless room, as dingy and shabby as the street outside. But again, he hardly noticed. He'd spent his life in places like this – peeling wallpaper, unshaded low output bulbs in the light sockets. Hardly noticed the details, that is. But he certainly knew that life had more to offer than anything he'd had out of it. He didn't know what but he knew something had to be better, almost anything. And even though his sense of how bad it was had been dulled over his lifetime, and his vision of how much better it could be was as limited as the view of the horizon from his bedsit window, he did have a vision. Deep inside, he knew it could all be better, deep inside, implanted and shaped and nurtured and updated by the images he had assimilated from countless television advertisements – a vision of a better life than this one – a sort of Kellogg's Cornflakes- family heaven, all bright ultra-white Colgate smiles, breakfasting outdoors in a beautiful Dulux green field on a permanently sunny morning in the grounds of an expensive executive 'home'…the vision which inspires a million lottery ticket sales every week. And tonight was going to be a giant step towards making that dream come real for Frank Carter, the first step up and out – it was going to give him at least enough money for a down-payment on a slice of the great big pie, not the crumbs he'd been living off all his life. The truth was that Charlie had chosen instinctively well when he'd linked up with Frank. Once upon a time, perhaps there'd been a chance for him as a human being, to develop, to flourish, no one is really born under a bad sign, but then again, there had never been a moment when he'd had a clear escape route up or out.

But while there certainly wasn't any gene wriggling about inside him that was responsible for him having become the totally nasty little shit that he had become, but that was what he now was, alright, a sly, vicious bastard. And while he'd certainly had a grim time of it all his life, so had plenty of others who had managed to come through it without turning into the nasty bit of work that was now Frank Carter. Though it must be said, he was no worse, no more ruthless or violent or lacking in moral judgement than many from much more privileged backgrounds with less excuse. But even so, in Carter there was a touch of genuine 24 carrot unpleasantness – he had become a complete thug, brutalised by life, but now undeniably brutal. A lifetime of petty crime, a tendency to self-pity, a ruthless, tormenting bully if he thought he could get away with it, and a grass – the sum total wasn't a character that anyone could ever warm to – or would want to. He lit a cigarette. From now on, he thought, his life would all be different. This was the big one, the sort of job people dream about, people like Frank that is. Money up front. And working for a copper, too. It was watertight, a doddle. As long as he didn't fuck it up. No, no way. He'd not even had a drink since Charlie had phoned him. He picked up his cigarettes from the arm of the tattered, light brown plastic armchair and thought back to the conversation they'd had.

"Hello, Frank, this is Charlie here. Is there anyone with you?"

"No, no one."

"Good. Now listen, there's been a slight change of plan involving that job you were helping me with. In fact, it could do you a bit of good if you play your cards right. We'll meet tomorrow, usual place, usual time. And don't go getting pissed and forgetting or any other stupid fucking tricks, right? It's a big one this, Frank."

"No, course I won't." Coppers! Who the fuck did they think they were, eh?

And they'd met and that bastard really had come up with the goods this time. Two grand up front, the other eight after the job – and already it was burning a hole in Frank's pocket. He could get out of the bedsit, out of these streets. He didn't exactly know where, but he could do things, go places. It wasn't enough to retire on, but you can go a long way on ten thousand quid, cash in hand, all in one go. Ten grand and all with no risk. That was the beauty. Charlie had seemed worried that his little nark wouldn't want the job, but Christ. It was easier than most of the small-time jobs out of which he had made what he laughingly called his living up until then. When he'd grassed up people, well that was much more risky than this and just for peanuts. When he'd been out thieving, he could've gone down for years – and all for piss all – a couple of hundred quid a time if he was lucky. But this. Just bump off some bloke he didn't know and there was no connection for the old bill to trace back to him. And all for a copper who had to be his guardian angel from then on in, because the last thing he could afford would be for Frank to get caught...

He heard the horn down in the street announcing the arrival of the taxi, making him jump. He put out his cigarette, took another and lit it, noticing for the first time that his hands were shaking, sweaty – not from any moral qualms about his task, but just from nerves at the remote but potential danger of being caught in the act. He checked the gun, the silencer. And the knife. Charlie had said to do it with a knife and take the bloke's wallet, make it look like a mugging. But the gun was just in case. He wasn't going to fuck this up. Nothing was going to fuck this up.

***

Derek pushed away his empty plate. He was feeling relaxed, expansive at last. Normally he felt at ease in this sort of situation – drinks in a pub, meal in a restaurant. It was home territory for him, something he'd done so many times with so many women that it had long since lost any edge of excitement or romance for him. But as in all other things recently, tonight had been different. The nerves had come back once they'd sat down in the pub worrying all the time what to say if there was a lull in the conversation, dreading a pause in case the pause went on and on to the point when neither of them would be able to break it, locked into an eternal silence from which they would never recover. But once he'd ordered the drinks and the alcohol began to work its age old magic, he began to relax, and by the time they'd moved on to the restaurant, everything began to flow more smoothly, with him turning on the tired old charm that just didn't seem tired or routine to him anymore, because this was invigorating, stimulating…fun. Val wasn't going to take all the bland clichés that he normally passed off as interesting conversation. Their exchanges were beginning to rush along like an express train, and, much to the mild disquiet of one increasingly isolated part of Derek's brain, possibly a runaway express train. There was a mutual excitement and enjoyment reflected in the gradually increasing volume of their conversation which did not entirely, or even mainly, derive from their increased and increasing intake of alcohol. It was as if they had both been waiting for a long, long time to talk to each other, as if they had been in solitary confinement for years and this was their first day out.

"Oh for God's sake spare me all the platitudes, It's always the same with you so called liberal men. Scratch the surface and you're all the bloody same. You agonise about your tortured, sensitive souls, but when it comes down to it…well, what was it Tolstoy said – 'We'll do anything for the peasants except get off their backs'?" He stared in mock horror at the fork she was now brandishing at him and they both laughed and she put down the fork and took hold of his hand and squeezed it and grinned at him. And he felt like a walking cliché from a teenage magazine – dizzy, excited. And Tolstoy, for fuck's sake, where did that come from? She was so bright, so sharp, so sparkling and …well-read, thoughtful – in fact absolutely dazzlingly brilliant and bloody gorgeous as well. He poured another glass of red and ordered another bottle.

***

Fresh was certainly not how Carter was feeling as he waited, he was cold, colder than he'd ever thought possible, shivering. Even during the day, the bus and tube station area behind the Stratford East shopping mall is desolate and intimidating. At night it is aggressively threatening, a dangerous place. The aggression was a gift from the architects – a maze of concrete tunnels lead from the chilling eeriness of the mall itself. On one side was the three lane 'ring road', which lets the city slickers drive as smoothly as possible out to their dormitories in Essex without ever having to see too much of how the rest of the world is getting on. The tunnels converge and emerge at the back, where the tube and bus and railway station stand bleakly surrounded by the desolation of the delivery service area for the Mall shops – the dark underbelly of the opulent consumer frontage – all bleak open concrete spaces and giant litter bins and broken glass and litter that hadn't quite made it into the bin. At night, the area is filled with hard white light and sharp black shadows, a cutting edge where they clash. And watching from the darkness, behind the Sainsbury's delivery area, Carter was waiting amongst the giant dustbins. It was one o'clock, Sunday morning. Any minute now. The geezer had been told to meet Charlie here, now – that it was urgent and very much in his own interests. When Carter saw him, he was to signal to him with a torch – three medium length flashes – what the fuck is a medium length flash, he'd asked Charlie.

"Oh for Christ's sake, use your imagination. I mean, there aren't going to be too many people out there flashing torches are there? This isn't a James Bond film, you know. I mean, he's hardly going to be spoilt for choice, is he? Just flash long enough for him to see, but not long enough to attract any attention if there do happen to be any other people around alright?"

He was right about not too many people around. One or two cars passed, but the late night 'rush hour' from the West End theatres had dried up to a trickle. A few gangs of lager louts from the local pubs had passed rowdily through a couple of hours earlier, doubtless looking for trouble, but they hadn't seen him in the shadows and all was quiet now. It was just a matter of getting it all over with. He'd used a knife before, but never cold like this. Before, it had always been in the mindless animal heat of a fight. But he had no time to think it all through again now. He noticed a car pull up at the far side of the bus station and his stomach tightened, he felt his breathing jump into a lower gear. He knew this was it.

Miller pulled in to the side of the road, just outside the bus station, and glanced around. He was pissed off about this, and more than a little uneasy. Why on earth had he picked somewhere like this? He looked across the road at the dark shadows around the base of the ugly buildings. He had to take it on trust, in the end. After all, he was dealing with a policeman and deep down inside, though he knew the guy was bent, he still retained the residual vestiges of …respect. And anyway, he didn't really have much – or any – choice. But he was way way out of his own territory here. There was nothing glamorous around here, and he sensed real danger, which didn't fit at all well with his usual little games. Still, the implication was that there'd be some more cash up front tonight, and he was a bit short of readies at the moment – embarrassingly so in fact – so he hesitated but only for a second and then thought, *Oh what the hell*, got out of the car and walked nervously through the empty bus station, his eyes stinging with the bright light. And then he was peering across the road into the shadows, waiting for Charlie's signal.

The man who got out of the car was vaguely recognisable to Carter from the photo Charlie had sent him, even from that distance and in the harsh white light of the bus station. The man closed the car door and looked around, then walked decisively through the bus station, almost directly towards Carter. Then, at the edge of the ring road, he stopped and peered across into the darkness. This was it. Carter pointed the torch – one flash; two; three. The man moved, briskly, almost straight towards Carter, who was fumbling, pushing the torch back into his pocket, getting the knife out of its sheath in the same right-hand pocket, feeling with his left hand for the gun. And then the man was there, on the edge of the waiting darkness, peering in, his eyes blinking in their effort to adjust.

"Charlie…?" Miller whispered. His voice was audibly shaking.

"Over here," Carter whispered in return, "behind the dustbins."

George Miller stared hard and managed to distinguish the dark shapes of the large commercial waste containers and he suddenly knew that something was badly wrong. The voice, the place… he'd been suspicious about this from the start and now he knew he had to get away from here, there was danger like he'd never known here, but at the same moment Carter realised that he had to act now. He rushed forward, grabbed Miller's right shoulder with his left hand and stuck the knife as hard as he could into his stomach. Miller doubled up with a sharp gasp of the blow, but Carter realised instinctively that the knife had not gone in or at least not gone very far through the thick overcoat. He grabbed Miller and shoved him further into the shadows, knowing it would be less than a second before he got over the initial shock of the attack and began screaming, or even recovered enough to fight back and run. Miller was still doubled up, winded by the first blow, and using both hands this time, he bashed the knife hard down into Millers exposed back and this time felt it gash through the coat and tear deep into him. The two of them tumbled to the floor, Carter loosing for a second his grip on the knife, Miller making a dreadful gasping, choking noise, trying to get up, trying to scream, but it was too late for him now. Pain and shock were strangling his efforts and somewhere deep inside him he knew he was already a dead man, knew there was nothing he could do and the sheer terror of death was gagging him. In an instant, Carter was back on him, straddling him, crushing him to the floor, leaning his whole weight through his two hands onto the knife until it in was up to the hilt and then twisting it and wrenching it around as Miller writhed and bucked, but more and more weakly, gurgling and moaning, gasping as the knife was finally jerked out. Carter gritted his teeth as blood splattered into his face and then he thumped the knife in again and out and in again and again, in a desperate frenzy to finish it all off, finish it, again and again until…there was silence. An edgy pause. Miller lay twisted, bloody, dead. Carter knelt staring, frozen, listening. And then the shaking began…He suddenly realised that he had to get away. It was over, finished and he had to get away fast. He looked round, dazed, to check that he'd left no obvious clues. Then he remembered the wallet, he had to nick Miller's wallet. He stood up, pulled the dead weight onto its back and, trying to avoid looking, even in the darkness, into the dead man's eyes, he rooted about awkwardly inside the overcoat, his gloves heavy and sticky with blood until he felt the wallet. He grasped it and was off, away from the body, still in control of himself just enough to walk not run and to know that he couldn't just march into the bus station, in his present state. God knows where the blood had splashed. He'd have to be very careful. He forced himself to go through the stages of the rudimentary plan he'd prepared. First of all, ditch the wallet. He opened it, took out all the money and stuffed the notes into his pocket. Then he just threw the wallet away. Now he could take off his sodden gloves and shove them into the inside pocket of his coat. Finally, he took out the hip flask bottle of whisky he'd brought with him and had a long swig. Then another. And then he poured some on his hands and wiped them over his face and hair, and poured some over his coat. That way, if he was to attract the attention of any coppers, they'd just think he was a drunk on his way home – he certainly looked dishevelled enough. Taking a deep breath and a last drink, he walked briskly and decisively across the now deserted road, through the empty bus station, over the railway bridge and into the welcome darkness of the narrow-terraced streets beyond, eager to get to the canal and be rid of the knife and gloves. And after that there was the long walk back to his bedsit.

***

Within minutes of Frank crossing the road, in one of those coincidences that would seem so unlikely if you read about them in a story, but which in real life constantly criss-cross through our lives, Derek drove past the same bus station on his way home to Woodford Green, past the shopping mall, past the still warm body of the man he'd followed up to Manchester on that increasingly fateful weekend. He was feeling warm, excited, pleased with himself, and very much alive. What an evening! He really couldn't remember having enjoyed himself so much for a long, long time. He felt waves of elation surging through him as different parts of the evening came into his mind – the meal, the walk to his car, the drive to her flat in a small, modern block on a sloping, tree lined road just beyond Dulwich 'village'.

He was feeling calmer now, but he recalled the nervousness that he had been feeling, despite all the drink (Christ, he shouldn't have been driving, he still shouldn't be.) He slowed down and checked his speedometer as he turned into the Leytonstone High Road, as dismal, dark and depressing an area as you could imagine.

They'd been talking about the environment, about women, about so many issues, and he realised just how little you see of people you work with. Val, the cool, controlled professional officer was the same person as this Val, passionate about social justice and the future of the world, about literature and art and poetry. He found himself able for the first time in ages to talk seriously with someone he worked with about how he really felt about some of these issues, without having to make jokes about them for fear of being laughed at by the lads at the bar with him. What's more, it had been stimulating and fun, there was a freshness to their conversation, and he realised now, as he reached the open spaces that marked the fraying edges of London, out towards Wanstead, that it was these exchanges, not the kiss they'd finally shared, that were the source of the deep feeling of intimacy between them which he sensed, sensed so strongly that he was convinced it had to be mutual, that it wasn't just him imposing his own feelings in a yearning of wishful thinking and that it wasn't just the drink – though as a drinker he knew there was always that possibility with alcohol.

He'd known she wasn't going to ask him in, it was perfect as it was. Everything else would come later. This was something so different and special it was relaxing and calming at the same time as being exciting and stimulating. It was like nothing else that he had felt since …well, ever. *And that kiss…for a moment he knew they could have both stumbled into her flat, into her bed but…it was better this way, the kiss marked the beginning, an unforgettable moment of itself, not to be lost as part of more kisses and all that would have followed, in itself not part of the foreplay that would have been the pattern of his past, but simply a kiss, full of its own complete sensuality…*

***

As Derek drove and Miller's corpse bled out and grew colder and colder, Val sat drinking a glass of brandy, as bewildered as Derek, but less elated. She knew that there was something between them, knew that when he kissed her there was a moment when it felt so good and so right that she could have pulled him gently inside, literally – God knows she'd had lots of boyfriends, more than she cared to remember, and she'd enjoyed herself with all of them to some extent, but there was something about this one that was definitely very different. She knew it wouldn't be worth analysing what it was – it could be any number of permutations – she was older and perhaps looking for different things now.

Derek was physically attractive, intelligent, sensitive, funny...vulnerable. She took another sip of brandy. But what on earth was she getting so uptight about? This was only their first date, for God's sake, it might not come to anything anyway. But she knew only too well what was worrying her – it was the thought that it might come to something, and if it did what would that something be? She sensed that she could really fall for Derek if she let herself, and had a feeling that he perhaps had already fallen for her. What would be the next stage? Well, the next stage was fairly straight forward and she felt herself thinking it was a close call that night – she'd been on the point of inviting him in, he'd had too much to drink to drive back for god sake – and she'd certainly been tempted. In fact, if they'd not been working together, she wouldn't have hesitated and she knew it would have been at least great fun. No, what she meant was, what was the stage after that? If it all went well, and why wouldn't it? Living together? Getting married and then what? Was she ready for all that yet, was she ready for any of it? He was older than her, possibly ten years...did that matter?

Once again, she found herself looking back to that first day at university, for the second time in relation to Derek. But it *was* a memory now, and she knew that things had changed – perhaps trying to hang on to that feeling could itself become a sort of tyranny over her life, holding her back from actions she wanted to take. And there was no doubt that with Derek she recaptured some of the freshness and excitement that she had not known since starting work at Customs and Excise. And he was interesting to talk to as well, amusing but not shallow. And then she caught sight of herself in the mirror on the opposite wall, and had to smile at how serious she looked. Play it by ear, see what happens and just enjoy it for whatever it was. She smiled again – and yes, after that kiss, she was definitely looking forward to the sex, very nearly dragged him in there and then.

She gulped down the rest of the brandy and got herself ready for bed – and with a final smile of pleasure at the evening, she sank into a deep and very peaceful sleep.

Outside in the shadows, a tired MI5 officer reached for his radio. "Well, it may be something we can use – certainly worth keeping a note of – Brown and the woman on the team, Henderson. Well, it looks like there's more going on there than a team meeting – yeah, they've been out for a meal and he's taken her back to her flat – no, he's left now, no he didn't go in, but he had his tongue down her throat when they were saying bye bye – like I say…might come in useful later. Over and out."

Chapter 11

It was late when he woke the next morning, and within minutes the drinker's doubts had set in as they always do when the real-world washes back in to replace the alcohol. The euphoria of the drive home was replaced by the first naggings of insecurity. Was she feeling the same as him? Last night, he *knew* she was, without any doubt. This morning he couldn't be sure – could it have been just been the drink after all – and his *readiness* for things to go well. Last night there had been the sheer thrill of being with her, touching her. Today there was just him alone with his hangover. To make matters worse, he wasn't quite sure what to do next. It was so long since he'd actually been interested in anyone or anyone had seemed actually to be interested, properly interested in him. So he wasn't sure what the next step would be or should be because he suddenly realised he hadn't ever taken the next step or even thought about a next step – he'd have stayed the night, had fun, driven home and…perhaps seen whoever again, perhaps not. But now he desperately wanted to do the right thing and he knew that nothing else in his life had quite prepared him for what that might be. And he was keenly aware that Val was complicated, wary, and that everything was less straightforward that it might have been because of work.

So he weighed up the options, through the tiredness and haze – Christ, had he really driven home in that state? He lit a cigarette, inhaled, coughed, inhaled again.

He could wait until he saw her again at work, but he knew that that might be quite a while – the main obs on the Carter character began on Monday. And anyway, he didn't want her to think that he was feeling at all casual about everything. But then again, the other risk was that he might come on too strong too fast for her, though he knew even as he was thinking about it that this was the risk he would have to take. He would never be able to live with himself if he lost her by being too laid back. If it didn't work out, well at least he would have tried. He picked up the phone, found her number and then paused. What was he going to say? Judging by last night, they wouldn't have any trouble talking, but this was without the drink and it was on the phone. Supposing there was just an embarrassing silence and they both ended up saying something stupid or even worse, nothing at all? He put the phone down, checked his diary and then picked it up again and dialled.

"Hello, Val?"

"Yes…"

"It's Derek… Derek Brown."

"Yes, Derek – believe it or not, you're the only Derek I know who'd be phoning me up on a Sunday morning."

"Well, that's a relief."

"And it's a relief to know you got back OK last night. Assuming this isn't your one and only phone call from the cells?"

"No, though I shouldn't have driven like that. I mean, I wasn't all that drunk or anything, but I was over the limit all right! Anyway I was phoning to say, well, how much I enjoyed it last night." There, he'd said it, it had just come out, almost naturally. But then the pause. And then "Yes. Yes, so did I. And I wasn't over the limit either…"

He smiled. Might as well keep up the momentum. Feint hearts and all that.

"So, I was wondering if, well, if you'd like to do something again, next weekend?"

"Yes, I'd love to." There was no hint of hesitation this time and he relaxed. "But I'm not sure when," she added, "I've just been working out the rotas for the obs next week and it's going to be hectic for me. Hang on a second and I'll check when we're both free… Friday night. Would you like to come round here and have a meal, carry on where we left off?"

"Absolutely, yes, that sounds a great idea. What time?"

"Well, come early, if that's alright – about half seven?"

"Fine. Right. Er, so I'll see you then. Well, I'll see you for your briefing Monday morning, good luck with that."

"Thanks, I'll need it. And Derek…well, I know you wouldn't, but…well, no sign of anything in front of everyone."

"No, no of course not."

"It's just…well, I'll be nervous enough anyway, being in charge and everything."

"No, don't worry. Of course, I'll just be looking forward all the more to seeing you on Friday."

"Me too."

There was a long pause, both realising that in some way they had passed a threshold, a tacit, intimate agreement that they were now involved, that it was going somewhere further.

Val took control. "OK, I'm going to have to go," firm but none of the sharpness of their earliest encounters. "Bye then."

"Bye," was all he could manage and all that was needed.

He put the phone down and realised he was shaking, as much with elation as with nerves. And now the doubts were gone. Her tone, the invitation, the 'me too'. For the first time since East Ham he really as if he was coming through, was sure it was all going to go well, Val and the job, Life. He could sense it. He lit up another cigarette, poured himself a glass of wine and settled down to read the papers.

***

That Sunday evening found Carter sitting beside the telephone, waiting as he had been waiting all day – second after second after second. The naked light bulb threw hard shadows onto the yellowing wallpaper. He stared at the tattered settee. The whole room had an air of impermanence, fleeting, transitory, like a waiting room at a bus station. How many other people had sat uncomfortably on the chair that Frank now fidgeted in, and how many more would do so after he moved out? But moved out to where? Up or down? He felt dreadful, worse than he could ever remember. It wasn't conscience. At no time during the whole thing did anything remotely like a twinge of conscience flicker through Frank's awareness. Not a hint of empathy for a fellow human being, suffering, dead. The nearest emotion to anything at all to do with last night was fear of being caught and this was the fear that was torturing him now. He was frightened and shocked, more than he had ever been before and far more than he had expected to be. He had had no doubts before, with the police on his side so to speak, and he'd even managed to get some sleep afterwards when he'd got home in the early hours – though that was as much due to the sheer amount of whisky he'd knocked back as it was to any feeling of security.

The most frightened person in the world would have slept the sleep of the just if he'd drunk as much as Carter had done. And he'd been drinking steadily since waking, so it was hardly surprising that it was now having the opposite to its normal soothing, soporific effect – this was the other side of alcohol to the one we mostly encounter, this was the devil not the friend, this was the poison, tormenting him with shakes and jitters and feverish paranoia. He couldn't shake off the nagging, nerve-wracking doubt that perhaps he'd been set up. You couldn't, shouldn't ever trust a copper, for Christ's sake. What the fuck had ever made him think he could? He'd been a fucking stupid idiot to get taken in and now he was in for it. If they nicked him, he had nothing to prove that Charlie was involved, nothing, sweet fuck all. They'd piss themselves laughing at his story. Charlie had abandoned him.

He picked up his cigarettes and lit one. It was his second packet of the day and there were only a few left, though he couldn't be bothered to count. He looked at the clock on the mantelpiece – 9 o'clock. He turned on the radio for the news, the same news that he'd heard every hour since he'd woken up. It had first been on the one o'clock edition and it had crumpled him up like you crumple up a cigarette packet. It was like a double whammy – at once absolute confirmation that he'd been successful, and at the same time, that meant he was now a murderer, so it was a sort of moral jumble of good news and bad news at the same time – but the bottom line was that he was in deep shit and his only hope of getting through it was a bent copper who hadn't even bothered to get in touch with him!

"…Police are still appealing for witnesses to the murder at Stratford last night of a man aged about 35 to 40. The body, which was discovered this morning, may be that of George Miller, a West London businessman whose abandoned car was found nearby."

He turned off the small, portable radio and poured another glass from the second bottle. The phone rang and he lurched to pick it up, spilling most of the whisky in the process.

"Hello…"

There was a long pause. It must be that bastard Charlie, pissing him about. Or testing him, seeing if his nerve was holding out.

"Hello. Look, stop messing about. Who's there?"

"Hello, Frank, it's me, Charlie. I was just making sure no one was within earshot of me at this end – I'm at work. Are you alone?"

"Yes, of course I'm fucking alone. Jesus, where the fuck have you been? I…"

"Now calm down Frank. You've done well, so just take it easy, alright? The reason I've left it so late is because I've been doing some sniffing around, on your behalf as you might say. And as far as I can tell they haven't got any clues at all, let alone anything that would lead them to you. So you can relax a bit now – not too much, though, eh?" There was a sinister edge to Charlie's voice, a harsh undertone which cut through Carter's whisky induced mental fog.

"What's that supposed to mean – not too much?"

"Well, your biggest enemy now might be you, Frank. You know how you like to talk when you get a drink inside you…and you're already sounding a bit slurred."

Frank took a deep breath and then spoke again, overcorrecting pace and pronunciation like a stand-up comic drunk. "Yeah, well I'm hardly likely to go out getting pissed up am I? I mean, I might be stupid, but I'm not a fucking moron. Talk about cutting my nose off to spite my face – and I've only got the walls to talk to here."

"Yeah, well don't forget what they used to say, eh – walls have ears, Frank. And that bit about cutting off your nose – I couldn't have put it better myself, Frank, though I'll just have to take your word for it on the moron bit. So now about the money, Frank. I'm surprised you haven't mentioned it yourself."

"Well, I've ..."

"Had more pressing things to occupy your mind, Frankie? Well, there's no need to worry now. It's all over, bar the ...paying. So, listen, enjoyable as this social chit chat is, it's business as usual now – do you remember we met once in 'The Gun' on the Isle of Dogs? Right, well, I'll meet you there next Sunday, that's a week today, at 12 noon. Opening time, Frank – and it'll be you buying the drinks, if I'm not mistaken – you'll have something to celebrate then, Frank, and something to celebrate with. You'll get all that's coming to you then, I promise you. But think on – you'll be all on your little own some after that, so you'll have to make your own plans as to what to do. Alright? Good. So repeat it to me – next Sunday, 12 noon, The Gun, Isle of Dogs."

"For God's sake, Charlie, I'm not simple..."

"So you keep telling me, Frank – but indulge me, say it anyway, just for me, eh?"

"12 noon, The Gun, Isle of Dogs, next Sunday. Have I passed?"

"Right. And don't forget – the only thing that can get you into trouble now is your mouth, so steer well clear of the booze – it'll be more than worth your while, you know that."

"Message received and understood, boss. And I have had a couple today, anyone would have done after... but..., I'm on my own, and I've been drinking here, not out in the boozer and..."

"Yeah, alright, calm down. More like a couple of bottles than glasses by the sound of you... I'm just telling you to be careful – it's your future on the line, don't forget. I'll see you next Sunday. Sleep tight – and pleasant dreams about what you're going to do with all that money, eh?"

Chapter 12

Friday night, seven o'clock. Derek looked at his watch again. He'd set off in good time because he wasn't sure of being able to find the place again, sober. But it had been easy enough, and now here he was, half an hour early and parked at the bottom of the road, feeling like a sleazy private detective out on a divorce case. In fact he wasn't sure what to do. He wasn't used to being in a situation where he was actually too bothered about the outcome, normally he was genuinely take it or leave it, win some lose some – but now it really mattered to him and he found himself overthinking everything again and he just couldn't help it. And on top of everything else, he had become increasingly aware of his age, worried about his looks, his clothes. He'd never spent so much time looking in mirrors – well, not since adolescence anyway. 'God, this middle age business is like dying,' he grinned to himself, 'I'm seeing my whole life flash before me'.

He looked at his watch again. He'd decided to go at twenty-five past – early enough to show enthusiasm, but not to cause any embarrassment. He took a last look at his hair in the driver's mirror, picked up the bottle of Cote du Rhone and walked slowly up the pleasant tree lined street to Val's block. He felt as nervous as if he'd been going for a job interview but by the time he walked up to the doors, he had managed to settle himself, only to be confronted by locked security doors. Shit! He couldn't remember that from his last visit. And he couldn't for the life of him remember her flat number. He remembered she'd said it was on the first floor, that would narrow it down if he could get into the building, but... he racked his brains for the number, and then thought what else he could do. Well, if all else failed he could find a phone box and telephone her, he had that number written down. Or he could just press one of the other flats' numbers and ask them to let him in, but unlikely anyone would in London. He stared at the doors and the bells and realised that there were only four flats on each of the two floors, eight all together. As hers was on the first floor, it would have to be number five, six seven or eight. Wouldn't it? So it narrowed it down. He looked at the keyboard and pressed 6. And waited, looking at his watch. Well, at least he wasn't going to be too early now – it had already gone half past. He pressed again and almost instantly the panel crackled into life and a voice said, "Hello, number six." Number six, not a name. It was female, but you really couldn't have told who it was, it was so distorted by the intercom.

"Hello, Val?"

"Yes, Derek?"

Bloody hell, a great omen. "Yes."

He'd have to start doing the lottery.

"Come on up."

The doors clicked open and he pushed his way through, into the clean, characterless lobby, smelling of everybody's cooking, as even the most clinically clean communal blocks always do. His heart felt like it was exploding as he walked the last few feet to her door. It was open. He hesitated for a second and then tapped and pushed it open

"Hi."

"Oh, hi." She came out of the kitchen and stood there, looking as awkward as he felt. The air was tense with embarrassment as they both just stood there. Should he literally continue from where they had left off last time, like she'd said on the phone - and kiss her? She looked gorgeous. He offered the bottle of wine instead.

"Oh, thanks. Come in, I've nearly finished in there. Come into the living room. Can I get you a drink?" He noticed that she was talking more quickly than usual and he recognised the same signs of nervousness that he was feeling, an observation which for some reason made him feel more relaxed.

"Yes, what have you got?"

"Not a lot, I'm afraid. Red or white wine, beer, whisky…"

"A beer'd be fine, thanks." The first impulse to make physical contact had passed along with the missed opportunity. He walked over to the window while Val fetched the beer. Then he sat down on the settee and, as he took his first sip of the fizzy, frothy canned beer, began to feel more at ease, almost comfortable. She came back in again with her own drink, a white wine, and sat in the easy chair almost opposite him.

"Right, about ten minutes and we can start. God, it's been hectic this week."

"Yes, well. Would you rather we'd have met tomorrow night?"

"Oh god, no, I didn't mean that this was hectic. I meant all the obs and so on. And no, I want an early night tomorrow – I'm on the six in the morning shift on Sunday, and I want to be there bright and early. After all, we haven't had much luck so far…"

"And Sunday's the first of the dates on the list! Of course, you want to be in on the kill." Derek laughed.

"Well, yes, I suppose I do. Though really, it's more that, well, if something doesn't happen soon, there won't be any case at all, will there? And that would be a real shame when we all *know* that we're so close."

"God, it'd be a bloody tragedy. Anyway, how does it feel to be organising the obs – I might tell you that everyone is very impressed."

"You condescending sod…"

"No, no look, I didn't mean it to sound like that. I'm serious, I've heard some very favourable comments. Bill has you marked down for great things." Derek saw that she was blushing, and he knew that for a moment he'd nearly blown it – he'd relaxed a bit too much, but – well, once they were talking, they seemed so easy together that it was hard to keep up the normal formalities. There *was* an intimacy between them that made it difficult to remember that they had only been out once before.

"Anyway," she said, "let's not spend the time talking about work – I'm more interested in catching up on us – now remind me, where were we up to last time?" – He looked startled and then before he could think she leaned over to him and kissed him, "About there, if I remember?"

And he needed no more encouragement. He kissed her and felt the excitement from her washing through him and over him, as they kissed and kissed and stroked each other. He started to undo her top but she stopped him, stood up and undid it herself and then everything else. For the briefest of moments he took it all in, her beautiful body, and then he stood up and began to take off his shirt, while she eagerly undid his trousers and then they embraced again, standing there holding each other and revelling in the pure, tingling sensuousness of naked flesh against naked flesh and then somehow they were both on the carpet, the softness of the white rug and she climbed on top of him and bent down to kiss him, lips, tongues exploring, bodies moving.

And then afterwards…they lay together, hot, sweaty, he stroked her hair, her neck, her back, gently, they held each other before she finally looked up and kissed him gently on the forehead and then the lips, just brushing hers against his.

And then she said, "Well, that was a great catchup now we've got that out of the way we can get on with the meal," and they both laughed as she stood up. "If you're still hungry?"

She picked up her glass of wine and wondered into the bedroom, emerging seconds later in a short, silk kimono, pearl coloured.

He put on his shirt and was about to get dressed when she said, "Hey, equality here…the shirt will do," and disappeared into the kitchen. "Good job it's coq au vin, just simmering and not burnt," and they both laughed.

**

The meal was delicious., the wine flowed, they touched each other's hand, face, hair as they talked and drank, wine then coffee and from that moment on for him their talk became just a sort of background music. Her physical closeness overwhelmed his senses again, he wanted to touch her, to hold her, to kiss her. As he paused in the middle of a sentence, she suddenly moved closer to him and again took the lead and again gently, firmly kissed him. And later it was she who suggested that he could stay over. "But I don't want you to think that I always let just anyone sleep with me on the second date you know!"

Derek was almost out of his depth. Her humour, her honesty, her control of the situation just swept him along. "I…I've not been able to get you off my mind. I …"

"It's alright. I know what you mean. Let's not spoil it with words." And she kissed him again and led him into her bedroom.

***

Hours later, Derek lay awake in the darkness, with Val, as far as he could tell, fast asleep beside him with her back to him. This was it, he was in love. There was no mistaking it, there was nothing else it could be, no other word for it. He thought of her undressing, of the sex, of her humour and sense of fun so quickly overcoming his anxieties and confusions. He closed his eyes and just hoped she felt the same – but again felt that he couldn't possibly be feeling the way he was if it wasn't reciprocated, that he'd have somehow picked up on it. As he slipped slowly to sleep, he dreamed a future, a real relationship, a whole way of life that he thought he'd excluded himself from –He found himself waking up again, stroking her back, feeling the hardness of her spine through her smooth skin, stroking down to her bottom, to her thighs, to the backs of her knees, then back up, slowly to her thighs, easing his fingers between her legs, sliding them back and forward, slipping them with a gentle rhythm in and almost out, sensing her breathing changing as she began to respond. Still with her back to him, she reached behind her and felt for his erection, rubbing it slowly up and down until both their bodies and heartbeats and minds were moving gently to the same rhythm, in and out, back and forward, up and down, as she pulled him to her from behind and he pushed slowly inside her, both lying on their sides, his hands now stroking her firm stomach, her breasts, her pubic hair, the front of her thighs…

Chapter 13

Saturday morning was as wonderful as everything else – more sex, more intimacy, more tenderness, more emotion, and all before breakfast and coffee and then she was ushering him out, reluctantly but keen to get on with the task ahead without distraction.

At the door, dressed and ready to go, they held each other and kissed, again, long, tender and for one slight second he broke off the kiss and looked into her eyes and very nearly said 'I love you' but before he could, she put a finger over his lips and then kissed him again. But it was there, he knew it as he drove back towards his flat, leaving her in hers. He felt simply elated, too elated to notice the dark blue Mondeo that was following him.

He was not on obs again until Tuesday but in the meantime, he was in charge of sorting out odds and ends in the office and continuing to look for any clues that the paperwork end of the operation might throw up. He thought that he might as well put in a couple of hours on his way back home – it would impress Val if nothing else. And it might help to settle him down a bit after all the emotional turmoil of the last twenty-four hours. He smiled as he thought of her, of kissing her good-bye, of their arrangement to go away for the weekend in two weeks' time, when all of this case was out of the way – as it would be by then, one way or another. After all, if nothing had happened by the last of the dates on the sheet of paper, they couldn't possibly sustain the case. And if something was going to happen, well, it would have happened by then and be all over bar the shouting, so either way, they'd both be ready for a break. But where should they go? She'd left it to him, 'delegated' it she'd said. And in between time, they were going to meet as and when they could. He was to ring her Sunday evening when she'd finished her stint watching Carter. Perhaps by then they'd know something more. God, he couldn't help smiling. It was all going to be good, so much better than he could have dared hope. It was going like a dream.

***

And for Val, too, it was like a dream, though as she lay in the bath, there was still lingering sense of uncertainty – not at how she felt – it really had all been even better than she'd expected. She'd sort of expected the sex to be good but she hadn't expected herself to feel so much emotion with it and to feel the same from him, the passion, the…love? Is that what it was, the coup de foudre? She was absolutely sure that he was about to tell her he loved her, when they were kissing as he left – and she knew she'd have said she loved him back…she sighed as she ran her fingers over her own body, enjoying the last sensations of her heightened nerve endings as they slowly subsided. For now she was happy to enjoy all of it and wallow in the dream of how good it could all be if it worked out well…and meanwhile she still had the responsibility of organising the obs on Salter.

***

While Derek and Val's lives had taken on the qualities of a dream, Frank Carter's had become an appalling, unremittingly unambiguous nightmare. He looked a complete physical wreck, in that state of self-neglect where appearance and mental well-being race each into the dark, bleak depths of total breakdown, a race to the very bottom. His nerves were really playing him up now and he'd had almost no sleep. Occasionally, images of the murder flashed into his mind, so vividly that he could see and feel it all again. There was still no remorse for the victim, no problem with the morality of the act. It was all complete self-pity. But the sheer physical detail of what he had done would not let go of him, it had got inside him like a virus he couldn't shake off. And the fear of getting caught, of being tracked down, of being double crossed by Whitcombe was always there, pricking at him. Charlie bloody Whitcombe of the C.I.D. And in the meantime, there was the waiting, hour after hour after hour.

He'd hardly been out of his room – only down to the shops for his fags and another couple of bottles of whisky, almost a bottle a night he was on, which meant he was never really sober at all. And just one more night to get through. Saturday night and then – the big payoff. He still didn't have any clear idea of what he was going to do with the money, except that he would leave London. Though where to exactly, he didn't know. He was London born, London bred, and had always felt out of place on the rare occasions he had been outside of the great city, as if everywhere else was just – nowhere. But as soon as he'd picked up the cash, he knew he had to be off *somewhere*. He'd made up his mind that he wouldn't come back to this place again at all and he knew the money would go a lot further anywhere outside of the capital. Straight to a station, and away. He didn't have many possessions anyway, one suitcase would fit everything, and he could take that with him when he met Charlie. And after that, a change of name with Charlie's help and he'd be free. He'd be free. He kept saying the words to himself, free, free, but somehow that didn't cheer him up at all. Escape – it was no longer a dream, an ambition, an exhilarating, tantalising fantasy, just a weary, dreary, depressing necessity, the word and the reality.

***

Sunday morning was a bleak, grey day, wet and windswept. On an open Derbyshire Pennine moor, it might have been bracing, uplifting, but in Limehouse it was claustrophobically depressing. Val looked at her watch – 7 a.m. – An hour since she and Ron McCartney had taken over their six-hour shift. The previous shift had nothing to report, but today was the 12th. of May, 12.5., and there was a feeling of tense expectation in the air.

By 11.30 that air of expectation had dissipated into numbing tedium.

Val wiped the misted-up windscreen. "Oh God, only another half hour and we'll be off. Bloody hell!" She thumped the dashboard in frustration. She had a real chance to make a name for herself with this job and yet it seemed to be stalling, fading, slipping away through her fingers with every second – though in fact. She knew that whatever happened, she was on the team, accepted, part of the crew. And there was Derek…

"Yeah, well I still reckon we've got the right bloke. I mean, nobody in the world stays in as much as this guy, surely? How many days have we been doing this, and he's not spoken to a living soul except for the bloke who serves in the off licence. Now we know he isn't a monk, and we know he usually hangs around in pubs. So…"

Ron's Liverpool accent struck just the right tone of logic and humour and Val smiled. Just then a taxi pulled up in front of Carter's place.

"God, you're right, Ron. Look… we're on, I bet you."

Ron started the car. "Right, let H.Q. know it's definite – here he comes."

They were parked about sixty yards down the street, well beyond discovery by the quick, cursory glance up and down that Carter gave before getting into the taxi. Ron pulled out to shadow the green Ford Orion diesel. There followed as grim a drive as could be imagined, in the stuffy car through the almost empty wet and windy streets of the East End, along Commercial Road, going East, away from the city. Then, just before the Blackwall tunnel, they turned right onto the Isle of Dogs. It was like an endless journey into the depths of a dark, half – remembered childhood nightmare – the old, dirty remains of the docks and the sweatshops, the exact same ones that had been there since Victorian Values had had their first, pre-Thatcher outing. Now they were filled with a new generation of ruthlessly exploited labour, new faces, new colours, same old grinding poverty, same long hours, same pittance in the pay packet year on year on year – if they were lucky! And the new blocks of flats where the workers were packed for overnight storage ready for another day's service, were like something from a cliched dystopian science fiction film. Here, in these dreadful places, sensitive, caring, hoping human beings struggled for dignity and fulfilment amidst the planned squalor – the nightmare we all want to push out of our minds as long as we don't have to live there.

A gust of wind lashed the car to the left.

"Hey, watch out, Ron, I want to get out of this in one piece."

"Sorry, wasn't concentrating."

They drove on, over an old iron bridge, past a wall proudly proclaiming 'Welcome to the Isle of Dogs' and then down a slight slope.

"He's turning left," Val said.

"OK, I've got him."

There was only one car between them and the taxi now. Ron slowed down, indicated left and turned to follow the taxi. They found themselves in a short, cobbled, very narrow street, at the end of which was a pub. It looked like a dead-end, the pub facing straight towards them.

"Oh bloody hell, he's bound to spot us now," Ron muttered, gripping the wheel tightly as they crawled along towards the pub and the now stationary taxi, both their hearts pounding. But as they got closer, they both realised at the same time that it was not a dead end after all. The road continued round to the left, at right angles, but the taxi was still blocking their way past. They pulled up right behind it just as Carter was getting out. He was putting his change into his pocket and looking around. He looked straight at them and Val gripped her seat tightly, so nervous she thought she might scream. She could see Ron's knuckles white on the wheel. It lasted only for a split second and then she knew what had to be done. She leant across Ron and pushed hard on the horn.

Ron jumped. "What the fuck…"

"Put your window down and tell him to get a move on, be aggressive. Quick!"

Catching on, he wound the window down and yelled, "Come on mate, get a bloody move on."

The taxi driver stuck two fingers up out of his open window and pulled away down the street. Carter turned and went into the pub, unruffled and with not even the vaguest suspicions aroused by the encounter – and they drove on past. The street they found themselves in was also cobbled and narrow, but there were no houses, though once it had been lined by grim, red-brick warehouses, which had now been knocked down, leaving a desolate wasteland. On either side of the road there was a thin strip of pavement, fenced off from the wasteland by large sections of faded green corrugated metal boarding. They pulled up opposite a gap in the fence where a section of the boarding had been ripped down and through the gap Val could see an overgrown vacant lot and beyond, a glimpse of the river. McCartney switched off the engine. For a second they both just sat there, looking straight ahead.

"Wow. Now that was a close one." He turned and looked at her. "And that was really inspired, Val. Nice one. God!"

They both grinned at each other and then started laughing. It was Val who brought them out of it, only just this side of nervous hysteria. "Right, come on, we'd better get into the pub, as soon as I've reported in."

She picked up the microphone and turned around in her seat to look at the name of the pub. As she did, she saw Charlie Whitcombe arrive, on foot.

"Christ, stay in the car. Look – it's that shady character we saw in that first photo – the bloke Bill Haggart and Derek thought they'd seen before but couldn't place. He's gone in now – did you see him?"

"Well, not clearly, but I'll take your word for it. Ooooheee, something big's happening here. Look, I'd better go in on my own. If we both go in and they decide to leave and go on somewhere else we'll be stuck. But if you wait here, you can follow them on your own. Radio for support, get them all down here – there should be at least two cars available now, and it shouldn't take more than twenty minutes to get here. I'll get in straight away. God, this is great." He opened the door and got out. "See you later, alligator."

Val pressed the transmit trigger. "Control? Car eighteen. We're outside 'The Gun' pub on the Isle of Dogs and there is definitely something going on here. How much support can you give us? Over."

"Hello Val, its Bill Haggarty here. There's four of us, in two cars. As it happens, I know 'The Gun' – a delightful place. We can be there in less than half an hour, easy. What's happening?"

"Carter's gone inside, and so has that bloke on the first photograph, the shifty looking one that you and Derek thought you'd seen somewhere before. Ron's gone inside, I'll stay in the car until you arrive. Over."

"Great stuff. So we know we're definitely on the right track. We're on our way. See you soon, Val. Don't let them get away, eh? Over and out."

Val put the mike back and sat back in her seat, relaxing down with a sigh from the stress of the last few minutes. She decided that it would be safe to stretch her legs for a minute or two and get a breath of fresh air. She needed to think clearly and four hours of boredom followed by such sudden action had clouded her mind. And even more pressing, she realised she needed a pee. She looked across the street at the hole in the corrugated boarding. If she was quick, maybe she could nip in there – god knows when she'd get the next chance – she could end up following people all afternoon at this rate. She stepped out into the wind and now quite light rain and took a deep breath. She walked across the street and looked through. Inside she could make out a large brick strewn open space, with patches of long grass, and at the far end, a low wall. Beyond that, there was the grey, stormy Thames, and then the south bank – but emphatically not the South Bank of Melvyn Bragg. This was a south bank of factories and refineries and gasworks and the mean terraced housing of Deptford, as depressing a scene as any city anywhere could offer. But no one around and she did need that wee.

*****

Inside the pub there was a pleasant, cosily panelled bar overlooking the river, complete with a terrace for summer drinking but it had that stale smell of last night's beer and it was still too early for many to be out drinking yet. As soon as Ron walked into the small bar, he spotted Carter and the other man sitting in the far corner. He ordered a pint and sat down at a barstool. There was a mirror behind the bar in which he could see the two men talking. He took a gulp of his pint and noticed that his hand was shaking. And no bloody wonder, eh? He was raising his glass for a second mouthful, when he saw both of the targets stand up and head for the door, leaving their half-empty drinks on their table.

"Oh God. This really is something," he said to himself, almost out loud, "thank God Val's still out there." He forced himself to stay put. He'd drink his pint as slowly as he could before he ventured outside. It was the only safe thing to do to avoid being noticed, and Val was more than up to handling the situation.

*****

As they stepped into the street, Frank felt pleased with himself. He had kept his appointment, he was sober, or at least as sober as anyone could be after the amount he'd drunk in the last few days, and now he was going to be paid off, get his money and be off out of this city, out of this sordid existence.

Charlie spoke first. "This way, Frank. Christ, this weather's bloody awful, isn't it? Still, we're better off out here – like I said on the phone the other day, walls have ears, eh? It'll soon be over, Frank, don't worry." His eyes kept flitting up and down the street, force of habit.

"Yeh, well it can't be too soon for me. Let's just get all this out of the way, eh?"

182

"Right, Frank, my sentiments exactly. And I've seen just the place up here where we can do it and no one will see us." He pointed up the street, but neither of them saw Val dodge quickly back into the empty lot. There was no way now that she could get back to the car. Frantically cursing herself, she looked for somewhere to hide and moved into a corner by the fence, kneeling in the long, wet grass. Then to her horror, she heard them approaching. So they were definitely making a move. God, if she was to lose them because she was stuck here!

And then, with even greater horror, she realised that they weren't going off anywhere. She heard one of them say, "In here, Frank. This is just about as secure a place as anywhere in London. Let's get it over with." And the two men climbed through the same gap that not two or three minutes before she had climbed through. She couldn't believe that they wouldn't see her crouching there, but they walked straight past her, not fifteen feet away, over to the low wall that looked out across the Thames. What a bloody mess – if they saw her now, he'd know they'd been rumbled and the whole operation would be finished, and after all that work. She quickly realised that she had two options. She could stay put and hope that they didn't see her, or she could try to sneak towards the gap and chance that they were too involved in their conversation to spot her. It was highly unlikely they'd fail to see her if she stayed put, so she took a deep breath, made up her mind and began to edge towards the gap in the fence, slowly, crouched, carefully edging, watching them all the time.

They both had their backs to her, looking out to the river. Beyond them, she could just see a passing tourist boat. She could tell from behind which one was Carter, but she couldn't hear what they were saying. She glanced again towards the gap and then back at the two men. As she concentrated on them, she saw something happen that at first she could not take in. It seemed to be happening in slow motion and yet at the same time with incredible speed. She saw the man with Carter take out a gun with a silencer attached, bring it swiftly and without hesitation up behind Carter's head and pull the trigger. She saw it kick almost soundlessly back against his wrist, saw Carter's head jerk savagely to the right, while his legs slumped to the left, and he buckled heavily onto the low wall. The man fired two more shots into the body and then turned suddenly and looked straight at her.

Without realising it, she had stood up straight with the shock at what she had just witnessed. For a second, the two of them stood staring at each other and, in that second, Val took in every detail of his face, his eyes wide with fear. It was still the same second when she noticed that he was pointing the gun at her, saw the black silencer glistening wet in the rain. But a second was more than long enough for Charlie to make his decision. He pulled the trigger for the fourth and then the fifth time in less than a minute. Both shots hit Val in the chest. She was dead before her head smashed onto the ground, before she had any time to feel anything at all.

Fighting down the sheer blind panic, Charlie turned back to Carter and heaved the body over into the murky river thirty feet below. Then he went over to Val. He had no time to think who she was or what she was doing there but he did know that he had to get rid of her quickly. He could sense that she was dead rather than just unconscious and he was about to drag her over to the wall to follow Carter into the Thames when he heard a car arrive in the street outside. He peered through a gap in the fence and saw a grey Ford Sierra stop just a few feet away.

Further along, nearer to the pub, he could see a green Cavalier just arriving. Both cars had two men in and all of them stayed put in their cars. Well, now he knew that his worst fears had been realised. He'd been a copper long enough to recognise a stakeout when he saw one, and this was one. And that fucking woman must have something to do with it. On the edge of complete mental collapse, he jumped back from the fence as the grey Sierra's engine suddenly revved. What the hell was going on? Who the fucking hell were they? From the sound of the engine, the car was turning round. He risked another furtive look through the fence and sure enough, the car had executed a three-point turn and was now parked facing the pub. And in a flash, Charlie saw his way out. They were *watching the pub,* watching the pub not an anonymous piece of wasteland. He knew he might only have seconds before the girl was missed and a search instigated, so with no further precautions he simply stepped through the large gap in the fence, turned left, away from the pub and its watchers, and walked briskly along the street. About sixty paces further on he saw a T junction with a road to the left, which he took. Now he was out of sight of the watchers and he increased his pace, knowing that he was finding it harder by the second to control his panic. He took another right turn further along, recognising the street in which he'd parked his car. He was well out of breath as he opened the door of his dark green Rover, his hand shaking so much that he had difficulty getting the key into the lock., and even more difficulty with the ignition.

Eventually, after what seemed an eternity, the engine fired and he managed to negotiate his way out of the row of parked cars without problem. As he finally drove out into the traffic of the Commercial Road a few minutes later, he knew that for the time being he was safe – being caught there, red-handed, that was the biggest threat. Now that he was away from the scene, there was nothing to tie him in with the killings. But for how long? What on earth were he and Salter going to do? And it *was* going to be Salter as well because there was one thing about which Whitcombe's mind had remained absolutely clear, through all the whirling confusion of the last few minutes – without any doubt, Salter was going to be in the frame with him on this, if it came to it. Charlie Whitcombe wasn't going to be anybody's stooge. He also knew that he had to get in touch with Salter before the inevitable announcements came over on the radio, because otherwise there was a good chance that he'd be off out of the country like a shot, leaving Charlie to face the music. Well, Charlie was going to make sure that if Salter decided to do a runner, he'd be buying two tickets to wherever he had in mind, and no messing.

**

"Control, come in."

"Control, go ahead."

"Christ, the shit's really hit the fan. Henderson, the woman officer on the team? The one having it off with Brown, for Christ sake, there's only one. Well, she's been shot, yes, shot, dead I think. And it's that bloody copper Whitcombe, shot her and Carter. The rest of the Customs team have just turned up, but they haven't found her yet. Look, I'll give you the details when I get back, but I want to get out of the way before the plods start trampling around everywhere. But the point is, the Customs people must be putting some of the jigsaw pieces together to have been here at all."

"Jesus that's all we need. Right, we'd better pull everything out, get well back – leave the wire's on for now, but get everybody back in – the last thing we need is to get caught up any deeper in this. Come straight back to H.Q. – and keep any messages on the scrambler."

Chapter 14

Derek was lounging on the settee in his deep blue dressing gown, sipping a glass of lightly chilled Beaujolais and glancing through the Observer colour magazine. Finally, revelling in the sheer luxurious decadence of a whole day off with nothing to do except think of Val, he let the magazine slip to the floor, lit a cigarette and lazily stretched out his legs. He began to doze, lost in a place he had once been but had almost forgotten, on a beach, no movement, no sound, the sun already down, the darkness coming, the daylight gone, complete stillness on land, in the dark flat sea, in the sky, and then a solitary movement, less than a wave, more than a ripple, swelled along the line where sand and sea met and then – everything just stopped still for one single still point in time and space.

And then the telephone rang.

Chapter 15

It took Derek less than twenty minutes to reach the Isle of Dogs. He in fact coincidentally knew 'The Gun' from a late-night drinking session there some years ago, when 'open all hours' had meant just that on the Isle of Dogs. It was a night he'd tried unsuccessfully to forget the boozing, and then, what made it such a repellently memorable night, the disgusting spectacle of a bare-knuckle boxing match in an alley just outside the pub. He recalled the sound of fist on face, the blood, the disturbing excitement on the faces of the crowd, like medieval devils in a Bosch painting. And then he was feeling sick with it all, with the complete and utterly degrading brutality of it all, a deep sickness that had made him fear for civilised life, if all this hate and violence was so near the surface. If even some of us somewhere inside themselves had the capacity to hurt and enjoy hurting and enjoy watching people being hurt, then it was small wonder that Bosnia and Rwanda could happen. All it needed was some buffoon on the right to get a bit more mainstream to unlock it all, all the bile of the disaffected, of the empty and left behind. Yes, it was that enjoyment on those leering faces that had made him shudder. Just like with fox hunting and the other blood sports, it wasn't the deaths so much that worried him, perhaps farmers might need to shoot foxes from time to time to protect their flocks. No, it was the fact that human beings could *derive pleasure* from the fear and suffering, dressing up in their ridiculous costumes for hurting and killing animals – all for a bit of fun. That was what dismayed him, made him feel sick, just as he was feeling sick deep in his gut now as he neared the pub, sickness and anxiety, desperate to get there but happier if he never had to arrive.

He parked carefully, just behind the small crowd that had gathered where the police had cordoned off the street with orange plastic ribbon. He paused after switching off the engine, to compose himself for the final few yards' walk but he realised he wasn't feeling at all emotional. It was more like he'd been anaesthetised, his senses frozen in that vulnerable numbness you get at the dentists, after the sharp pain of the injection and just before the drilling starts, but knowing that it is going to start, that the drilling will start, that it always starts. For the moment, though, there was a still point after the injection, before the drilling and he was thankful to be without feeling, except for surges of adrenaline that sent his heart galloping, and that awful lurching sensation in the pit of his stomach. He physically braced himself, took a deep breath and got out of the car, easing his way through the crowd. Each detail of the scene, the faces, the police checking his warrant card, the ambulances, the flashing lights, were like colours being added one by one to a black and white photograph – everything was becoming more real, tint by tint. And with each new colour came increased dread, as if the detail was breaking through like lasers, burning their reality deep into the dark, warm recesses of his being, the places we go to hide when it all becomes too much out there, chasing him in relentless pursuit, forcing light and colour painfully in so deep that he could not escape seeing and confronting the images they burnt into his brain. It *was* all really happening, it wasn't a nightmare, and when he reached the end of the street he wasn't going to wake up, or be told it was all a mistake and he wasn't going to find Val waiting for him, perhaps nursing a Hollywood flesh wound, huddled in a blanket, shivering, but smiling bravely. She was going to be there alright, but dead – cold and horrible like all corpses, like that girl on the stair at East Ham. Oh God.

He knew it was soon that the pain was coming. He could remember this sensation once when he'd cut his hand very deeply with a Stanley knife – for a split second there was no pain, only the appalling knowledge as he gazed uncomprehendingly at the terrible deep gaping gash in his flesh that it was on its way, the blood and the pain and that when it arrived it would be with a vengeance. And at that moment, the expectation was almost worse than the pain – almost but not quite, because there is nothing, absolutely nothing quite as bad as pain, real pain and when it does come, you'd give anything to be back in that moment before it came. Derek knew as he approached the group of police at the end of the street, milling about around an ambulance, that what he was about to endure was sheer physical pain.

It was still drizzling as he neared the ambulance. Just before he reached it, someone caught his arm.

It was Bill Haggart, looking pale and tired. "Derek, come here, laddie."

Derek turned and stared at him. "What the fuck happened, Bill?"

"It's just an awful, terrible business. We don't know exactly what happened yet. What I do know is that we were right about the case all along, something big is going down and now I wish we hadn't been. God, I wish we'd been wrong and we could have all just shrugged away our bloody pride and got on with another case. I knew it would be a dangerous one, this, I just felt it."

"And Val? The message I got said she's been shot…"

"Shot? Yes. She's dead, Derek, shot twice. Just so awful, and her so young and …" He shook his head.

"Where is she?" Derek manged to get the words out but wasn't sure he could stay on his feet

"In the ambulance. They've only just finished all the photographs and everything. I've given them a preliminary identification – hey, are you all right, Derek?" Derek could feel himself swaying lightheadedly. He felt Bill grab his shoulder to steady him. "Christ, come on, let's get away from here, there's nothing we can do, it's all police work here. I've sent everyone else home for the time being, except for Ron McCartney – he was with her and he'll have to stay around to help with their immediate enquiries. But everyone's in a state of shock." Derek moved towards the ambulance. He didn't want to see her there, but he knew it would be the last time he would ever get a glimpse of her, literally forever. They were just closing the doors.

"Just a minute, hold on," and before anyone could stop him, he hauled himself in and pulled back the blanket covering her face. For a moment he didn't even recognise her – she was so grey, her lips were caked in dried blood, one eye was frozen slightly open. And then he could look no longer. He stumbled out of the van, nearly knocking Bill over. "Hey, steady on Derek, steady on. I reckon after this and East Ham, you and I and Ron are in need of some extended leave. Seriously."

"Bill," Derek looked down at the drawn face beside him. He felt so utterly destroyed that he knew he had to tell someone about him and Val, and it had to be now. "I think you should know that she, Val... we... me and Val..." She hadn't wanted anyone to know about it when she was alive, but he knew he wouldn't be able to cope at all in the days to come if the others on the team didn't know. Mourning a dead colleague was one thing. But this...And he couldn't finish the sentence because he didn't know what to say – "we were having an affair", "we were going out together"? None of it sounded right, none of it came close to how they'd been to each other in those brief moments together, so he just stopped. There was a pause as Bill stared at him, the full meaning of the words only slowly sinking in.

"Oh, Christ, Derek, I had no idea, no idea at all. I wouldn't have sent for you like this if I'd have known. Jesus Christ! Come on, let's get back to your place, there's nothing we can do here for a while. My car's just around the corner. We can get yours picked up later." He led Derek to the car, shouting over his shoulder to Ron, who was standing near the ambulance, talking to a police officer, "Ron, I'm taking Derek back to his flat – I'll explain later. I want you to stay here and liaise with the police. Give them any info they want, OK, full cooperation."

Ron, pale, drawn, gave a thumbs up, and Bill and Derek drove off. Derek was feeling now as if he was clinging to a piece of driftwood, only just keeping his head above a vast, cold ocean of pain which was all but drowning him, sucking him down, down, down. He knew that if he moved at all he'd slip under the icy water into the darkness. He held himself completely rigid. "Well, what did happen, Bill?" Talk talk talk, his old escape route.

"God, we don't know, Derek, not exactly." Bill hesitated for a second, trying to decide what sort of approach was the best in the circumstances, wondering what sort of line to take for the best, and deciding that he might just as well go straight through it all as it stood. "Val and Ron followed Carter to the pub. Ron followed him and our other mystery man inside, while Val waited outside in case they made a move. She made a call to us for support, to me in fact, and the four of us at the office got down here quick. It was obvious that something was going down. Anyway, before we got there, Val must have left the car for some reason and gone onto a nearby patch of wasteland, next to the river. And Carter and the other bloke must have surprised her there. By the way, we know why Carter and the other bloke went there – we found some blood on the wall overlooking the river and two spent cartridges. It looks as though one of them was shot as well – they're searching for a body in the river just down from there, they can sort of work out the drift, apparently. So Val must have surprised them or something. May 12. God knows what the 16th has in store."

"That bastard Salter. We've got to get him, Bill."

"Well, it won't be as easy as that now, will it? He's almost certain to call off any deals he had planned, or at least postpone things for a while. And there's nothing at the moment that can tie him in with the murder, not as far as we know. Perhaps when we get an identification of this bloke…"

"Well, he's not going to get out of this one, not this time. I'll make sure of that." Something inside Derek, some missing piece of the jigsaw, slipped into place or out of place. Bill hardly noticed the hardness of the tone, his mind on how to get Derek through the next few hours. If he'd been more observant he would perhaps have sensed something deeply unnerving behind and beyond the distress, something profound, disturbing and dangerous in his tone.

As soon as they got back to Derek's flat, Bill found a bottle of scotch and poured two very large glass full. They both just sat there in complete silence, drinking. Derek was trying to fix a picture of Val in his mind, trying to pin down some of the brief time they had had together so that it didn't slip away like a dream after waking. But the images were random and many, though for some reason one particular snatch of conversation kept coming back to him. They were at their first meal together in the restaurant, and he had been teasing her about her optimistic, liberal outlook, him playing the world-weary cynic to her naïve idealist.

"The trouble with you," he'd said, "is you assume that everyone is as thoughtful and sensitive and caring as you are, you assume that inside, everyone is just like you," and, very seriously, she had said, "Of course I do. It's the only safe thing to do, because the minute you start to think that they're not, the minute you start to think that other people are somehow not quite as human as you are, well," she had grinned and pulled a finger across her throat, "you can justify doing anything to them."

Well, she was right and she wasn't right, Derek thought – he didn't feel he needed any justification for anything he did to Salter from now on. He would get that bastard in a cell and God help him then. Why should the bastard get away with it? And then another image came into his mind, something he had said to Val in her flat, only two nights ago. "Of course," he'd said, "You want to be in on the kill." And that was when he began to cry, starting with a great, heaving sob that seemed to tear itself from the lining of his lungs and burn its way up his throat. Bill just sat with him, unable to offer him the physical comfort they both knew he needed, both of them, as Val might have said, locked into their male emotional strait jackets. And she'd have been right.

***

Philip Manson waited anxiously in the small reception area outside the room of the Assistant Chief Investigating Officer, David Maloney. He was feeling apprehensive about the interview and chewed another indigestion tablet. He had been in the service for most of his working life and he was near the end of his career now. Well, it would be more accurate to say he was already at the end of his career because he wasn't likely to get any further promotion. He was fifty-three now and would probably take early retirement at fifty-five if he could get it – there was nothing to keep him in the job anymore, even before this wretched incident. He looked at his watch and sat back, thinking how much things seemed to have changed since his early days in the job. When he had started with Customs and Excise, there had been a sense of camaraderie and purpose but now all that seemed to have gone, replaced by time serving and cynicism. He wasn't a stupid man, and he realised that he was tired and disillusioned and perhaps it was him that had changed, perhaps, in reality, it had always been as it was now, and he'd just not realised it when he was young and naive. But as he had risen in rank, his growing experiences of the bureaucratic civil service politics had at first surprised him, then appalled and disgusted him, and finally left him feeling completely worn out, frustrated and purposeless. All that kept him going now was that he did still believe in the job, the *real* job, at the nitty-gritty level. But now, this business with Salter – and Val Henderson. He'd felt from the beginning that it was going to be different, though not for a second could anyone have had any idea just how dreadful a form that difference would take. In a strange way the job had rekindled something of those early days in him, a spark he'd caught from the enthusiasm of the team, from Bill Haggart, from Derek, from all of them. Yes, poor Derek – this would be enough to finish him. He'd been in the doldrums for so long and then the case, even without his personal involvement with the girl, it had seemed to put new life into him. And now it had taken such a new life.

He looked at his watch again and glanced questioningly at the smartly dressed secretary, busy behind her desk. *She'd look more at home in a bank*, he thought. She looked up and smiled sympathetically at him, but said nothing. The appointment had been for ten and already it was quarter past. "I bet the sod is keeping me waiting just to wind me up. Probably something he learnt on one of his management courses." Philip knew what the meeting was about – whether to continue with the Salter investigation or not. He knew that on balance the team's emotional instincts were to see it through despite the likelihood that Salter would postpone everything – at least they could see it through the original dates, just in case he had the sheer nerve to call their bluff and go ahead after all. But he also knew that there would be pressure to drop it cold. It hadn't been a popular case to start with, not 'up there', and the galling thing now was that, emotions aside, it was clear to everyone including the team that it was, on any rational assessment, utterly pointless to continue with it. But, older and more weary, he wondered why emotional considerations should be set aside so easily. What the team wanted really was just to stay on the case until the final date on the sheet, just in case, and as a sort of catharsis, a grieving. Otherwise they'd never know for sure…

The door opened, interrupting his thoughts, and Maloney popped his head out. "Sorry to keep you waiting, Philip, come on in now. No calls, please, Jean." The secretary nodded and smiled her vacuous smile, a product of the emptiness of her job.

As soon as they were settled, Philip, partly from his nervousness, partly because he thought being direct was the best policy now, opened the interview.

"Well, what do you think we ought to do now – sir?" He sounded more brusque than he had intended, and he could tell from the tone of the reply that he had put Maloney on the defensive. Philip knew in his heart of hearts that his position was an untenably weak one and was overcompensating in making the case for continuing with it all. He looked at Maloney, dressed in his sleek grey suit, sitting behind his desk in his soothingly decorated office, watched him smooth a hand through his neatly trimmed grey hair, and knew that there was a gulf between them that would never be bridged, and understood more than ever the antipathy that always existed between them, the crackling of static that seemed to spit between them over any and all issues.

"Now look, Philip, I made it clear from the start that this was a touchy business…"

"That's one way of describing a murder, I suppose…" Philip knew he was being unreasonable now, but just he couldn't help himself.

"Oh, don't be so crass, Philip. You know damn well I feel as bad about that as anyone, and it's bloody cheap and arrogant of you to even imply anything different. But what I'm saying is that we are all accountable – you to me, me to the Collector and beyond. And right now they're all on my back."

"So you're going to climb up on mine?"

"I'm going to throw your question back at you – do you think that there is any point in continuing with the case now?"

"Come on, Philip, just tell me straight, are you coming around to ordering us to drop the case? Is that what all this is about?"

"No, you come on, Philip. You know damn well that it's not as simple as that. As I said, I feel as strongly as anyone about this incident, but I will not allow the department, the team, to make a bloody mess of itself because of an emotional reaction – which incidentally, I understand better than you perhaps think. But I want a clear-headed, rational assessment of the situation. Do you, as a professional officer, think that we should go ahead with this case or do you think that we should call it off? In particular, I'm thinking, as you must be if you are honest, that there is almost no chance now that the deal will go ahead at all, and certainly not as planned."

The word 'honest' sounded hollow coming from Manson, but Philip knew that he was completely right, to a point, on one level. "No, that's true, but…well, obviously I've talked to the team about this, and we think…*feel*… that we should carry on, at least until after the 16th. If we're dealing with someone who can stay cool, they may just think it's worth a chance to go ahead as planned. I know that's a bit farfetched, and I know that there is almost no chance that the buyers will still want to be involved but on balance I agree with the team because – because I think it's important for team morale. They've been badly shaken by this whole business, especially coming so soon after East Ham…" he trailed off, feeling out of his depth, outmanoeuvred and essentially wrong. Lamely, he played his last card, "And it's only a couple of days to the next date on the list…"

"Yes, yes, I'm sure…but what you are saying is that the whole case is now unlikely to come to anything, which is my conclusion exactly. And while I do appreciate how you must all be feeling, it is my duty to come to conclusions on more objective criteria than the ones that you, quite rightly, feel compelled to take into account. So on balance, nothing you've said has made me change the conclusions that I'd come to from studying the case so far. Which means, I'm afraid, that we, you, the team, will be dropping the case. I think that the best thing now is to leave everything to the police with their murder inquiries and see where they lead. Apart from any other considerations, it is possible that continuing our case at the same time as the murder investigation would needlessly complicate the whole affair. There'll be so many cops around there won't be any room for us, and they're bound to be putting an obs on Salter – we'd all end up tripping over each other. It's just not on, anyone can see that."

"So you are ordering us to drop it?"

"Well, for God's sake, man, I didn't think I'd need to do anything as formal as that – surely you can see the sense of not proceeding. I suppose we could leave it on file rather than close it completely, pending the police inquiry…"

"I'm sorry, sir. I can understand the reasons, but I know that despite all that, the team will want to carry on, alongside the police investigation. If we could get Salter for the drugs and tie him in with the murder, it would, well, it would sort of make more sense of Val's death, wouldn't it? Or even if not making more sense of it, it would at least mean it wasn't totally in vain. I'm not expressing this very well, but look, I'm not saying to carry on because of the dead, I'm saying carry on for the living. That team is one of the best we've ever had. And if this is called off it will be the end of them. I don't know if they'll actually resign back to normal duties or not – some of them have mortgages too big for the cut in salary – but you'll never get the same standard of dedication out of them ever again. And that's for sure. And I'll have to consider my own position very carefully."

"Bah, this is complete nonsense, Philip, and I don't like being threatened – I won't *be* threatened. And I'm not fond of this sort of melodramatics. Those men – and you, incidentally – are paid very well to do a tough job. If any of them shows the slightest sign of not giving one hundred per cent to that job, it won't be a case of them applying to go back into routine work, I'll boot them back there so fast they won't know what's hit them and make no mistake. The case is off and that's that. I do think Bill, Ron and especially Derek should be given lengthy leave, incidentally – and access to our staff support team if they feel they need it – say three months? Not open to discussion, with immediate effect. Full pay.

"So, thank you for discussing it with me, Philip. And a word of advice before you go. You are too close to retirement to go around making ridiculous gestures now – you'd be a fool to risk your pension at this stage. Now I'd like you to go and tell the rest of the team that I want them to take three days leave, compulsory for all of them, and report back ready to start a new case. And the three months for the East Ham three.

"OK, Philip?"

Philip paused for a second, deflated. There was nothing he could say, Malone was right. And even if the case had been kept going, Ron and Derek and Bill would have to have been taken off it, for their own health and well as for the safety of the rest of the team. He stood up, nodded and left.

Chapter 16

Bill pushed his way through the crowded, smoky public bar to the corner where Derek was sitting waiting for him at a table already filled with empty beer and spirit glasses. He carefully placed the two pints he was carrying on the table and sat down opposite Derek, who lit a cigarette, throwing the match in the vague direction of the already full ash tray.

Bill stared at the mess of stubs in genuine if deliberately overstated disgust. "My god, I'm glad I've stopped that revolting habit. Mind you, sitting this close to you, I don't suppose it makes much difference." He grinned, nearly adding the standard 'you really ought to try and give it up, you know', but he was sober enough to know that it wouldn't have had any effect at the best of times – and this was definitely not the best of times. Stopping smoking was obviously not high on Derek's agenda just at the moment. Bill took a sip and decided that now was as good a time as any to break the news that the case was being dropped.

"By the way, Derek, Philip went to see Maloney this morning, to find out what was happening with the case, and…"

"They've decided to drop the investigation and leave the whole thing to the police murder inquiry. It was obvious, for fuck's sake, Bill. Surely you weren't surprised? And for once I agree with Maloney – and I can understand why he's doing it. What else could he do? Salter's not going to move anything now. The deal will be off – even if he wanted to chance his arm, no one in their right mind would want to buy anything off him at the moment. He's stuck with the bloody stuff but as long as he doesn't go anywhere near it, there's nothing we can do. He'll just sit tight until he thinks it's safe – a few months, a year…"

Bill stared down into his glass, avoiding Derek's eyes so he could hide the relief he could feel flickering across his face. Breaking this news had been the short straw job on the team today. Everyone had been pissed off by Maloney's decision, mainly because it was Maloney rather than because of the decision itself. But they could see the reasoning was strong, but there was still the question of how Derek would take it and it had fallen to Bill to tell him. Now that it was over and so painlessly, he could relax a little. He lifted his pint glass and took a deep drink, the first that he had really enjoyed since everything had kicked off, now that the onerous part of the afternoon was out of the way.

'And there's good news as well, at least *I* think it's good news – you, me and Ron are on full pay leave for three months. We can still go in and out to tidy things up, it's not like a suspension or anything, obviously. But it isn't voluntary either. And it's probably a very good thing, especially for you'. He heard Derek mumble something but didn't quite catch what he said. "What's that, Derek, I missed that?"

"I said, there's more than one way to kill a rat. The bastard won't get away with this one, whatever happens." He smiled as he spoke, and it was the smile that really caught Bill's attention. There was something wrong with it, like the smile on the face of one of those down and outs that wander the underground begging – empty, but at the same time, behind the emptiness, something more disturbing.

When he saw that smile, he knew for certain that all was far from well. Taking another gulp of beer, he forced himself to ask, "What on earth do you mean, Derek?" By way of an answer, Derek's smile widened across his pale, tired face and he tapped his nose with his forefinger. Bill felt the hairs on his neck stand on end and he gulped down the last mouthful of beer before making his excuses and leaving.

***

Derek half walked, half shuffled along the dark, damp street, a shuffle familiar to anyone recently bereaved, with their whole system overwhelmed and barely functioning. He felt a tiredness that was beyond the help of sleep, draining all life from him, as he forced his feet heavily forward, deeply involved in an apparently endless and intense dialogue with himself. He was going over and over what was happening to him, one part of him talking, the other listening, dazed by the mumblings and mutterings that were sometimes in his mind and sometimes spoken under his breath. He'd lost all awareness of the barrier between external and internal, it was all just going round and round, his mind, the world.

It wasn't just Val, he knew that, though God knows that was bad enough. But after all, when you put it in perspective, he'd been involved with her for such a short time, intense though it was, so highly charged with the promise, the certainty of more to come. Val and this job had given him new meaning, a new vision of how things could be different – and her death had snatched it all away. He felt now that he had to make some sense of it. Part of him realised that it was all about him, the downward spiral, the collapse into darkness and dysfunction – he'd been on the very edge of it when East Ham happened but Val had offered salvation. The visit to Manchester had been the rounding off of his past, and the beginning of the new, the fulcrum, the cusp between the stale and the fresh, the dead and the quick. The return to London had brought freshness – Val, the chance to get Salter, no more darkness, no more losing. He had a role he could believe in, a role that reconciled his beliefs with his work – and that role was, he now realised, to get back at the big boys, to use his position to bring the likes of Salter to justice. To play a small but effective part in undermining the rotten edifice that he loathed, it all seemed to be making sense, a real purpose to everything. But now, her death had tilted him into a darker, distorted vision, where he could see only one way of fulfilling that purpose, with him as the champion of the oppressed, David against Goliath, a terrible and fiery avenging angel. His life was no longer a seemingly endless loop of wasted time, meaningless drifting, squandered chances. He had once seen Ibsen's 'Peer Gynt' and been particularly struck by the part where Pier has to face the fact that he had been destined to be someone great, a 'shiny button on the waistcoat of the world' but in reality he had walked on the earth and 'left no footprints,' or some such phrase. That was how he'd seen his own life. If he was to die, he thought in his darker moments, he had done nothing at all to show that he had ever been alive. He was back to that darkness, that emptiness – he did not even have any children, which is the way most people affect the world, the footprint they leave. Val had given him the promise of personal meaning, the case had shown him that he could at least play a part in the wider world – a very small part but an honourable one, relentlessly pursuing people like Salter, Establishment People, the very people who, directly or indirectly were behind the police smashing up peaceful crowds and worse, in their ruthless and grasping craving to preserve their power and privilege – and he'd seen in all this the chance for him to leave a small but distinct footprint.

But now, with Val, they had snatched it all away, Salter had got away with it – the drugs case was being called off, and the chances of tying him in with the murder were probably zero – he surely wasn't stupid enough to have left himself exposed on that count.

And it was clear to Derek, as far as anything could be through the drink and exhaustion, that he must now hold to a new and fearful role, the last chance to make sense of everything, to give it all a meaning and see justice done. His own existence was worthless now, there would be no more opportunities, nothing for him, no looking forward. He was already dead, had already crossed over an invisible rubicon and there was no going back. What other explanation could there be for the fact that he was now walking to a meeting that no sane or rational person would ever get involved with. He glanced around, one small part of himself clinging desperately to life, and suddenly realised he was talking out loud. He looked along the dark street, its edges softened by the steady drizzle that stuck to him like a heavy sweat, running down his face. He was unsteady on his feet, too much drink, too little sleep, too many amphtimines - but not for much longer. Ahead was the back-street pub he was looking for 'The Duke of Wellington'. The directions he'd been given had been accurate enough, but it had taken him longer than he'd thought. He'd decided to leave the car some distance away and walk – it was more anonymous – but he'd underestimated the distance and he was tired now, so, so tired. He looked back the way he'd come, peering into the shadows. For the last five minutes he'd had the feeling that there was someone following him through these dark streets of old warehouses and boarded up shops and narrow alleys but… there was no sign or sound of anyone. Paranoia, eh? Not him – he *knew* the bastards were out to get him. He grinned again and shrugged his shoulders. Seriously, who would be interested in him, anyway? No one knew what he had in mind, after all. No matter how paranoid he might be, he knew for certain, for absolute certain, that no one else could possibly know what he was going to do. But the police might have an interest in him. They knew now about his relationship with Val and they might put a tail on him, for a variety of reasons, not least that the last thing they'd want would be a maverick nosing around in the middle of their investigation.

The street was perfectly quiet, he'd not seen anyone at all for the last ten minutes. The area was mainly industrial, old warehouses and small factories. The new estates were further east and even the few locals who still lived in the area seldom ventured along these streets unless they worked nearby, and never at night. The pub was probably busy at lunchtimes – as he drew nearer, he saw a sign outside advertising 'Hot and Cold Food 12 till 2' – but he was surprised it opened at all in the evening. He paused again in the pool of light at the entrance and gave a glance in both directions, a glance which would have marked him out as suspicious in the eyes of anyone watching. As indeed it did.

Once in the lobby he had a choice of saloon or public bar. As arranged, he pushed open the door of the public bar. It was small and empty, apart from a scruffy looking man, in his early thirties, who was sitting opposite the door – the man he had come to see. As Derek approached the man, an informer he'd used many times in the past, he felt a sudden apprehension as if normality was trying to assert itself, to make him see sense but was too exhausted for anything other than a tired, limp gesture. It was one worth making, though because Derek was about to break the law and take the first step along a path which he knew would lead inevitably to his own destruction and there would be no going back.

"Hello, Mr Brown. Are you alright?" Derek looked distinctly unsteady on his feet and the man felt instinctively that something was not right in a situation already fraught with danger for him.

Derek ignored the question, brushed it aside. "Hello, Jimmy. What are you drinking?"

"No, I'm fine, thanks, Mr Brown."

Derek couldn't see anyone behind the bar anyway, so he sat down opposite Jimmy. Normally he'd have been in control of this situation, manipulating his informer with a mixture of bait and bullying. Snouts lived dangerously in their dark world and they were exploited pitilessly. But tonight there was no natural hierarchy of power to hold the relationship securely in place, it was open, volatile, and Derek had sensed the same hint of shakiness in the man's voice as he knew for certain must have been in his own. There was no indication that Jimmy would seize the moment to dominate proceedings – the lack of certainty, the lack of authority ran deep and it probably frightened him more than anything else and nothing in his existence had prepared him to take advantage in a situation like this.

Derek, aware of the nuances of the relationship, finally took the initiative and asserted himself to re-establish the natural order of things. "Have you got it?" He looked round with the shiftiness of the amateur wrongdoer.

"Yeah. But I don't like this, Mr Brown. I mean, I ain't never got involved wiv shooters before. I don't 'old wiv 'em, if you know what I mean."

For a second, Derek nearly burst out laughing – the accent, the clichés, the whole scene suddenly surreal but he knew if he started, he'd never stop, not ever. It was just that Jimmy Green was a snout and for both sides of the law and order divide, snouts are the lowest of the low, though both sides use them like pawns for their own ends. Derek had always felt a bit sorry for this one – he looked as if he'd not had a good hot meal in years – but he was repelled by him as well. Still it just went to show how little you know people when your job brings you into contact with only one dimension of them – and now here was Derek on the receiving end of a disarmingly naive morality lecture about firearms, from his holiness, Jimmy the fucking Snout. And then the urge to laugh tipped into an urge to cry. He knew that he was barely in control of his emotions or his mind, knew that he was only just managing to hold himself this side of hysteria, and the sincerity of this reptilian creature touched him to the quick. He couldn't speak but just sat there concentrating on not bursting into tears.

Jimmy was becoming more alarmed with every passing second. It was a situation that could be one of life or death to him. He looked at Derek, saw the drawn paleness of his face, the redness around his eyes, noticed the edginess of his movements. "Look, are you sure you're alright, Mr Brown? You look fucking dreadful. Let's get on wiv it. Now, you sure you want this?" Derek nodded. "Right, 'ere it is." Jimmy had now usurped the authority and grasped the initiative just to resolve it. He could have tried pushing up the price, knowing Derek was desperate and vulnerable but all he could think about was bringing the whole thing to a close and getting out of the place. He pushed a brown paper parcel onto Derek's knee. Derek pulled himself together, like putting himself onto auto pilot, and shoved it clumsily into his anorak pocket. Then he took out the plain, grey envelope that contained the money – £150, a bit over the odds nowadays, but Derek hadn't felt like haggling and he had wanted extra ammo – fifty rounds he'd asked for.

"It's all there, count it if you like? Did you get all the…"

"Yeah, at least. I didn't count 'em, but there's at least what you asked for, 9 mm."

Jimmy stared at him, with genuine concern in his eyes. Derek met the gaze and looked away.

Jimmy began to speak and Derek knew what he was going to say – he was going to ask what he wanted the gun for, or worse he was going to ask if he was sure he knew what he was doing. Derek looked straight at him and got in first. "Right, Jimmy, thanks. That's all, then. I'll be off – there's no way this will be traced back to you. I've not even got a car out there. No one will ever know where I got this." He stood up and suddenly felt a pang of loneliness and isolation and gripped the edge of the table, swaying. "Christ," muttered Jimmy, standing up and glancing around nervously as he took hold of Derek's right arm.

"It's OK, I'm alright." Derek pushed off the helping hand, afraid that this human contact, with its suggestion of tenderness and caring, might finally push him over the edge of his emotional abyss.

***

Safely back in his flat, barely aware of how he got there, Derek carefully unwrapped the parcel and sat staring at its contents. He had no real plan as to what he was going to do, but he felt better now he'd got the gun and he began to relax, to give in to the dreadful tiredness that he had been fighting off for what seemed to be forever. But just as he began to sink into sleep, he jerked himself awake and stood up, shaking his head. "No, it's got to be now, now, before I have a chance to think too much about it, before he has any more time to get away, if he hasn't done already. I've got to do it now."

He picked up the gun, loaded the magazine and pushed it firmly home, feeling that satisfying click as it locked into place. He'd done all his firearm training, though he'd never fired a shot in anger – but he'd been very good at target shooting. And he'd enjoyed the feel of the handguns, solid, heavy – and he was confident handling the weapon, checking the weight and balance of it. He scooped up most of the remaining bullets and walked unsteadily towards the door, aware for the first time that he had to act on the assumption that he was being followed, just in case, even if he wasn't. It would make sense if he was serious about all this. He had the feeling all the time now that he was being tailed, and although he knew it could just be the mental state he was in, he couldn't take the chance.

Chapter 17

In his office, late on Wednesday night, David Maloney sat waiting for the promised call from his opposite number in the Met. He felt exhausted by this murder business and the whole Salter case, exhausted and frankly pissed off with the whole affair. He knew how the teams under him felt about him – the desk-bound bureaucrat who'd completely lost touch with the day to day realities of the job – and he could understand that it was only natural to feel like that about 'the boss', it all came with the job and the salary. It was part of the role once you got promoted beyond a certain point. After all, he'd felt the same as a young officer, but with each new promotion had come new insights and perspectives and he'd never let criticism bother him because he'd convinced himself that he always tried to do the right thing, whether it was popular or not and he really did believe it. He knew that his role was as vital as that of the field officers, neither could function without the other, and he knew that it was his job to take a strategic view which sometimes clashed with the tactical approach of the teams. But what really worried him was that he was now having to confront some aspects of his character that he'd hoped he wouldn't ever have to face, ask questions he had hoped he'd never have to answer. Most alarming of all was facing up to the possibility that perhaps, over the years, he had actually *become* the role he had taken on. He knew many of his own weaknesses, but he also knew his strengths – he was good at his job, an efficient administrator and extremely able at playing the political game for the benefit of Customs and Excise and in the long run for the benefit of all his officers – and the public. But he had always felt that there was a clear divide between Maloney the Assistant Chief

Investigations Officer and David Maloney the person. He'd always tried to keep the two things separate, his role and his private life, full of family and interests. He genuinely saw his job as what he did, ultimately, for the money to pay for his real life and didn't see that as a drawback. Quite the opposite, he understood that this was what was meant by being professional – or so he had always convinced himself. But now he just didn't know where the boundaries were or what had become of that person he saw as *himself*. And more than anything now, only three days after the murder, he felt drained and confused because he couldn't be sure how far his feelings about the case and his role were to do with genuine upset at the death of one of his officers and how far they were to do with the repercussions of what could appear to be a monumental cock up…which he feared was going to reflect back onto him. God knows where it was all going to end. The phone rang and he jerked it off the hook. "David Maloney here, yes, ah, hello Stephen, good to hear from you, how are you?"

The voice at the other end was quiet, cultivated but with a hint of roughness, "Well enough. It's been a long time, David. I've not seen you down at the lodge for many a month. Not going off us, I hope, David, you never know when you might need us." The voice chuckled softly and before Maloney could reply, continued, "I suppose that you're really in touch because of this Val Henderson case aren't you? Well, I can tell you that we're making headway, though I think it's one of those cases where the shit is going to hit the fan if and when it all comes out."

Maloney could have well done without this little piece of news, which he didn't fully understand, though he got the gist of it clearly enough. "What do you mean, 'exactly'?" He fought hard to control a tone of increasing panic in his voice "Is there something we don't know – I mean, I know that Salter is well connected, I could hardly forget that, but…have you tied him in with the murder?" He didn't really want to ask these questions and he didn't want to listen to the answers, because somewhere deep inside he knew there was going to be no reassurance, no way out, no comfort.

"Well, it's worse than just Salter. That photo you lot gave us, with Salter and another guy? well it was pretty soon identified – he's one of ours, a D.I. from Stepney, one Charlie Whitcombe. We've put a tail on him, he's on leave at the moment – he suddenly went sick yesterday. We think he must have stayed on duty for a couple of days to find out if we were getting close, but we don't think he knows about the photo, so he's got no reason to think he's in the frame, literally in this case. Anyway, he hasn't bolted, we know where he is, and we could pull him in at any minute. What we thought we'd do is give it twenty-four hours and see if he makes contact with Salter – or anyone else, come to that. The picture you have of him with Salter, it ties them together, but not in any meaningful evidential way. It convinces me alright, after listening to your team, but it won't do any harm to try and get something more concrete to link them both, you know what the CPS is like if it means prosecuting someone like Salter – this isn't some miner nicking a few lumps of coal you know. So there it is, I'm afraid – not much more than circumstantial at the moment, but taken together, I'm sure we'll get there. And we do want to get there, I couldn't care less how well-connected Salter is, this time around – we're treating this as if it was one of our own officers that copped it. Straight bat on this one."

"Yes, thanks, it's really good to hear that, Stephen and I very much appreciate it, believe me. It'll be more bad press for the Met. though, won't it?" He felt a sudden sense of relief in the reassurances of progress, with the focus elsewhere than on him.

"Well, for a day or two, but we have our own hacks as well you know, and we'll be able to spin it into 'it proves how squeaky clean the rest of us are when we get one of our rotten apples so quickly' routine. And we've got broad backs in the met, have to have. But it will stink for a while, especially if some smart arse Pilger wannabe starts sniffing around about corruption in general. The worse thing is that Salter and that D.I. are both in the same lodge, you know."

"As each other?"

"As each other and as us, David."

There was a long pause as Maloney grappled with the implications of this.

"Oh Christ, Christ. Well, I knew Salter was a mason, of course, but I didn't know he was in our lodge, and… I really can't recall this Whitcombe bloke."

"No, well, Salter has only just transferred in, but if someone wanted to make something of it…Still, I'm sure no one will make the connection anyway, but I thought I'd better warn you just in case. I'm hoping that the fact we've got him so quickly will mean the end of the whole matter. Anyway, look, I'd better get off – oh, by the way, what can you tell me about Henderson's boyfriend, this Derek Brown, I think he's called?"

"Brown?" Maloney was still shaken by images of tabloid headlines about Masonic connections and had to force himself to concentrate. What the hell was coming next? "Well, not a lot really. He blotted his copybook with a lot of headstrong union activity a few years ago and won't ever be promotion material, but he's solid enough as an officer. Thinks he's a bit above the rest of us, with his Oxford degree and working-class background – but generally OK. Why? He's not in the lodge as well, is he?"

"Very funny, David, glad to see you've not lost your sense of humour."

"Christ, Stephen, I wasn't fucking joking."

"OK, OK, let's not get over excited. It's probably nothing, but we're not the only ones interested in this case – apparently the funny boys have been keeping a watching brief, given the sensitivity of some of Salter's connections, and they put a tail on Brown and the team…"

"What?" gasped Maloney, who was now unable to disguise the growing alarm in his voice, "Why on earth…?"

"Oh don't worry, I think it was just to keep tabs on you all – don't forget they had to cover all possibilities, especially now – we don't want anything screwing up the murder investigation and rocking the boat, do we? Anyway, apparently, he made contact with one of his snouts earlier tonight. You have definitely and officially called all your teams off the case, haven't you? The last thing we need now is everyone tripping over each other."

"Yes, of course I have, and in no uncertain terms. If he's working on it, it's entirely off his own back, and he'll be for it if he is."

"Well, I just thought I'd check, but I don't suppose it matters too much now. By this time tomorrow night we'll pull Whitcombe in, and hopefully Salter – though as I said, we still need something concrete to tie it all together. The Scene of Crime guys have got some footprints from near the shooting – that's going to be our best bet, if we can place Whitcombe there, we've as good as got them both. I'll bet you anything that once we pull him in, he'll cough Salter to us. But we'll keep a watch on Brown all the same, just in case he is thinking of blundering in and ruining everything. MI5 guy says he's not in good shape, drinking very heavily, stumbling around, literally, so better safe and sorry. But we've called off our tails on the rest of you, though."

"The rest of us." There was another pause as this latest bomb exploded its high explosive meaning into Malone's mind "…what do you mean…does that…" he hardly dared finish the question… "does that include me as well? You've been tailing me?" he felt indignant and frightened at the same time and somewhere in the back of his mind he registered that the 'they' which he'd taken to refer to MI5 when Stephen had said 'the funny boys', had blurred into a 'we' and 'our'.

"Something like that, David. Oh come on, you'd do the same for me, I'm sure. That's life. Listen, I'll get you a G. and T. at the next lodge meeting, though on second thoughts it might be better if we both stayed away from there for a while. No hardship for you but I still do a bit of networking there. No, my club, we'll get together there, soon. I'll have to go now. See you, David." He hung up. Maloney slowly put the phone down and stared at the wall opposite, trying desperately but unsuccessfully to organise his thoughts.

***

The radio informed Charlie Whitcombe that it was nearly midnight on Wednesday 15th. May. Less than three days since the murder but he sensed he had very little time left to make his escape. Just call it a copper's instinct. Monday and Tuesday, the two days following the crime, had been spent almost in a trance. He had not dared get too close to the investigation, but he had listened to the grapevine without arousing suspicion through over interest. The last thing he'd heard was that the investigating team were onto something really hot, and then it had gone completely quiet, complete shutdown. And at that point, he knew that he couldn't take any chances, couldn't do any more digging, ask any more questions and definitely couldn't afford to delay any longer. There was no actual panic in his decision to move now, he just sensed from years of police work that to delay would be fatal – literally in his case because if they did get him and send him down, he was a dead man, or he'd wish he was. Life for an ex CID in jail…didn't bear thinking about. But the one thing that kept him together at the moment was that if he went down, Salter was going with him. This one fact meant that he effectively had Salter's vast wealth and network at his own disposal and this was the only chance either of them had now. They had made outline arrangements on that dreadful Sunday – Salter would leave the backdoor of his house permanently unlocked so that Whitcombe could get in at any time without being too obvious, though if anyone was watching the front, they'd almost certainly have someone at the back as well. But Salter had shown him a way into the large back garden through a neighbouring house. There was a very narrow, almost unnoticeable alley at the side of next door but one, that ended in a gate. Salter thought it was probably technically a footpath but no one seemed to know it was there and it hadn't been used for years and years. Anyway, it it was like in the

'Secret Garden', and led into the grounds of a big house whose garden was in an L shape, so that part of it ran along the back of other gardens in the row, including Salters, so once into the garden it was a simple matter to turn left and then over a low wall into his place.

So they agreed that as soon as Whitcombe gave him the nod, Salter would book two tickets to Sao Paulo on the next available flight. Whitcombe would call round to pick up some cash for himself, enough to get by on for a while if they became separated or if by any chance the police picked up Salter but not him – after all, without Charlie, they wouldn't be able to make anything stick against Salter, so it was in Salter's interests that he was well provided for in any event. And now was the time. Whitcombe picked up the phone and rang – it was risky, but they had agreed on a code that would need only a few words to be spoken, so the risk was kept to a minimum. Salter answered, as arranged, "Hello, 685789."

Whitcombe gave the reply they had planned, "Sorry, I wanted 686789, wrong number," and put the phone down. It was now or never. He picked up his overnight case, checked that he had his passport and set off for Salter's place. He had carefully planned the best way of getting there without being tailed, based on his long experience of being on the other side of operations like this. He would walk from his house to Wood Green Underground, where he could hail a black cab to take him to Leicester Square – it would be busy there even at this time of night – and then walk through the square, in and out of some of the narrow back streets on the edge of Soho, and into another taxi. He was aware that they might well already have a watch on Salter's place, depending on how much, if anything, they already knew, in which case his precautions would be a complete waste of time. But there was always the chance that they hadn't a clue about Salter's involvement yet, or even his own, so it was worth making the effort.

As he left the house, the detectives waiting in their car outside radioed base. "Something's on – he's moving, on foot. What shall we do?" Their controller understood the difficulty

– at this time of night, in these deserted streets, a pedestrian tail would stick out like the proverbial sore thumb, especially to someone as experienced a copper as Whitcombe bloke must be.

"Whatever you do, don't lose the bastard. If you think you're going to, nick 'im straight away. Do you understand, pull him in, over?"

"Yeah, well it might come to that. You'd better warn the stakeout at Salter's place – he might well be heading that way. He's going toward the main road at the moment. What we'll do is, we'll drive past him onto the main road and wait somewhere along there, see what he does."

"OK, but be careful – the DCI'll have your balls cut off if you cock this up."

"Too late, Sarge, Mrs got there first – said if I didn't get down the clinic, she'd do a Bobbitt. Over and out." He turned to his driver, "Right, you heard all that. See which way he turns…OK he's gone left, take the first left just here and then right and right again – that'll bring us onto the main road, ahead of him."

"That's near the tube station isn't it, Wood Green? We'll have to watch that he don't nip in there."

"Right, if it looks like he's going to do that, I'll get out and nick him straight off."

Charlie heard the car start behind him just as he was joining the main road, a long way behind him, about as far back as his house. So they *were* onto him, then. His heartbeat trebled as the adrenaline flooded into his veins. Were they going to nick him now? He carried on walking, waiting for a car to pull over, doors opening…but it seemed to have gone a different way. Perhaps he was just getting jumpy. All the same, he had a real sense of threat and urgency now, only just this side of panic. *I must stay calm, make the adrenaline work for me, like they tell you in training.* Ahead he could see the tube station and the black cabs waiting outside. His breathing slowed up a little and he forced himself to walk more casually. Amongst the busy traffic, he didn't notice the dark Ford pulling into the side of the road just beyond the station, but the two detectives in it had him in clear view. As he neared the station they moved into action.

"He's going for the tube, radio in I'm going to nick him."

As he reached the brighter lights of the station entrance, Whitcombe saw a man getting out of a car further along the road, saw him and knew instantly that this was it. He hesitated for a second – run back, run into the tube…and then he pulled open the door of the first black cab he came to and jumped into the back. "Leicester Square, now and fast, seriously, get going." The car was in gear almost before he'd finished speaking accelerating out into the steady stream of traffic. "OK mate…"

Charlie thought he was going to have a heart attack. His chest was so tight he could hardly breath and his hands were shaking so much that he had to sit on them to keep them still. He didn't look back, and didn't see his pursuer start to run after the cab and then give up and run back to his car; didn't see the car desperately trying to get into the main road, but being blocked for vital seconds by other black cabs all setting off at once, and a crowd of pedestrians coming out of the station. He would never know how lucky he had been in timing his movements to coincide with the last train out of London. By the time the detectives were underway, their blue flashing lamp in place on the roof, there were half a dozen black cabs between them and him, and there was no way of knowing which was which, or where he had given instructions to go. As soon as they realised this, they switched off the flashing light and pulled over to the side of the road.

"Shit, shit, shit," the driver spoke for both of them. "There's no point in just driving, he could have gone anywhere. All we can hope for is that he *is* heading for Salter's, otherwise were for it."

"Christ, we're for it anyway. I didn't even get the cab number, for fuck's sake. I was just so sure he was going to dive into the tube station. One thing is for certain, he's not on a routine visit – he's definitely making a run for it, and if he wasn't sure we were onto him before, he bloody well is now. Bastard. We'll get an APA out asap."

Salter sat waiting in the empty house, in a dark room, lit only through the half open door by the light in the hall. He was nervous as he waited, edgy and irritated that he was at someone else's beck and call, something that he had not been for a very long time, ever in fact. The seriousness of his position had not escaped him, or the fact that he had only himself to blame for having got into all this, it had not yet acquired any reality in his brain. It was outside his imaginative powers to visualise himself being put into the dock, being found guilty, being sent down for years and years. In the vague perceptions of the outside world reality that his mind allowed in, he could see it only in terms at worse of a short sentence in an open prison – and if the murder hadn't been involved, he was probably right – open prisons…so convenient for when the rich and powerful were ever actually held to account and more than a good ticking off demanded, (by the public outcry, rather than by the seriousness of the offence) as Archer and Aitkin would find out.

He wasn't unusual in this. Time after time we've seen government ministers and public figures blatantly flaunt the advice they give to the public, even to the point of breaking the law and then look like startled rabbits when they're caught in the headlights, because it has never really occurs to their consciousness that anything really applies to them. So even now, real fear of the future in terms of gritty punishment eluded Harry Salter – except …except for the fucking murders. That was where it had all unravelled and now, on the fringes of his self-aggrandised delusional world view, a wider, harsher reality was pricking at him and there was the beginning of a realisation that everything he had built up, his life, his wealth, – was all going to change. Well, his family had built up, of course but which he's expanded beyond their wildest dreams and probably beyond anything they'd have actually wanted. He wouldn't lose it all if things now went to plan because he'd long moved money to untraceable accounts all over the world, to avoid taxes, mainly, but also just in case

- but it would all change profoundly now. He would have to leave so much of it behind. But his ego would never let him fully admit any real responsibility, of course that idiot Whitcombe, that bloody interfering Excise girl – they were the real culprits. He drummed his fingers on the table in front of him. Because he also knew that his initial impulse was to have acted out that reasoning about Whitcombe and had him taken out but he knew, really understood now that it was a good thing he hadn't because – he actually needed him more than Whitcome needed Salter. Whitcome had the experience, the knowledge of the real world – and the worst aspects of the real world at that - which might just enable them to get out of the country. So they were stuck with each other. He just hoped Whitcombe hadn't reached the same conclusions of the subtle but profound shift in their relationship.

He poured himself another brandy.

And waited.

***

The fear that Charlie Whitcombe was feeling was anything but academic – it had his throat and chest in a tight, cold grip that was still making it difficult to breath, even though he realised he had, at least for the moment, got away. But it was all so close and he knew exactly what the future would have in hold for him. And there was nothing of the fantasy about his vision of what the future would hold for him if they were caught. It wasn't just that he was an ex-cop but he'd murdered 'one of their own', a law enforcement officer. He knew what to expect, alright, and his mind couldn't shut it out, try as it might. And it had been so fucking close at Wood Green.

***

Derek too was in a heightened state of emotion as at that very same moment he was also heading to exactly the same destination – Harry Salter's house. Unlike Whitcombe, though, he was no longer feeling wrecked by his fears and uncertainties. A strange calm had descended on him as he drove through the empty streets, but with an underlying restlessness, a dangerous sense of power and invulnerability deriving from the fact that he no longer cared less about what happened to him, fuelled by alcohol, amphtimines and exhaustion he had gone way beyond any thought of physical vulnerability – easy to say and not mean but he really had reached that point. Now he had one single purpose in life and nothing else mattered and he sighed at the simplicity of everything once you let go and accept that you are going to die. He wasn't just cruising these streets, he owned them. He didn't just own them, he had created them, they were merely an extension of himself, a dark avenging angel. He parked, carefully, taking care not to do anything that might attract more attention to him because the only thing that nagged at the back of his mind was that only risk he did fear was that they might stop him, deliberately on randomly at this time of night, acting suspiciously. But then he felt the weight of the gun in his pocket and once more realised that nothing could stop him and nothing would. He walked as steadily as he could toward the street that ran behind Salter's row of houses, conscious only of the gun in his pocket and the determination to go through with his plan. He remembered from the previous case with Salter that the house didn't have direct access from the back but there was some sort of access through the back gardens, which quite possibly the bill weren't aware of. But he didn't care anyway and was too self-absorbed now to notice a thin grey figure dart into the street ahead of him and disappear in through the gap between houses. So he had no idea of how good this was going to be for him, the chance to could kill two bastards with one magazine of 9 mm bullets.

***

Bill Haggart locked his car up and looked up and down the dark street, dark in a way that mirrored the deep sense of Celtic foreboding that clung heavily on him. He wasn't frightened, not in the sense of fearing a physical attack on himself, but he was fearful of what his present errand might divulge. Earlier, when the almost incoherent message from one of Derek's informers had been passed on to him, he could tell that it was urgent and genuine and that something awful was happening. Luckily, Bill was the only officer that Jimmy knew, through an earlier case with Derek and so it was him he'd asked for. Bill already knew things were seriously awry with Derek, but he'd hoped they would settle down with the prospect of the three-month break. But that now seemed unlikely and he knew he was about to find out just how bad it was. The message had said he needed to speak to him, urgently and said to meet at The Black Lion in Plaistow.

From inside the pub, the friendly sound of human conversation and laughter drifted into the otherwise silent street. Despite it being two hours past closing time, the door was still open and, when he walked in, there was a casual if not friendly atmosphere extended to him, despite the fact that he must have had Law written all over him. He ordered a drink and sat down, to be joined immediately by a thin, shifty-looking man.

"Look, I don't want to hang about. It's not easy this – your Mr Brown…" he hesitated.

Rather impatiently, Bill said, "Yes, get on with it."

"Well," he paused, "he's bought a gun and loads of ammo, and he just doesn't look right to me and…"

"Oh Jesus fuck." Bill's voice was loud and his accent aggressively coarse enough to attract watchful eyes from the bar.

"Look, no trouble, don't want no trouble. I'm off." He half got up, but Bill gently caught hold of his arm, mindful of how his actions might appear to the others in the pub.

"Yes, yes, look I'm sorry, I'll be quieter, I'm sorry." The man sat down again, but looked agitated. Bill spoke calmly again, gathering his thoughts. "Look, I'll see you all right for this – you've done exactly the right thing, a genuinely brave thing and I'll make sure you get your due reward, but I've no cash on me and I don't suppose you take cards." He smiled, but the man didn't. "Give me a ring on the number you used tonight, next week, and we'll sort out a payment. You've done really well and I appreciate it. By the way, do you know who sold the thing to him?"

"No, sorry, mate, and if I did, I wouldn't tell you, but I know he's got it and it's a 9 mm semi-automatic. And I'm going. I'll ring you." And he was gone. Bill stood up and left a few seconds later, all eyes watching him now in a way they hadn't when he'd come in, as if to say, 'we've seen you, mate, if you try anything with our friend'. He went straight to his car and picked up the heavy new mobile phone they'd recently been issued with and he'd left on the seat. He had to get on to someone senior – well, it would have to be Maloney, he'd be the best one to do whatever had to be done, it was beyond anything he could patch together himself now.

The phone was ringing. "Come on, come on, for fuck's sake answer the bloody thing." He looked at his watch – one thirty.

"Hello, David Maloney here."

"Sir, its Bill Haggart here."

"Bill, what on earth is it, this is highly irregular, you know…"

"It couldn't wait, sir, and I thought it had better come straight through to you. It's about the Salter case…"

Maloney's heart sank and he felt sick. What the hell was it with this bloody case? "Yes, well…"

"Well, Derek Brown – I think he's going to do something stupid."

"Stupid?"

"Worse than stupid – look, I have it on pretty reliable authority that he's just bought a gun…"

"A gun? Jesus Christ what the bloody hell are you telling me…"

"I know it sounds …unlikely…but I think he's going to try and kill Salter. We've got to do something bloody quick, for everyone's sake, if only get someone round to Salters and pull him in for questioning. It'd be worth the fuss he'll kick up, but at least we'll know he's safe. Then we'll have time to get Derek – we wouldn't need to involve the old bill..."

"Not involve them? One of our officers is running around London like some sort of fucking John Wayne with a bloody gun in his pocket and you seriously expect me not to tell the police? For God's sake, Bill, this isn't covering up for someone who's had a few too many on duty or something. You'd better get around and pull in Salter all the same – that's definitely the safest thing in the short term – I'll send two of our officers round to meet you at the house. I'll get down there as soon as possible – actually I'm sure the bill have got the place staked out anyway, so I'll contact them directly, let them know what's going on and get one of their senior officers down there. Hopefully they'll be able to stop Derek getting in, or take Salter into protective custody straight away. I'll bring a warrant down with me for the drugs involvement – enough to hold him for a few hours. Now get going, Bill, and perhaps we'll still be able to salvage something from all this. As quick as you can...when did he get the gun?"

"Not sure but he hasn't had it long."

"Right, well if he really is going to do it, he'll do it as soon as he can, he won't risk the police getting there first and he must know that the longer he's in possession, the more vulnerable he is. Get going – and well-done Bill."

Bill pushed the car into gear and accelerated hard, the back wheels swinging wildly as he shot the clutch out. He had to get there before Derek. At this time in the morning it wouldn't take more than ten, perhaps fifteen minutes to Salter's.

***

The MI5 team on the case sat in the bare room at HQ listening to the tape of Haggart's call.

"Jesus." It was the tall man, the who had done most of the talking to the civil servant Henry Thomson. "This is getting well out of hand. We've got to take him out. There's nothing to tie *us* into any of it, but if this guy goes blasting away...I know we said we might be better pulling out altogether but thank god we didn't. We kept Johnny on him, didn't we? – Get through and tell him to do it ASAP. We can have a clean-up team down there straight away."

"Not good news, sir, lost sight of Brown – he's given him the slip, which probably means that Brown knows we're onto him…"

"Oh fuck, why is nothing ever fucking straightforward. Right, get onto the bloke at the Met who's running the murder inquiry, no not the DCI, that bloke Stephen whatever his name is, he's sort of one of ours – get him and sort out some transport to Salter's place now." He paused, deep in thought. "You know, there may be another angle to this. It occurs to me that this could work out OK, look, what if we just pull back and let Brown take out Salter and that bent copper? You say they're both definitely in there now? Then we could take out Brown, legit, in a shootout. Hey presto – no questions, no loose ends."

There was what seemed like a long pause as everyone tried to think through all the angles.

"So you want us to just stand back and watch the fireworks. Machiavelli eat your heart out. Chris, how have we ever come this?"

"Alright alright, I'm just thinking aloud. What I will say is, just don't rush in – use your professional judgement."

"Which is another way of saying if it all goes wrong, it's all down to us eh? Understood."

Chapter 18

Salter heard the movement in the hall. In the darkness, he had noticed that the house was never still, never actually quiet. Always, in the night, there was a restless muttering, so that he couldn't tell if this was an intrusion or just another floorboard creaking conspiratorially to the darkness. "Whitcombe, is that you?" His voice sounded empty, disembodied, curiously gothic, like a Vincent Price voice-over in a '50s' black and white 'B' movie.

"Yeah, where are you?" Whitcombe's tone, breathless, frightened, a hint of desperation, was far from the firm reassuring presence Salter had somehow hoped for in these dark hours of vulnerability.

"I'm in the last room on the left, switch the light on as you come in."

Charlie did as he was told and as he entered the room the two of them stared at each other for a second or two, each appalled by the drawn, pale tiredness they saw in the other, both aware that the physical deterioration they observed was a reflection of their own. It was Whitcombe who broke the silence.

"Well, have you got the tickets and the money? They're onto me, definitely – they tried to arrest me on the way here, so we haven't got much time – don't worry, I'm sure I gave them the slip."

"Gave them the slip? You bloody idiot, you've only gone and given them what they want – concrete proof that I'm involved – they're probably outside now."

"Well, you'll forgive me for not being too heartbroken, Harry. I mean, it was your fucking bright ideas that got us into this mess in the first place. And don't you forget, if they get me, they get you, alright?" The conversation was doing nothing to reassure Whitcombe and he realised that the sooner the two of them were apart, the better for them both. The next fifteen minutes were going to be the most crucial – if they could get out of the house without being nicked, they'd stand a pretty good chance of getting out of the country. He looked at his partner in crime and realised instinctively that while Salter could still do the pompous bluster and sound sort of commanding, the balance of power and authority between them had indeed shifted. Whitcombe struggled with himself for a moment, knowing that now he was the only chance either of them had of getting away. If he could pull himself together, focus, they might still be OK From the murky depths of his inner self, he managed to dredge up some vestiges of calm and authority. "Right, well give me my money now. We have to get to the airport, do you understand? Will I be able to pick up my ticket independently of you?"

"Yes, I explained the situation, that we'd be arriving separately. We have just over an hour to check-in."

"Good, good, the sooner the better. How much have you got for me?"

"Ten grand – if we do get out together, we'll need to pool our resources, I mean once we're settled somewhere I'll be able to access more but…"

"Yeah, I know, what you've managed to draw out won't go very far until we can get hold of your hidden stuff – especially once they freeze your assets over here – still, better than freezing your arse off in some prison cell eh? And that's the alternative – no little cash for questions 'we 'll get you off this time, matey' from the powers that be. I'm the only friend you've got." He sneered, couldn't help it, his instincts those of the servant who has broken the power and authority of a hated oppressor, too bitter for benevolent forgiveness. But there was no time to relish the moment. "Right, the money?" Salter pointed towards an executive briefcase on a chair in front of Charlie, with an apathy that in another context may have looked like an aristocratic gesture of elegant nonchalance but in this case was simply bewildered shock and exhaustion. Charlie immediately grabbed it, without elegance or nonchalance. There was no time to waste now, they both knew he had to be off straight away. "Right, give me ten minutes, and then you set off – what was that? Is there someone else still here?"

Before Salter could answer, Derek pushed open the door. He was used to making arrests in situations like this, knew the advantage of speed and surprise, but he was so physically wrecked by exhaustion now that his movements were clumsy and uncoordinated. The frightful look on his face, however, more than made up for any other dramatic shortcomings in his entrance and Whitcombe and Salter could read in that face, in a text older than words, that whoever the fucking hell this was, he was *very* dangerous. Seeing the gun in his hand, Whitcombe, eyes wide as he struggled to stop himself finally going hysterical, backed away towards the window and then stopped. Salter, already in shock at so many intrusions breaching the walls of his 'reality', stood up as if he was going to say something, but no sound came out of his mouth, only a trickle of saliva which Derek noticed dribbling over his lip and down onto his chin, but which he didn't dare to wipe. Derek stared at them, waiting for one of them to move or speak, ask who he was or something. He'd vaguely had it in mind to go through a 'trial' for Salter, or at least read out a list of his 'offences' before executing him, but whatever it was he'd planned to say had gone completely out of his mind. All three of them stood, completely silent, completely motionless, Salter and Whitcombe aware on an instinctive level that they were facing a wild animal, the slightest sound or movement would trigger the attack. For a second, perhaps two or three at the most, the three of them were held, frozen in time and space by an ancient spell cast in the depths of human prehistory. There was no movement, no sound, no thought – Derek had not even consciously registered the identity of the third, unexpected participant in this motionless dance. Then the tightness of the atmosphere became just too much and it snapped. Salter coughed, Whitcombe tried to throw himself at Derek, and Derek, stepped back and fired, first at the moving

Whitcombe, who collapsed in a crumpled heap at his feet, and then at Salter, fired and fired and fired.

Outside, the two detectives watching the front of the house had just finished radioing in the news of Whitcombe's arrival, and then the more dramatic report of a second, unidentified intruder. They were calling for more support, convinced that now was the time for the knock, and that three of them were barely enough for the surveillance. The radio crackled back at them, "OK we're sending in three more teams, should be there in about four minutes – D.C.I. says go in fast, and hold them all there. And don't forget, they are almost certainly armed, and you definitely have the authorisation to use your guns." And almost on cue, the bangs of the shooting rang out, sharp and clear, even out there in the car.

"Shit, it's kicking off, sounds like world war three. What shall we do now?"

"Nothing, no action except contain, support E.T.A. one minute – but it is imperative that no one leaves – use all necessary force to prevent anyone leaving, over."

Both the detectives checked their guns and got out of the car, ready for action should the need arise. A few lights were already being switched on along the dark street and the noise of the arriving support teams would no doubt wake even more. Inside the house, Derek stood absolutely still again, staring first at one body, then at the other. So much blood, he had not expected so much blood, and the noise, the sheer intensity of the action had left him stunned, disorientated – but he was gradually becoming aware of his first real feelings, and was able to register a vague surprise to find not guilt or horror, but… disappointment. It had all been over so quickly, after such a build-up –He should have somehow prolonged the moment, made them suffer more, like he had suffered, he'd wanted them to feel his suffering, to hand some of it over to them but all done in an instant all over so quickly. Without thinking, he took the empty magazine from the gun and began to reload it. As he did so, he remembered something he had read, years before, in one of Orwell's essays, that the contemplation of revenge is far more satisfying than its final execution. It is always over too quickly – you spend hours, days, months, years, plotting, planning, rehearsing your revenge, until slowly, insidiously it becomes an obsession, it becomes the central to your existence and then, one day, you get your chance and … bang bang bang, it's all gone, everything, your planning, your plotting, the thing that had become your reason for living, all over and done with – and then what? What were you left with then? Well, for him the long term would have to wait, but he knew what he had to do now, and that was to get away, though get away to what? There was nothing left for him to get away to or for, but the shooting had jolted a deeper level of self-preservation, and it was more a thoughtless move to do *something* rather than *nothing* than a real urge to escape which now drove him to seek a way out. He gave one last look round the room and then turned his back on the scene and went out into the hall. He couldn't remember exactly the route back to the rear entrance and, seeing the front door immediately to his left, decided that it would have to do – if the place was under surveillance, the front would be no worse than the back, especially after all the shooting. He opened the heavy door and walked down the steps to the street. Before he reached the pavement, he saw two men on the opposite side of the street begin to move purposefully toward him. He pulled the gun out of his pocket and at the same time began feel his way back up the steps towards the still-open front door.

"Armed police, freeze…" It sounded so hollow and almost comical. None of this seemed real to Derek anymore insofar as his conscious mind was functioning at all. He paused on the steps, smiled at the awful futility of all this, and then fired, not really at them, just in their general direction. At the same time he was aware of two, perhaps more cars screeching to a halt over to his right. He turned, and began to run back up the steps when he was hit by the first of the return fire, just knocked flat by a great fist and, as he tried to get up, dazed and winded, he was flattened again.

He was lying half in the hallway now and beginning to feel the sharp, sour pain of his wounds. He tried to move but the pain got worse, making him wince at the sharpness of it. He wanted to die now, but paradoxically the wounds had kicked his physical body into primal survival mode. He knew that if he stayed where he was, he was finished, so whimpering with agony, he drew his legs inside the doorway and managed to kick the heavy door shut. Breathless, gasping, he knew that he had gained some time – they wouldn't come straight in in hot pursuit now they couldn't see him, they'd have to be circumspect, turn it into a siege, any other course would be too risky now that he could be anywhere. But he also knew that he had to get to a more secure position, had to get somewhere as soon as he could, make it as difficult as possible for them.

And there it all was, that was how he'd got here, dragging himself along the hall, away from the door and then seeing the wooded cellar door, which managed to open and crawl inside. God knows how he'd shut the door or got down the stairs or how long had passed, but that was it. And now what? He'd put it all in order, sorted it out and here was where it all led, just here where he was dying, that was what and was too weak to be frightened about it. For a moment he was still trying to cling on to some sense of achievement but it was fading with his consciousness. Had he at least made a scratch, if not a footprint. But he also knew with a strange clarity that there would be not even a scratch and it had never been about three minutes of fame, just making some sort of difference, just righting some wrong and at least what he had done was worthwhile, he was convinced of that. It was a source of real gratification to him to discover that despite what had happened to him, he didn't regret it for a second but at the same moment he knew with equal clarity that an individual action like this achieved nothing truly significant. He sat back, able for a moment to contemplate what had happened. And then, his own life...so this was what it was all about. And then, the last temptation, he thought that just perhaps – the story would have to get out – Salter's drug connections, his friends in high places, it would all come out now, if only gradually, there was bound to be some young ambitious reporter who'd see it through. If only he'd left something in writing, a sort of manifesto or battle cry, something to make it clearer that this wasn't just a simple case of personal revenge. He wanted everyone to know that he was trying to do something more than that, that he was sending out a warning to 'them' that they weren't going to just get away with everything all the time, that there was always going to be someone who was going to get back at them. Well, it wouldn't be him, not now, this was his first and last, but perhaps someone else – propaganda by deed they called it, didn't they? perhaps someone else... if only he'd written it down, he could have existed after all this, but no, too late, too late, and anyway, ...

The room seemed to suddenly get darker and his thoughts became even more random and incoherent, a series of images and phrases beneath which he felt for the first time a wave of primal fear and a deep, deep painful longing for someone to come and take all this dying off him, someone to come and make it all better, to cradle him and soothe him to sleep, all tucked up in clean sheets and warm blankets.

But no one would come and his fear slipped away with his sense of narrative as he finally lost his grip on meaning and significance, let go of everything and felt himself whirl deeper and deeper into a maelstrom of cold, jagged darkness, nothing cosy, not the warm darkness of childhood sleep that he had craved, just the cold darkness of pain and confusion and aching emptiness.

Outside, Derek had imagined the scenes that had so often been on television screens during sieges like this – roads sealed off, hundreds of police, sharpshooters on the rooftops, banks of cameras – television, press, the works. But not this time. Outside, in the pale light of approaching dawn, at the very moment when Derek faded out of existence, there were in fact only three, unmarked cars, an unmarked operations van in a now perfectly quiet street. Around the corner were three ambulances, their crews sitting around in one of them, smoking and joking and waiting, voices quiet. There were also two police cars and some uniformed officers at each end of the road, taping off the entrances but there was nobody out in the street. Bedroom lights that had been switched on in alarm had all been switched off and everyone who'd popped out to have a look at what might have been a major incident had long gone back to sleep – just another hot London night of distant police sirens, obviously no big thing, find out what it was tomorrow. They'd kept it deliberately low key, playing the waiting game.

Crammed inside the van, as well as the driver and radio operator, there were four other people sipping mugs of coffee amidst the seemingly chaotic jumble of monitoring equipment. Behind the house there were two more plainclothes officers, from MI5 now, replacing the police officers of earlier. No sharpshooters, no cordoned off-street, no uniformed police, no television cameras, not even a hack from the local gazette. The world was already moving on, sneaking quietly past on the other side of the road, eyes averted from the corpses in the house.

Inside the operations van, Stephen Butler stared at the floor.

"Well, it shouldn't be too long now, we know he was hit at least twice – give it another hour and we'll go in – he can't be in much of a state now."

"No, I suppose not…" Maloney felt uneasy being there at all. He was shocked, deeply shocked by what had happened to Brown, the way everything had somehow exploded around this case, splintering the normality of life for so many people, including himself, because, above all he felt appalled by his own personal position. There were so many splinters left from this, ready to cut and prick, shards of glass everywhere. Cut fingers, gashes, blood, nowhere you could just sit quietly and anonymously now for fear of being sliced by splinters of glass. Even if they managed to somehow keep the lid on it all, and he knew that was still a possibility, it would have put pay to any hopes he might have had of reading his name in the honours list, this year – and for a long time to come. And the bugger of it was that he hadn't been involved, none of it was a result of anything he'd done or said. Just sheer association with something like this was enough. Still, it could have been a lot worse. Thank God that Stephen had been able to convince his superiors that there was nothing to lose and a great deal to gain by keeping the siege low key. He'd been motivated by a desire to keep himself and the Met. out of potentially embarrassing situation rather do the Customs and Excise any good turns, but that was the effect, by default and he had to be grateful. And he was alive, so many were dead. Yes, he *was* alive and so many really were dead.

"So what's the story, then?" Bill Haggart broke the silence, his rough accent making the other two jump. He eyed the two men he didn't know, unsure of who was what in the confusion of the last hours, but well aware that this was not an ordinary police operation. It had 'funny boys' written all over it and he knew that the two men Maloney had pointedly not introduced to him were deeply involved. And he was frightened of them, frightened of what might now happen to him. He'd reacted without thought in getting involved in all this, instinctively and against his better judgement, but now, with some time to reflect, he realised just what a fraught situation he was in. A Talking Head's song kept repeating itself in his mind, 'This ain't no party, this ain't no disco, this ain't no fooling around'. Dead bodies, real dead bodies and he knew more than he wanted to know and more than was good for him.

Butler answered, as cool as you like, as if he was giving a straightforward factual briefing on some insignificant topic at a local press conference.

"There really isn't much to worry about with rogue individuals like this, you know. A bit of a headache admin wise but if Derek thought he was going to shake the foundations and bring everything crashing down he was sadly deluded. Organised labour is more of a problem for us, especially like the miners when they've got a leader with integrity, vision, and genuinely wanting to mobilise against the whole system – but most of the time, most of the unions are led by human beings who just want a quiet life, on big fat salaries sat in posh offices a long way from the shop floor – so even they're not really a threat. But then we get things we can't plan for like the poll tax riots – grassroots, no leadership as such and resonating wider than you'd think, that sort of thing can keep us awake at night because we simply don't know where it's going…but Derek…not a problem – in fact he's done us a favour with Salter, he was becoming a bloody jumped up nuisance. So to answer your question, well, we've prepared a story of a minor underworld shooting incident, just straight police and thieves stuff, nothing to excite any special interest. The local rag haven't even bothered to send anyone yet – but if anyone asks, they'll just put the press release straight in, it'll only be worth a small paragraph at the bottom of the page, but it's all so tidy I doubt if there'll be any interest at all."

"Yes, but what if someone does pick up on it?" Maloney couldn't get rid of the feeling that if the cover up were exposed, it would be far worse than having played it straight in the first place. "I know what you're saying about all that stuff about bringing down the system – I couldn't care less about all that, but what about all of us if it does all somehow get out?" What he meant, of course, was 'What about *me*?'

"Well, I think we're pretty well covered – after all, there are no civilian hostages, and we're pretty sure that everyone is dead, or damn near it by now, so you could argue we're doing it the best way anyway. Where we've really scored, where your bloke really did us a favour, was in cleaning it all up like this for us."

Haggart looked up again, "Cleaning up! What the fuck are you talking about?"

"Bill, that's no way to talk to a senior police officer." Maloney was clearly out of his depth. He sounded unconvincing and looked bewildered, and was feeling a growing sense of unease at the look of anger and distaste on Haggart's face.

Butler, with the cocky arrogance of one now totally secure in his surroundings, warmed to his subject. "Well, he's saved us the trouble of a trial, hasn't he?" He looked at the silent man next to him, who nodded his approval to continue the explanation.

"Well, bloody hell, who knows who's involved with him somewhere down the line – it doesn't bear thinking about, what might have come out in a trial. Incidentally, Mr Haggart, I hope you are not going to give any of us the impression that you might do something er… irresponsible with all this information to which you've become privy." Maloney saw the anger flash across Haggart's face, saw his body tense, as if about to move into action, then saw it relax. He recognised, as Bill lowered his eyes, the same fear and confusion that he was feeling himself and he noted with surprise that it gave him a kind of strength based on some sort of basic tribal sympathy for one of 'his', a protective urge towards one for whom he felt he had some responsibility. Before anything else could happen, and despite his fear, he said, his voice hoarse with stress and tiredness, "Look, I'm sure there's no need to adopt that sort of a tone, Stephen. I hope that none of us relishes this situation and we're all at a low ebb at the moment. Bill, why don't you go home, there's nothing you can do now, nothing any of us can do for Derek now. And then report to me tomorrow morning and we'll sort everything out. I know I can reassure Chief Inspector Butler here that you are the last person to behave in any way irresponsibly. Isn't that right?"

It wasn't much in the history of heroic interventions but it was all he could manage and it was better than nothing.

Bill stared at each of them in turn and stood up as far as he was able to in the back of the van, thankful for the chance to get away. He stumbled to the back of the van, fumbled the rear door open and climbed into the street, his eyes blinking in the growing light. He turned to look at them, crouching still in the back of the van, "God, you know, I think Derek's big mistake was in thinking small, he should've got a machine gun and done for the fucking lot of you." and then slammed the door shut on them and walked over to his car. Back in the van there was silence for a few seconds, broken by the coarse voice of the man from MI5, speaking into a radio microphone. "Alpha watch, come in."

"Alpha watch, go ahead."

"Target has just left the van. Please keep under twenty-four-hour total surveillance, phones, the lot, until further notice – and apprehend immediately should he make any attempt to contact anyone connected with the press. Over."

"Understood. Over and out."

Butler smiled at Maloney, who's already drawn features had turned deathly white. "What on earth…"

"Oh, come on, David, it might not be in the national interest, but it's sure as hell in yours and mine – I might put a tail on you too again if I think you're going to go soft on me. No harm will come to him, if he's as sensible and reliable as you say… but just in case…"

"Oh god, poor old Derek, poor all of us, we really are rotten to…"

"The core? Come off it, Maloney. It's just the way things are."

"Sir…" the man who was monitoring the sound and heat levels in the house took off his earphones and turned to the huddled group at the back. "I'm pretty sure that we can go in now. I don't think we'll find anyone alive."

"Good, well that's the end of that, then, hopefully." Butler sighed.

"Amen," said the man from MI5.

Chapter 19

Outside, Bill walked away from the van, trying to clear his head in the cool freshness of the early morning air. He was angry, he was confused and he was frightened. Across the street he could see the entrance to Salter's house and was startled by the sound of engines starting up – then the three ambulances appearing around the corner and pulling up outside. *Must be all over,* he thought and found himself crossing the road towards them. As he approached the ambulance crews were already going up the path to the front door, each pair with a stretcher. One of the spooks spotted him and shouted, "Who are you?"

"Customs…" He waved his warrant card and that seemed to do the trick. He knew it wouldn't be long before the controllers realised he was there, but he decided to risk it and walked up the path in the wake of the stretchers and into the hallway.

Inside it felt crowded and chaotic – the entrance to the cellar was narrow and the stairs steep, so only the first of the stretchers had gone down and the rest had to wait until they were back up – strictly one at a time.

One of the crew turned and spoke to Bill

"There's a bit of a problem down there apparently, don't know what – those police guys seem a bit confused. Are you with them?"

"No, not exactly but I'll see what I can find out."

Bill squeezed past the stretchers and through the doorway into the cellar. As he reached the bottom, he could tell there was some kind of altercation going on between the spooks and the two-ambulance crew. They all stopped and looked at him.

One of them raised his eyes. "Christ, Uncle Tom Cobbley and all. Who the fuck are you?"

"Customs team. Same one as him…" he pointed at what he took to be Derek's body, slumped in a chair.

One of the ambulance men looked at him.

"Well, thank god for that – these two don't seem to be worried about him at all…"

"Worried, what do you mean, he's, he's …dead, isn't he?"

"Well, that's just it, we don't think so but he won't last long if they don't let us get him out to intensive care. We think he's got a pulse…"

For a second, no one spoke and then the full understanding hit Bill like a physical jolt. "Christ. You two," looking at the ambulance men, "get him out now. And you guys from MI5 or 6 or whatever you are, get out of the way, now, or we'll all have to report you formally for your actions.' He glanced at the ambulance crew. 'Ambulance – radio in now and log one survivor, make sure they're ready at the hospital. Go, now."

Both of the crew jumped into action and within what seemed seconds had secured Derek's limp and ashen body onto the stretcher and we're beginning to haul him up the stairs, shouting, "Clear the hall, casualty coming through."

The spooks stood completely still and silent as the stretcher disappeared out of their realm and into the real world beyond their control. They glared at Bill but knew they'd lost control and run out of options, there were just too many witnesses.

"So I guess you two were just going to try and wait until he really was dead, eh, surprised you didn't help him along before the crew got down here."

There was a pause before the taller of them answered with a sort of wry grin

"Absolutely. We just didn't realise he was alive until one of them examined him. I'm not convinced he is, as it goes, but we'll see. Nothing we can do now."

"No," said Bill quietly, "and I'll make sure he has a 24-hour watch on him from our guys, even if it's just volunteers. Protect him from our protectors, eh?"

He looked around the cellar properly for the first time and noticed a trail of blood leading into the shadows – 'He's lost a hell of a lot of blood', sensing they might be right about Derek's chances of survival

There was another moment of silence.

"It isn't his," said the tall one.

Bill blinked. "What do you mean, not his?"

"We only found one body upstairs…"

"Who?"

"Whitcombe, the bent copper."

"And Salter?"

"He's not here. It's a total fuck up – we didn't know there was a door out of here, leads into the back garden. There's so much blood, he must be badly wounded, but we don't know where the fuck he is. He must have somehow crawled down here before Derek and got out through the back"

"My god, you guys, with all your resources and confidence and accents and everything and you couldn't organise a piss up in a brewery. And we rely on you for our safety and security. God help us. What a fucking mess. I just hope for your sakes that Derek makes it through because if he doesn't, I'm going to do everything I possibly can to expose what's gone on here, for what good it'll do. You stupid bastards."

Back in the command and control van, Butler had reached a similar conclusion. "Well, that's where we're up to. If Derek is only just alive, let's just keep our fingers crossed that he doesn't make it through the night. Otherwise things might well get a little bit more tricky for a week or two than we imagined. And with Salter somewhere out there…yes, all a bit tricky. Nothing ever really ends, you know' he said, philosophically, 'there's always something unpleasant that bubbles its way up to the surface through the earth, no matter how deep we think we've buried it, something that needs sorting out or smothering or just watching out for – keeps us all in a job, though, I suppose, and I don't honestly think this one will disturb very much in the long run, whatever happens tonight.'"

He looked up but everyone else was looking down at their feet. There was nothing more to say. Just an edgy, restless silence.